PENGUIN CRIME FICTION

ICE BLUES

Richard Stevenson lives in Massachusetts and is
the author of two previous Donald Strachey Mys-
teries, *Death Trick* and *On the Other Hand,
Death* (Penguin), which *The New York Times*'s
Newgate Callendar called "a lively book . . .
thoroughly realized characters and skillful
plotting carry the reader straight along. Highly
recommended."

ICE
BLUES

A Donald Strachey
Mystery

RICHARD
STEVENSON

PENGUIN BOOKS

PENGUIN BOOKS
Viking Penguin Inc., 40 West 23rd Street,
New York, New York 10010, U.S.A.
Penguin Books Ltd, Harmondsworth,
Middlesex, England
Penguin Books Australia Ltd, Ringwood,
Victoria, Australia
Penguin Books Canada Limited, 2801 John Street,
Markham, Ontario, Canada L3R 1B4
Penguin Books (N.Z.) Ltd, 182–190 Wairau Road,
Auckland 10, New Zealand

First published in the United States of America by
St. Martin's Press 1986
Published in Penguin Books 1987

LIBRARY OF CONGRESS CATALOGING IN PUBLICATION DATA
Stevenson, Richard.
    Ice blues.
    (Penguin crime fiction)
    I. Title.
PS3569.T4567I3   1987   813'.54   86-18672
ISBN 0 14 00.9403 2

Printed in the United States of America by
Offset Paperback Mfrs., Inc., Dallas, Pennsylvania
Set in Caledonia

ICE BLUES

ONE

THE ATTENDANT AT FAXON TOWING AND Storage looked surprised to see me back so soon, and a little wary.

"You all set?"

"I need to use your phone."

"There's a pay phone over to the station."

"I haven't got a dime."

"It's a quarter now."

"I haven't got a quarter, and the Albany police department doesn't accept collect calls from people they don't want to hear from. I know, I've tried it."

He had a broad fatigued face with heavily bagged eyes, one blue and white, one blue and red, not the result of patriotism but of a burst blood vessel in the corner of the right one. He smelled of grease and cold sweat, and this mixed with the stench of the kerosene heater and the Mr. Coffee machine, whose crud-stained pot contained two cups of a substance the EPA probably had on a list somewhere. Wet snow was starting to thud sloppily against the windowpane.

"You want the cops? Somethin' wrong with your car?"

"Somebody left something in it," I said.

"Oh yeah? Well, you could leave it here, case somebody calls."

"That wouldn't work. It's too hot in here."

He looked at me as if I might be one of the deinstitutionalized, a new social class that merchants and tradesmen feel compelled to gingerly indulge up to a point.

Shrugging, he said, "Phone's yours. Just make it quick. I got calls coming in." He lifted the filthy apparatus—no Trimline—off a pile of oil-smudged documents and set it on the counter. I dialed.

"Detective Lieutenant Bowman, please. This is Donald Strachey."

"Hang on, I think he's still here."

The snow was pounding down hard now in the last light of the January afternoon. I said, "This entire section of the North American continent should be declared unfit for human habitation."

"Huh?"

"It's snowing again."

The attendant shook his head. "That's Albany for ya. Winter gets some people down. Me, I don't mind."

"You must be half penguin."

"English, Irish, German, Norwegian—yeah, there might be some penguin in there somewhere."

There were squawking and banging sounds at the other end of the line, then a voice: "This is Bowman. Who's this?"

"Don Strachey. I'm calling about a police matter."

"Hey, it's my least favorite fruitcake—the wimp of Washington Park, the Georgie Boy of Crow Street. I was heading out the door, but I'm always happy to wait around and accept a call from the only man I know who went to Kentucky for an artificial-wrist transplant." He chortled inanely.

I said, "This is not a social call, it's police business. I'm at Faxon Towing. My car was hauled out here last night, and now there's a problem. You should drive out."

"What the hell are you talking about, Strachey? This is the homicide division, and you got a beef with traffic you won't get me involved, oh no, I'll not act as an impediment to those officers. Anyway, it was plainly announced on the medias which streets were gonna get plowed last night, and if you're too dumb or too contrary to move your car out of the way, I've got no sympathy. The snow removal crews have a job to do, and—"

I cut him off. "There's a man in it. He's dead."

"There's what? In what? What's there a dead man in?"

"In the back seat of my car. Timothy Callahan—you know Timmy—he drove me out here to pick up my car. Timmy dropped me off, I paid the extortionate towing fee, and I located my car. When I opened the door it caught my notice that the rear backrest had been lowered, and a man was curled up back there. His eyes were open wide, but he didn't say 'Cold enough for ya?' or 'What do you think of all this snow?' or 'Ciao, baby' or anything else at all."

"What man? This man was dead, you say?"

"Under the dome light I could make out little icicles of blood extending down from his mouth and nose and ears. I did not check his vital signs, but when the human body temperature falls below thirty-two degrees Fahrenheit, death ensues. He's gone. I thought you ought to know."

"Is this some stunt of yours?"

"No."

"It better not be. I'm driving out there."

"No rush. I shut the heater off. But I'll need my car, or a ride downtown."

"Don't you touch *any*thing till I get out there, you got that?"

I hung up and handed the phone back to the attendant, whose blue-and-red eye was twitching.

"You shittin' me? There's a dead guy in your car?"

"Yep. Did you put him in there?"

"No! Holy Christ, no!"

"When was my car brought in?"

With a jittery hand he leafed through a stack of forms, leaving a black thumbprint on each one. "This here one's yours, ain't it?"

I examined the form, in the boxed spaces of which were handwritten my license number, the make and model of my car, and the notation that it had arrived at Faxon's at 3:20 A.M. and had been checked in by "Pert" or "Fert."

"This is it. Who's Fert, the truck operator? Or is there somebody here who checks them in?"

"That'd be Ferd. He was driving last night, I know."

"What's Ferd's last name?"

"Plumber. Frederick Plumber's his right name. Hey, you're not the cops. Maybe I shouldn't be telling you this. Are the cops really on their way out?"

The door opened and a woman wearing a coat crafted from six endangered species strode in brushing snow from two of them. Atop the grimy counter she dropped a receipt from the traffic division showing that she had paid her fine, along with two fifties. In a voice as icy as the evening, she said, "I—want—my—car."

"No problem," the attendant said, and started messing with some papers.

As I went out the door, the woman said to the attendant, "Don't you *ever* wash your hands?" If there was a reply, it was not immediate. Maybe he'd placate her by offering her some coffee.

I walked back to the car through the gobs of blowing snow. With a gloved hand I lifted the hatch where it had been jimmied. The body was frozen in a fetal position, and I reached up under its peacoat and pulled a wallet out of the back pocket of the man's faded Levi's. The driver's license belonged to John C. Lenihan, Swan Street, Albany. The other two cards showed that Lenihan had been a member of the Albany Public Library and was eligible for discounted admissions to the Third Street Cinema in Rensselaer. Otherwise he had not been a joiner. The portion of Lenihan's estate left in his wallet amounted to six one-dollar bills.

The wallet contained one photograph of a middle-aged woman. Also stuffed in a small slot in the wallet were three scraps of paper with names and phone numbers, each in a different script, presumably but not necessarily that of the person whose name appeared. The names were those of men prominent in Albany community affairs.

I got out my notebook and copied all this down and replaced the wallet in the pocket of the cold Levi's. I had thought the man's face looked familiar, and the name was one I'd heard before too, but I couldn't connect either of them to a time or place. I checked the front pocket of the man's Levi's and found some small change but no keys. Nor were there keys hung from his belt.

From the glove compartment I took out the flashlight, banged it against my palm, and shined the half-watt beam around John C. Lenihan's face and head. He had been a more-or-less young man—thirty-six, according to his driver's license—but prematurely bald, and the downy brown hair at the back of his head was caked with frozen black blood where the blows had been struck, repeatedly and with force. His face was unmarked except for the red-and-black stalactites and the wide-eyed grimace. There were two tiny mild abrasions on either side of the upper bridge of his nose. He'd worn glasses, but I didn't see them anywhere.

Back inside the office shed I asked to use the telephone again.

"Ain't the cops here yet?"

A CB radio on a shelf crackled and a voice came out of it. "What'd you say, Roy? Guy's got body damage? I was outta the truck and couldn't make out what you said."

Roy ignored this, and I said, "They're not here yet, but I have to get in touch with a friend."

"A lawyer?"

Crackle, crackle. "Hey, Roy, you in there yankin' yer wanger, or what? Roy, you there?"

"He's a lawyer, but kind of a cute one. Not a criminal lawyer. I won't need that."

"Cute?"

"The phone, please. If there's a charge for the call, Lieutenant Bowman will take care of it."

"You work with the cops?" he said, and hoisted the reeking appliance onto the counter.

Snap, crackle. "Hey, Roy, I'm comin' in after I get this Caddy out to Conklin's. Where's Pat, up to Route Seven? Roy? Hey, Roy?"

"No, I don't work with the cops. I don't work against them either, except a couple of times a year, but you don't want to hear about that."

He backed off, and I dialed.

"It's me. I'll be late."

"I just got home. The roads are a freezing mess again. Where are you?"

"Still out at Faxon's. There's a dead man in my car."

"Right. I'm heating up some chili and I picked up some George's bread at Lemme's. How long will you be?"

"I don't know. Ned Bowman's on his way out here now. He'll want to fling some insults, twirl his truncheon around, maybe ask a few pertinent questions. Forty-five minutes to an hour, I'd guess."

"How did a dead man get into your car?"

Flashing blue lights appeared through the volleys of blowing snow. Beneath them a blue Dodge materialized and halted outside the shed's window, on whose surface a finger had written CITY HALL SUCKS in the steam that came up from a pot of water on the kerosene heater.

"I don't know yet how he got there. I assume he was placed there by whoever killed him—he died violently, I think. Though he might have crawled in there on his own because the evidence suggests that he drew his last breath while curled up in the back of the car. If he did that though, first he would have had to jimmy the hatch lock and disengage and lower the backrest, and the man's wounds look as if he was in no condition to manage that. So far, it's all speculation on my part."

A pause. "Are you making this up? I wouldn't put it past you on a night like this. Or any night."

Roy the attendant had gone outside to meet Bowman,

and I could see Roy shrugging and shaking his head through the UC in SUCKS.

"Bowman's here and I should go. It's his problem now, not mine. My only pressing problems are cabin fever alternating with cold feet. I'm sick of this snow. Let's get out of here—fly to Puerto Rico or the Dutch Antilles. Tonight."

"You've been whining about winter since the first leaf dropped on Labor Day. But you'll have to suffer ignobly for another month. You know I can't leave now. The people of the State of New York need me."

"We can take out a second mortgage on the house and lease a beach cottage at Luquillo for a month. Just you and me and a houseboy named Fernando who's lackadaisical but has fifty-eight great teeth and the immune system of a steam locomotive."

A familiar silence—he was the only man I knew who could roll his eyes over the telephone. "You're at the Watering Hole, aren't you? Happy hour at Gloomy Gulch. Should I put on my WCTU sweatshirt and walk over and rescue you?"

Bowman was moving toward the door, followed by Roy and a uniformed cop.

"Gotta go now. Who's John C. Lenihan?"

"You mean Jack Lenihan? You know Jack Lenihan. He's Warren Slonski's lover—a friend of Herb's. They were at Herb's pool party last summer. Is he over there with you? I haven't seen Jack since—"

"Gotta go."

I hung up as Bowman shoved at the hinged side of the glass door. He remarked on this error in his terse, unequivocal way, then pushed at the unhinged side, which yielded him up into the stinking hut. Bowman was unchanged since I'd last seen him except that he was suffering from what appeared to be a severe case of athlete's foot of the nose.

"Ned, what's wrong with your face? I don't think you've been drying thoroughly between the folds and interstices."

He looked as if he would have liked to beat me severely about the face and head, and snapped, "Where's your car? You lead the way. Now. I was just on my way home for supper."

I led the way. The phone rang and Roy stayed behind. Flapping sheets of snow swooshed around under the floodlights as we moved up the rows of cars. We came to mine and I lifted the hatch.

"Do you know him?" Bowman said.

"No."

"Probably a wino or mental case. Crawled in to sleep one off, and died. Poor slob."

"Look closer, at his head."

The uniformed cop shined his Rayovac at the dead man's face and head.

"Jiminy Christmas!"

"I'd say a lead pipe or maybe a tire iron did that."

"That will be up to the medical examiner to decide, not you or I. Holy Mother! So, where's your tire iron, Strachey?"

"Unless it was removed by the killer, it's under the rug beneath the body, with my spare."

"Well, I intend to have it examined and retained as possible evidence. You know I have to do that."

"What am I supposed to do if I have a flat, use my teeth?"

"It wouldn't be the first time you put something filthy in your mouth. In fact, I'm confiscating your entire car. You'll get it back when I say so. Now I have to make a couple of calls and get a crew out here to ID this guy, and then I'm going to interrogate you. I think you're in trouble, Strachey. Real bad trouble."

"No, you don't. But you'd like to think so."

"Well, you've got one hell of a lot of explaining to do, that's for damn sure."

"Let's make it quick. I've had enough of winter in this godforsaken outpost, and I'm leaving tonight for the Dutch Antilles."

"No, you're not. You're staying right here in Albany, Strachey. You're not going anywhere at all until *I say* you can."

"People I'm fond of keep telling me that."

TWO

I MADE MY ENTRANCE WITH A SHRIEK-ing wind hurling snow at my head and shoulders, like W. C. Fields in *The Fatal Glass of Beer*, then shut and locked the door behind me. Timmy was in his thermal underwear and was holding a steaming mug full of something that smelled like the mouth of the Brahmaputra at midday.

"You weren't there. Neither was Jack Lenihan."

"Weren't where? How about a slug of that smelly stuff?"

"The Watering Hole. I slogged all the way over there, and all I found were two pharmaceutical salesmen from Utica feeding gin to a pimply youth with staples in his ears and poster paint on his eyelids. I asked him if an art supply store had blown up, but his gentlemen friends told me to buzz off, so I left. The bartender said he hadn't seen 'Miss Donald' for days."

I removed my boots, which were making fog, and dumped them on *The New York Times Magazine* spread out for that purpose in the front hall. "I didn't say I was at the Watering Hole, and anyway, that bartender is an idiot. I can't stand this town any longer. When are we leaving? Is the airport still open? We could be on the beach at Grand Cayman by dawn."

"Come on, you don't really hate Albany, except in winter, what with your having grown up in semitropical New

Jersey. We go through this every year, and then spring comes and you go chirp-chirp, 'Isn't the Northeast grand? How tedious it must be in those tepid places with no change of seasons.' You can't have it both ways, lover."

He led the way back to the kitchen and ladled out two bowls of chili.

"Of course I can have it both ways. I can spend November through March in Guadeloupe, then you wire me when the annual ice age alert has been lifted and I rush back to pick you a daffodil and unclog your frozen fuel lines. I'll be warm, and you'll be glad to see me."

"Generous of you."

"Why aren't we rich? Did you buy a lottery ticket today?"

"Yes, but you won't like it."

"Don't tell me. You played eighteen-eighteen again. This chili's good. I like it when my head sweats into my dinner."

"That number's going to come up someday, and I'll be the only winner. A million flat, and no going halvsies with a corset manufacturer from Garden City."

"Tell me again what eighteen is—your Aunt Moira's shoe size?"

"On her eighteenth birthday Aunt Moira played number eighteen on a punch board at the Poughkeepsie Elks lodge and won a twelve-pound Spam. Since then eighteen has always been a lucky number for the Callahans. It's simple mathematical probability that eighteen-eighteen will come up sometime in the next five hundred years. Some Callahan is going to get stinking rich, and with a little luck it'll be me."

"Do we have any Molsons left?"

"The refrigerator is right over there."

"My question concerned inventory, your department. I wasn't suggesting we play Ozzie and Harriet."

"I never know with you. You have all these residual heterosexual inclinations."

"Male presumption of entitlement, Timothy, has nothing to do with sexual orientation. It is a characteristic of certain moody, confused men—homo or hetero—who never left their mommies. I am not one of them."

He got up and brought me a beer. I grunted benevolently. He sat down again and picked at his chili.

"Let's make a deal," he said after a moment. "You quit acting churlish with me and I'll quit acting churlish with you. I understand that you hate the cold weather, and you're between cases, and you're bored with Albany, and with me, and with yourself—and that the AIDS situation has put a crimp in your normal abnormal outlets. But all this tension is getting me down, and there's no point in both of us being miserable. I know you feel too rotten to act sweet naturally, or even just civil, but do me a favor and fake it part of the time. I'll be grateful, and I'll bet you'll feel better too."

"What? What's that you say? You want me to periodically hide my precious inner feelings? As if after all these years Dr. Joyce Brothers' column turned out to be simpleminded charlatanry?"

"Yes, bottle up your negative emotions in a neurotically unhealthy way. For my sake. Just off and on until spring. Your springtime emotions I like a lot."

I took a long swig of beer. "I don't know, Timothy. I have to tell you, this is a bolt out of the blue. Your proposition is not something I ever dreamed I'd be faced with when we began sharing hearth and home and Vaseline jar. I'm going to have to give this one a lot of thought."

"Don—I'm serious. Really."

I ate the chili and drank the beer and grimly considered what he had said. As usual, he had me. A student of Jesuits, Timmy could play fast and loose on the larger matters, up to a point, but on the conduct of human affairs he was pathologically astute and rational.

I said, "Look, I know you're right. I hate this town in winter with its wind and cold and sooty snow, and all those moral pygmies in charge of the place. But taking it out on you is unfair, and I'll try *moderately* hard not to do it anymore. *Try*, I said. A small maniacal outburst once in a great while is still okay, right?"

"Of course. It's all right with me if we both remain human. Thank you."

"You're welcome. Now get me another beer."

"Get it yourself, Kramden," he said, and laughed but didn't get up. I got myself another beer.

"Where were you this evening anyway? Were you really out at Faxon's all that time? You let on as though you were at the Watering Hole."

"Unh-unh. You drew that demeaning inference, but what I said on the phone was the truth. That I was at Faxon's waiting for Ned Bowman to show up because there was a corpse in my car. Which there was."

"What? You're not really serious. You look serious."

I was loading the last of the chili onto a slice of George's famous whole-grain wheat bread, using a second slice of George's famous whole-grain wheat bread as a bulldozer. I said, "This stuff is good and good for you."

Timmy's mouth was open but he wasn't eating. "Who was it?"

"Jack Lenihan."

"No."

"It was."

"Mother of God!"

"That was my thought, or the Presbyterian equivalent thereof."

"He was dead?"

"Oh yes."

"How did he die?"

"On purpose, though not his own, I think. He'd been conked with a tire iron or something."

"Holy Jesus! And he was in your car when you went to pick it up?"

"In the back, atop the lowered backrest."

"But—how did he get there?"

"I have no idea. Ned Bowman is handling the investigation."

"Is there more to this than you're telling me?"

"A lot, no doubt. But I don't know what it is, and my interest in it is only a little more than academic. Nobody has paid me money to look into the matter, and anyway I'm not taking on any job—especially a cop case—that would require my moving around out of doors any time before Easter. I've been thinking about it, and I might do some security stuff to pay my share of the mortgage and distract me from morbid self-absorption. Maybe sit behind a mirror in a drugstore rereading *One Hundred Years of Solitude* with one eye and spotting elderly shoplifters with the other. But that poor guy in my car is Bowman's problem. It's got nothing to do with me."

"But you *knew* Jack Lenihan."

"I met him once. I remember him vaguely."

"Herb's pool party, the Fourth of July."

"Right. We talked for a few minutes. About politics, I think."

"Really? I thought Jack never discussed politics. He was embarrassed about his family and its sordid past."

I cleared the table while he ground the coffee beans. Until I met Timmy I'd always thought coffee was a mineral that occurred in nature as tiny crystals and was mined like coal. I said, "Who's his family?"

"The Lenihans—the Lenihans of Albany. Pug Lenihan is his grandfather. You didn't know that?"

"Pug Lenihan, the Boyle brothers' bagman? He's dead, isn't he?"

"He's in his nineties and still lives in the North End somewhere. But I doubt whether Jack has anything to do with him—had. Jack was a notorious druggie for a while, using and dealing, and the Lenihans were as unfond of him as he was of them. Did he mention Pug to you?"

"As I recall, it was just before the Democratic convention and we talked national politics. What was he, a rich kid snorting the family fortune away up his nose?" I set the dirty dishes in steaming water and made a plastic bottle spurt something pink into it.

"No, the Lenihans are bust. Pug lives like a pauper, and his only son—Jack's dad—died a drunk twenty years ago. Jack has a sister, I think, but the money's gone. The Boyles must have accumulated plenty, but what they didn't hand out at the polls they gave away to charity and North End down-and-outs. Jack must have seen a lot over the years, or smelled it, and he hated the Boyle machine with a cold passion. God, Jack was the last of the Lenihan men. Talk about a famous family going out with a whimper." He dumped the ground coffee in a paper filter and poured hot water over it.

"Lenihan may have hated the machine," I said, "but he did not avoid all contact with political personages. His wallet had three slips of paper in it with a name and phone number on each one. What would Lenihan have had to do with Creighton Prell, Larry Dooley, or Sim Kempelman?"

Timmy looked perplexed. "That's a pretty weird combination. Politically those three have nothing in common. Prell is the Republican county chairman and the mayor of Handbag. Larry Dooley, as you know all too well, is an Albany city councilman and a real ambitious pain-in-the-neck nitwit. The word is Larry's going to buck his machine pals and run in the mayoral primary as a populist reformer, which is a bizarre joke. And Sim Kempelman is head of Democrats for Better Government in Albany. You know about them, don't you? Sort of a local Common Cause, except with half the balls Common Cause has."

"That would be about one eighth of one ball. Why would Lenihan be carrying their phone numbers around? Could they be tricks?"

"That's doubtful. They're all straight, so far as I know. Maybe it's something else personal. It's odd."

"What about Lenihan's lover, what's-his-name? Have I met him?"

"Warren Slonski, sometimes known as the irresistible Warren Slonski. He wasn't at Herb's with Jack, so you might not have met him. Maybe they were on the outs last summer. They've had their ups and downs, I know. Slonski's very straight, nonsexually speaking. He's a chemical engineer of some kind at Schenectady GE. You'd remember him if you'd met him."

"Why would I?"

"Because, as I said, he's irresistible. Or so it is told."

"I wonder if he's been notified of Jack's death. The cops are often sloppy about that sort of thing."

He poured more water over the coffee, making slow circles around the inside of the filter, washing it down so as not to waste any. "I suppose you're thinking of driving out to break the news and offering whatever consolation seems appropriate."

"That's not what I was thinking. Not exactly."

"Right. These are new times. No more of that."

"Absolutely. Out where? You said 'drive out.'"

"Colonie. They live in some development out on Shaker Road, I think."

"Jack's last address was on Swan Street. It's on his driver's license."

"Maybe they moved. Or split up."

"What did Jack do for a living?"

He served the coffee and proceeded to dump half a cup of skim milk in his. "The last I knew he was working at an all-night quiche parlor on Lark Street and going to business college in the daytime—computers probably. If the abacus ever returns, twenty thousand Albany twenty-five-year-olds are going to be back dropping buns on the belt at Burger King."

"Lenihan was a few years beyond twenty-five. You said he dealt drugs. How recently and in how big a way?"

"Big enough. Two or three years ago he was hauled in on a coke bust that involved mid-level wholesalers. Three other guys went to Sing Sing, but Jack was acquitted for lack of evidence. He escaped by the skin of his nasal passage. Jack was really a very smart and decent person, and I think the drug stuff was probably some anti-Lenihan-family acting out. But I didn't know him well enough to know exactly what went on in his head. I suppose you could say that after a certain age you don't call it acting out anymore."

I drank my coffee and tried not to look at Timmy's, which resembled the water in a creek below a paper mill. "He must have been dealing again," I said. "He must have diddled a supplier, who had him killed. All the earmarks are there. Those people are savages. Awful."

Timmy screwed up his face. "I don't know. Jack seemed pretty straight that last time I saw him. But you never know when people are going to revert."

"People do it."

"Why your car, do you think? Coincidence?"

"Sure. I suppose so, yeah."

"When was the body put there? Out at Faxon's?"

"No, on the street, it looks like—last night, before the car was towed. Or maybe the road crews were involved. Though that's unlikely, because Bowman is sure to bang their heads around, and big-dope entrepreneurs aren't that dumb. Hell, I should have moved my car when you told me to."

"You got distracted and forgot."

"Then fell asleep. In fact, I wouldn't mind sleeping right through until April. The bears have the right idea. They're the only mammals who know how to live in this dreary, desolate place." He grimaced. "Sorry—I backslid. There I go again. Sorry. Really."

"Maybe if you'd make an *effort* to enjoy winter, you'd do better. There are alternatives to cabin fever. For example, let's both learn to ski. How about that? It'd be fun and it'd be healthful."

"That would require my moving about out of doors. My idea of a winter sport is knocking around on a sunfish off Virgin Gorda."

He sighed very deeply. "I'm going in and sit by the picture of the fire and read. How much more snow are we suppose to get? Have you heard?"

The "picture of the fire" was a framed photograph of the San Francisco fire given to us by a friend as a housewarming gift a year earlier when Timmy and I picked up our tiny Federal-style town house on Crow Street for something in the neighborhood of two-point-six billion dollars and discovered that the "working fireplace" described by the realtor didn't.

I said, "We're supposed to get another five inches or so. That will bring the season's total to four hundred feet, five inches."

"You're exaggerating slightly."

"But not much."

We cleaned up the kitchen, went in and saw the snow sloshing down the living room windowpane, put on some Thelonius Monk, and spent the evening by the picture of the fire. At eleven-fifteen the bright-eyed man who soft-shoed in front of the Channel 12 weather map said it now looked as if the earlier snow forecasts had been too conservative and "a lot more of the white stuff" was on the way. Timmy shrugged.

"I hear bells, ringing and ringing."

"I'd better get it, it's after one. Shift, this way." I groped for the phone.

"It's never been this way for me before. The electric mattress pad moved."

"Don't give me quotes from *Wings of the Dove* at a time like this." I found it. "This is Strachey."

"You got something that doesn't belong to you."

"Come again?"

"Who is it?"

"Shhh."

"I think you can tell that we are serious people, Strachey."

"No, I can't tell that at all. Rude presumption is not the same as seriousness. May I ask who is calling, please?"

"We'll be in touch tomorrow about the delivery. We just want you to know that we know you got it. Keep yourself available and do *not* leave Albany."

"Mr. Strachey isn't here. This is the chimney sweep. If you'd like to leave your name and number—" Click.

With two fingers I shoved the receiver toward its cradle and it rattled down into it.

"I sense that you are suddenly preoccupied. Who was that?"

"He didn't say. It was a man with a handkerchief over his mouth, or a large tablecloth. He said I have something that doesn't belong to me."

"What is it?"

"He didn't mention that either."

"Public libraries are starting to crack down. Do you have a book overdue?"

"He said I could see that he was a serious person. 'People'—he said 'serious people.' And he'd be in touch about the delivery."

"Floral?"

"No, I think I'm the deliverer. Of this thing I have that doesn't belong to me. He had a hard voice—nasty, even through the hankie."

"Hell, then give it to him."

"I haven't got it. I *think* I haven't." I extricated myself and reached for an imaginary cigarette.

"Maybe this has something to do with Jack Lenihan. Are you going to call Bowman?"

I struck an imaginary match and took a deep drag. "In the morning. Ned's unconscious at this hour."

He straightened out the covers, looking solemn. "This thing you're supposed to have—maybe it's what Jack Lenihan was killed for."

"That passed through my mind."

"Are you still interested in Guadeloupe? We could drive down to Kennedy and be there in time for an early morning flight, be on the beach by noon."

"No, now I'm curious."

"Nnn."

"Look, let me spend a few days clearing up this obvious misunderstanding, and then it'll be the weekend and we can get the hell off this ice floe for a couple of weeks—fly away and really thaw out. Were you serious about that?"

A little silence. Then: "I guess not. I can't now. Not while the legislature's in session. You know that."

I stared over at him for a few seconds, and then I physically assaulted him. He fought back, in his way, and I didn't mind. Hudson Valley winters were not a total loss.

THREE

THE SCHOOLS WERE CLOSED, THE CAP-itol and state offices shut down. Eighteen inches of new snow had fallen overnight on top of the foot that had dropped the night before. WGY described a front that had stalled unexpectedly. I called them up and said it certainly hadn't surprised me, and they thanked me for my interest.

While Timmy fixed his Wheatena I ran my three eggs through the blender with a pint of orange juice. Each of us found the other's early morning culinary habits nauseating, so we stayed on separate sides of the kitchen.

I phoned Ned Bowman at Division 2 headquarters, where he'd just come in. "What have you come up with on Jack Lenihan's death?"

"No, no, Strachey, *I'm* the police officer, *you're* the material witness. I want you in my office at one P.M. promptly. I want to run over this thing with you one more time at least. Lenihan was one of yours, you know, which gets me to thinking. Oh yes, he was definitely one of yours."

"I'm childless, so far as I know. Briget, my ex, liked to confide in me, in spite of everything, and she would have mentioned that."

"You know what I mean, damn well you do. You met Lenihan at some swish tea party last summer at Mr. Herbert Brinkman's house in Niskayuna. You knew the body was Lenihan's last night, but you didn't mention it to me, and I demand to know why. One o'clock, on the dot."

"You're wrong about my recognizing Lenihan, but otherwise, Ned, you've been quick and you've been thorough. This is unprecedented and I'm impressed. Is there anything from the medical examiner yet?"

"No, except that Lenihan is certifiably dead. Fucking geniuses look at a six-foot icicle and say, 'That man will never bowl again.' I'll get a report later today that might have a little more in it to go on."

"Has Warren Slonski been notified? He's Lenihan's lover, or was as of last summer—which, incidentally, was the first and last time I ever saw Lenihan."

"You mean has Slonski been *questioned*, and the answer is yes. I caught him early before he left for work this morning. Of course, he'd already heard about it on the media, he says. Sort of a stuck-up prick, this Slonski—Mr. Pretty Boy. He claims he hasn't seen Lenihan since Christmas, but I'll be checking that out. He was not what I would call entirely cooperative."

Bowman's idea of "entirely cooperative" was a man who brought along a certified stenographer to take down his own confession. I thought, I should have gotten there first. To break the news in a decent way, to find out what I could before Slonski got turned off by the clubfoot crew, and of course to cast eyes on "Mr. Pretty Boy."

I said, "I received a phone call that might be connected to Lenihan's death. I'll tell you about it when I see you at one."

"You'll tell me now."

"No, it can wait. Are the roads passable? I might need to do some moving around today. When can I get my car back? If the city of Albany wants to lease it for five bills a week that's one thing, but—"

"What do you mean, you got a phone call? This is a criminal—"

"One o'clock." I hung up. The phone rang fifteen seconds later. "It's Bowman, but don't answer it. I don't want to talk to him again until I've checked on a couple of things."

Timmy shrugged and went back to meditating over his Wheatena.

"May I use your car? You're not going to work today. Nobody on the public payroll is." He nodded. "Don't answer the phone at all, if you don't mind. I'll call my service and they can pick up there. You deserve a day of peace and quiet. Or are you going out to play with your sled and enjoy winter?"

"I might go for a walk in the park. It'll be really lovely. Want to join me later?"

"Sure, if you'll pull my Flexie-Flyer."

"Yeah, I'll pull your Flexie-Flyer. Isn't that all we're supposed to do these days?"

"And look—if Hankie-mouth should show up at the house, tell him to leave a message with my service and I'll make myself available later today."

Despite the Wheatena clogging his veins, his eyes grew alert. "He might come here? You think so?"

"It's possible, yes."

"Maybe I'll just walk down to the office and spend the day clearing up a few things. It'll be as quiet there as it is here."

"Good idea."

"I'll shovel the walk first."

"Lift with your arms and not with your back. That's what the radio said. You're past forty now and might have a heart attack."

"Nah, I'm twenty-seven. I'll always be twenty-seven."

I kissed him on the little bald spot on the back of his head and left him to his bowl of mush.

The blizzard had moved off into northern New England, leaving a churning gray sky that still spit occasional teasing showers of snow. Cold sunlight broke through in a few places and I brought my shades along for when the sky cleared and the city turned into a million-watt icecap. Instead of digging out Timmy's car, a white lump, I hiked over toward Central Avenue, crunch-crunch, crunch-crunch.

Most of the cars out were blue Volvos with skis on racks heading toward the interstates and on to the Adirondacks and Berkshires—people who paid for their good times with numbed extremities and cracked lips, who finished off a day of fun by having to coat Vaseline on the wrong orifice. I'd always enjoyed the sweet variety of the human race in its pursuit of pleasure, however, and if a face full of ice was what turned on these LL Bean Vikings, who was I to care what they did in the privacy of their own mountains?

I walked up the middle of Crow Street on the hard-packed snow. The city plows had been out early, maybe due to the fact that it was a mayoral election year, when the Democratic machine tends to become visible, providing the odd useful service. At Crow and Lancaster a disabled city snow-removal truck had been abandoned in the center of the intersection forcing the Volvos and delivery vans to detour carefully around it. One end of its steel plow rested on the street where it had gouged out a section of tarmac. The driver's side door hung open, as if the driver had been driven off by attackers, maybe Republican terrorists, the Governor Thomas E. Dewey Brigades. Election years in Albany can be turbulent.

I headed up Lark, where some of the boutiques and spinach-salad joints were opening up, their owners apparently hoping the state workers would occupy their sudden leisure with some recreational spending. The street was cleaner than I had ever seen it and the few people walking along it looked happy to be out and taking part in a harmless emergency.

On Central Avenue I glanced through the frosted window of the Watering Hole, where a few of the regulars had already shown up for an early light brunch. I could hear the jukebox playing something pleasantly sordid, but it seemed a bit early in the day for that—or late in the decade—and I didn't stop in.

My office was locked up and unmolested. I turned the key and shoved the door open and nothing blew up. There was no evidence of forced or unforced entry, and I could see no sign of the "thing" that didn't belong to me having been left there by Jack Lenihan or anyone else. I half wanted it to be there. If a man hadn't been killed, I would have welcomed any distraction from my sour hibernation. As would Timmy, whose tolerance for lighthearted dishiness was high but for bitchiness low. I guess he'd learned from the Jesuits how to make distinctions like that.

I slid the pie tin out from under the leaky radiator valve and dumped the rusty bilge that had accumulated into the plastic bucket resting nearby for that purpose. I spilled about a third of a cup on my boots and wiped them off with the old T-shirt that lay along the windowsill as a puny obstacle against the winter wind.

Wednesday's mail was still on the floor where it had been shoved through the door slot the previous afternoon, which I'd spent tracking down my car. There were three invitations to purchase a sewing machine and win a free trip to Las Vegas, and an envelope with a dollar bill in it from a former client who was paying me off a dollar a week for three thousand weeks. The fifth item was a slip from the postal service notifying me that a registered letter was waiting for me at the main post office. I slid the slip into my wallet.

The Albany phone book showed a Colonie listing for John C. Lenihan. I called directory assistance and was given a new number for Lenihan on Swan Street, which I dialed. I let it ring for a full minute. Down on Central traffic was starting to build. Behind the beer truck double-parked in front of Jimmy's Lounge a rusty beige Buick sat idling with a man in a baby-shit-brown leather jacket behind the wheel. He was smoking something and looked settled in.

I hung up the phone, locked the office and went down the back stairs to the fire exit. Snow had drifted against the door, but I shoved it open far enough to angle my way out, then over a fence and through a backyard to Washington Avenue. Snow worked its way down into my boots, and I figured if I kept this up I'd have to stop off somewhere for a couple of bread bags and two rubber bands.

Back on Crow Street I opened the passenger door of Timmy's big snowball, retrieved the snow brush from the back seat—no body was on it—and went to work. The plastic handle snapped under the wet weight and I ended up swiping the rest of the car clean with my arms. Snow seeped into my gloves, and I thought again of the islands.

I warmed up the Subaru, rocked it to and fro for a time, then shot onto the roadway and over toward State, trailing chunks of flying snow like James Bond firing at a pursuing nemesis. My pursuer, undeterred, was the green Chevy pickup that had been parked across from our house when I'd passed it ten minutes earlier. I sailed down State on the hardpack, then left on Broadway. I drove around to the back of the main post office, through the gateway, past the columns of mail trucks, up a ramp, and into a loading bay. The green pickup did not follow.

"Hey, you can't park there!"

"Governor's office," I chirruped, and flashed my library card. "Special-delivery birthday greetings for Mario's mom!" I fled on into the building, signed for the registered letter, pocketed it carefully, strode out, drove down the ramp at the far end of the loading dock, exited through the gateway opposite the one I'd come in through, lined up on the north side of a CDTA bus about to cross Broadway, then stayed with it through the intersection. The pickup truck was nowhere in sight.

On Lodge Street I parked alongside the Hilton, went in and booked a double room under the name Hiram Nestlerode.

"But that's not the name on your credit card," the clerk pointed out. I'd seen him around, at the Watering Hole, the Green Room, Uncle Charlie's Far North.

I winked. "Look, I'm really Engelbert Humperdinck, here for a sold-out concert at the Coliseum, and I'd just like a little privacy, that's all, a little discretion on your part. You know how it goes." I winked again.

His experienced desk clerk's eyebrow went up. "My dear, you don't look the least bit like Engelbert Humperdinck. You look more like—Tom Selleck, except with a few years on him."

"That's who I am actually—Tom Selleck with a few years on him. Now just give me a room, will you?"

"Welcome to Albany, Mr. Selleck. If there's anything I

can do—anything at all—to make your stay more enjoyable, just let me know. Ask for Malcolm."

"You're too kind."

"Have you any luggage?"

"It's en route from the airport."

"I'll have it sent right up. Perhaps I'll carry it up myself. *Front!*"

The envelope, with no return address, was postmarked Los Angeles, the previous Monday, January 14, P.M. The letter inside was dated January 13 and was handwritten on two sheets of plain white inexpensive typing paper. Taped to the bottom of the second sheet were five tiny keys.

Dear Mr. Strachey,

We met one time last summer, and I am hoping you remember me. I was at Herb Brinkman's pool party and we talked about the Democratic convention which was coming up soon. You might recall that I was a Jessie Jackson supporter for the Rainbow Coalition and you said you were for Morris Udall. I argued that your vote would be wasted because Udall was not running. Do you remember me now?

Although I disagreed with your position on certain issues, I got the strong impression that you are a man of integrity who can be trusted to do the right thing when the chips are down. Other people I know said the same thing about you recently, even though you are rather weird in some ways, but I can relate to that.

Mr. Strachey, I need your help very much right now, and I am in a position to pay for it. A large sum of money has come into my possession, and my request is that you keep it safe for me until I can dispose of it in an appropriate manner.

You are probably wondering why I don't deposit this "fortune" in a bank—is this money "hot" in some way? I just want to say that what I am doing might be illegal, strictly speaking, but it is not immoral. *Not in the least way. On the contrary.*

I have heard about the way you think, and I'm sure you will agree with me. For the time being, it is in your interest if I do not explain the details of this project completely. This way you will be protected if anything goes wrong. Some people are very pissed off at me, but all you would have to do is show this letter bearing my signature to prove your lack of knowledge.

If you ask anybody, you might get an earful from certain people that I am a rotten apple. Well, I have had my ups and downs, good times and bad, this is very true, I admit. But all that is in the past, and for the first time in my life I am taking a positive attitude toward certain things instead of negative.

I have a chance to make up for a *very great amount of evil*, and don't you think I would be a "real shit" and a coward if I did not embark on this project?

You must be confused, but I am asking you as a gay friend and a concerned citizen to *trust me!!*

I will be back in Albany as soon as I clear up some matters and I will contact you. Please take what you charge as your fee and for your expenses. I hope you don't mind me doing it this way, but I don't have any choice. You are the only person I can trust right now who is "street-smart" and not connected with me in an "obvious" way.

When you find out the nature of the project you have participated in, you won't be ashamed. You will be proud of yourself, just like I will be proud of myself for the first time in my fucked-up life.

> Your friend,
> (signed)
> Jack Lenihan

I reread the letter, and then I began to forget about the weather.

FOUR

I PHONED TIMMY, WHO SAID HE WAS
alone in his office reading a book, probably *Nanook of the
North*.

"Don't go back to the house."

"Why?"

I described the morning's events and read him the letter.

"You talked me into it. I won't go back to the house."

"I've got a room at the Hilton. Come over here when
you're ready to leave. I'm either Hiram Nestlerode or Tom
Selleck, I'm not sure which."

"Your usual state of affairs."

"Or Engelbert Humperdinck."

"Nah."

I said, "What do you make of it?"

"It's obvious. Lenihan stole some big doper's payoff boodle, and he was going to use it to finance—I don't know
what—blowing up the Federal Building?"

"It wouldn't require a 'fortune'—Lenihan's word—to do
that. No, it's something big but less loony, something that
only a rigid mind would consider wrong or morally ambiguous. Maybe something with political implications—an act
against the machine he's known to loathe. He seemed so
certain that I'd approve."

"It wasn't morally ambiguous to *him*. But he might have
been nuts."

"Yeah, but you can be nuts *and* be right. It's happened in
history."

"*King of Hearts* must have come around again. Are you
going to show Bowman the letter?"

"I guess not. No, that letter is confidential. It's from a
client."

"A *dead* client. Your contract with Lenihan—which didn't exist when he was alive anyway because you'd never agreed to be a party to it—is breached upon his death."

"Is that the kind of so-called logic they taught you at Georgetown? I'd always thought the Jesuits had a finer appreciation for the moral potential in legalistic murk. Anyway, until I hear otherwise I'm going to consider Lenihan's *estate* as my client. His estate, and his good intentions. He really sounds in the letter as if he was about to climb out of the grubby pit he thought he'd spent all his life in. Maybe I can still help him do that."

"Don, he'll never know."

"Yeah, he won't. I want to meet the people who prevented him from knowing it though. That has nothing to do with contracts."

"Well, you're going to do what you're going to do."

"Short of getting my head bashed in, yes. Or yours. If it looks as if it's coming to that, the hell with it."

"Thank you."

"I'll give them the money and fly to San Juan. If I have it."

"Who's delivering the money to you?"

"Lenihan didn't say. I plan on asking the deliverer a few questions though."

"Maybe it'll never show up. Maybe *it's* on the way to San Juan or Bogota. Then where will you be?"

"Room 1407 at the Hilton. For the rest of my life."

"Well, you'll get to finish Proust."

I phoned a contact at the Federal Building and asked him if Jack Lenihan's name had come up in any recent narcotics investigations.

"Funny you should ask. Ned Bowman was just wondering about that too. I just got off the line with him."

"What frame of mind was he in?"

"He was the usual charmer. Hey, Strachey, what do you

think of all this snow? I figured you'd be off at Killington or Mount Snow. Half the younger guys in the office are out sick today—called in with the flu, but, hell, I know better than that."

"The snorkeling is poor at Mount Snow this time of year. So when Bowman asked about Lenihan, what did you tell him?"

"Lenihan was clean as far as I know, and I'd know. Evidence can take a while to develop—forever in too many cases—but names I've got plenty of. They come up, and Lenihan's is not one of them. I'd say he learned his lesson when he slipped away from us in eighty-two. That's rare, but it happens."

"Isn't it possible he'd just gotten back into it? Within the past couple of weeks?"

"Possible, yes."

"His killing has the earmarks, right?"

"From what little I know. But being clubbed on the brain is a real popular way of getting killed in America. Aunt Minnie, Cousin Bud—everybody does it. Don't you read the *Post*?"

"I'm just looking for a pattern here."

"I see it was your car Lenihan got dumped in. If it was dopers I'd say they were sending you a message, Strachey. Listen, pal, you got some kind of problem? You know what we're here for."

I said, "No, no problems of mine. I'm just trying to clear my car's good name."

"What's its name?"

"Rabbit."

"No investigator worth shit is gonna have a car named Rabbit. My car's called Fox. You really ought to get one of those, do your work a world of good. Look, if I can help out, let me know. And if you should hear about anything relating to my field of expertise that might interest me, I'd appreciate it."

"Sure, as always."

"Not always."

"Sometimes."

"That's more like it."

I spent half an hour phoning Herb Brinkman and other people who had known Jack Lenihan socially. I learned that he had had no known close friends other than Warren Slonski and that no one had even seen him socially for the past three months. He had pretty much dropped out of sight in mid-October. Everyone who had known Lenihan had been shocked by the news of his death and couldn't imagine that he had made such a lethal enemy—unless he was dealing dope again.

I lay back on the bed I'd rented for a night—or longer—and thought about Lenihan's letter. Outside, the gray sky over the Rensselaer hills was falling apart as if an icebreaker had chugged through it. White sunlight poured across my legs, was gone in an instant, then broke over me again. It was twenty till ten and I had time for one more quick call, to a friend at American Airlines.

"Don Strachey. I need some flight information."

"Where to, Donald? To warmer climes, I'll bet."

"I wish. But this isn't for me—yet. A John C. Lenihan may have been in Los Angeles on Monday. I'd like to know when he went out there and when he came back."

"I don't believe, sir, that you quite understand how our system works. What I will need is a flight number and a date."

"Listen, Alex, that's why I'm calling *you*. *You* have that information. You're the airline, I'm the inquiring consumer. Can't you rummage around in your machine? Let's say he went out Saturday and came back Monday or Tuesday. Try that."

"He might have gone United or USAIR."

"From Albany you've got the most flights and the best

connections. Just shake that thing a couple of times and see what drops out, will you?"

"Hang on, I'm putting you on hold."

"Don't play any music."

He did—a mononucleotic string arrangement of "Good Golly, Miss Molly." It went on for minutes.

"Donald?"

"Yo."

"A John Lenihan flew to LAX, changing at O'Hare, last Friday, January eleven, departing Albany five-eighteen P.M., arriving Los Angeles eight thirty-one. Mr. Lenihan returned on Tuesday, January fifteen, departing LAX at ten-fifteen A.M., changing at O'Hare, arriving Albany at seven-forty P.M. Lenihan—isn't that the name of the guy who was murdered, John Lenihan?"

I wrote the dates and times in my notebook. "No, that was John Hanrahan. This one's a friend of mine."

"I thought I heard it was Lenihan. They found his body in a car somewhere—at a garage, frozen solid."

"Say, how's Joe doing?"

"Fantastic. He finishes his residency in June, and then we might get to spend half a day together."

"What will you do to celebrate?"

"He'll probably sleep. I'll watch some TV."

"Well, cheers."

"Thanks."

I removed the five small keys from Lenihan's letter. Each had a number painted on it, one through five, with what looked like fuchsia-colored nail polish. The numbering was sloppy, as if done with a nail-polishing brush, and small bits had begun to flake off. I inserted the keys onto my own key ring, pocketed the letter, and headed out into the winter playland.

FIVE

I PUSHED THE BUTTON UNDER *J. LENIHAN* three times and got no response. It looked as if he had lived alone since his split with Warren Slonski. My Sears card popped the front-door lock on the old Victorian town house, now broken up into six small apartments. Sooty dun-colored paint was flaking off the stairwell walls, and the winding staircase itself hung ten degrees into the abyss and groaned as I moved up it. I stayed close to the wall.

My lobster pick got me into Lenihan's apartment, where lobster had not been served recently, just eggs, peanut butter and Wonder Bread. The kitchenette and one small drafty room were strewn with clothing, books, papers; the place had been turned inside out recently by someone, or someones, no doubt including the Albany cops. Whoever had done it had possessed keys, or at least a lobster pick.

Among the debris beside the rumpled daybed were a phone book, on the back of which were the word "Ma" and a Los Angeles area number, which I wrote down. I found no checkbook, phone bills, or other useful financial records—I figured Bowman must have waltzed off with them—but I did come up with a single stub off a week-old payroll check with Lenihan's name on it from Annie's Quiche Quorner on Lark Street. I knew the place.

The only other objects that seemed remarkable in Lenihan's gloomy quarters were a complete four-volume set of Morris Gerber's *Old Albany*, uninscribed and otherwise unmarked, and a battered RCA LP called "Opera for People Who Hate Opera." The other books were paperback bestsellers—Ludlum, Higgins, MacLean. Stacked up next to the discount-store stereo setup were thirty or forty 1960s rock

LPs—the Dead, Van Morrison, Janis Joplin, the Stones. I found no narcotics, no "fortune," and no clue suggesting that the occupant of this sorry little hole-in-the-wall had had recent possession of either.

I drove west on back streets, found an unoccupied snowbank on Jay, pulled up along it, and walked around to Annie's Quiche Quorner. With the state offices shut down the place wasn't busy during the lunch hour, so I was able to question Annie and her two waiters.

Once it was established that I was neither a health inspector nor a cop—Bowman had called on Annie earlier and left a poor impression—they talked a little, but only to say they knew little of Jack Lenihan's personal life, were horrified by his dying, and couldn't imagine what kind of mess he might have gotten into that ended in his being killed. I asked if Lenihan might have been dealing drugs, and Annie, an immense sloe-eyed woman in black pants, said, "I wouldn't know about that."

The two waiters—who, like nearly everybody else on jazzy Lark Street, appeared to be twenty-five and not wasting a minute of it—looked at each other.

"He got me some hash once," one of them said.

"Was it any good?"

"The best."

"Did he say where he got it?"

"Shit, no. And I didn't ask."

"Mister," Annie said, "within a hundred yards of where you're sitting you could probably find two hundred people who could get you any type of controlled substance your heart desires. Stand out on the sidewalk and hold up a sign that you want drugs and they'll crawl right up out of the manholes. Jack probably just walked around the corner and asked anybody on the street. That doesn't make him a criminal."

"Did Jack have visitors here?" I asked.

"There were a couple people who came in who knew

him," Annie said. "Neighborhood people, people he knew, I dunno. He didn't seem to have any real friends, not that came in here. Jack was nice, but he was a loner, I'd say."

"What about that guy last Friday," one of the waiters said, "who kept looking for Jack?"

"Oh, yeah, that spiffy one," Annie said, remembering. "He came in a couple of times asking for Jack when he wasn't here— Jack was mostly working nights. This guy looked more like lower State Street than Lark—La Serre or the Fort Orange Club. Good-looking older fella with an alpaca topcoat and a fifty-dollar haircut. I thought I'd seen his face before, but I couldn't place it. In the movies or somewhere."

"Did he mention why he was looking for Jack?"

"He didn't say. He sure was anxious to track him down, though—came by later the same day and said Jack wasn't home, he'd tried his apartment. I told him Jack had the weekend off and didn't say where he'd be. The guy seemed real itchy to get in touch."

"Did he leave his name or any other message?"

"Unh-unh."

"Has he come back at all?"

"Nope. Hey, you said you're a private detective. Who're you working for anyway, Jack's family?"

"No, did he talk about them?"

"Not a word. I was amazed when I saw in the paper Jack was Pug Lenihan's grandson. A historical family, he came from, and Jack never let on."

"Did Jack mention any sort of project he was working on?"

"Project? What kind?"

"Any kind."

"If Jack had a project I think it went on inside his head. I always had the feeling there was an awful lot going on in there the rest of us were never gonna hear about. Jack came to work for me last October, and he looked like he had a lot on his mind when he got here and he looked like he had a lot on his mind the last time he left. Three months is a long time to be wrapped up in your thoughts like that. I'd've had a headache myself. Maybe it was some kind of family thing or project, is that what you mean? I know Jack was close to his mom. He was just back from seeing her in California when he started here last fall. Maybe she knows more about his private life. Maybe you should talk to her."

"You're right. Maybe I should."

I had four eggs with sausage and home fries, and then Annie let me use the phone to call my service, which had four messages, all "urgent." Three were from Creighton Prell, Larry Dooley, and Sim Kempelman, each of whom had left a number and asked that I call back as soon as possible regarding a matter of the utmost importance. The fourth was from an unnamed caller who said the "delivery" should take place that night at midnight at the corner of Clinton and South Pearl, and that there would be "no hassle."

"If the mysterious one calls back," I told the service's operator, "tell him to leave a number where he can be reached, that I'm willing to talk about it."

Next I phoned Alex at American Airlines.

"I'm awfully busy, Don. We had to cancel two flights last night on account of the storm, and I'm up to here with people who'll die if they don't get to Chicago, though God knows why."

"When you've got a free minute, I need dates and times on an October trip that John C. Lenihan took to LA and back."

"When in October?"

"Right, when in October?"

"I mean, early, late, what?"

"I'm not sure. Early to mid, I think."

"Do you realize that could take me two hours? It's one thing to violate FAA regulations, something else to stay late doing it. Like I say, we've got problems out here."

"So you'll miss 'One Hundred Thousand Dollar Name

That Tune' this evening. Listen, I'll buy you a Molson next time I run into you on the avenue."

He fumed amiably for another minute before we struck a deal: two Molsons and a plate of the peppered beef with black mushrooms at the Peking in return for the flight information. Airlines never give you anything without a lot of conditions attached.

The thermometer in Annie's doorway read eleven degrees Fahrenheit, but the wind speed had dropped, so I donned my shades against the glare and pretended I was at St. Kitts on an off day.

"You lied to me, Strachey, you bald-faced lied. You acted like you didn't even know who Lenihan was, which made me suspicious right away, because it wasn't like whoever killed Jack Lenihan dumped him in just any citizen's car. No, it had to be yours, and you put on your 'What? Who, me?' innocent bullshit performance like you're goddamn Mother McRae."

"Carmen?"

"You're up to your pouf eyeballs in this thing, Strachey. You know it and I know it, and now I am going to hear all about it—how, and why, and what for, and no more bullshit-horseshit-crap out of you, or believe me, you are not going to walk out of this building today. I'll see to that."

Bowman still had his hideous nose disease. This might have affected his outlook, which never had been sunny, though I had seen him less fatuously airheaded on one or two previous occasions. As he spoke, Bowman's hand kept coming up toward his nose, but apparently he had been instructed to avoid scratching the gruesome appendage, because the hand always made a quick frightened detour of his face, then went restlessly back to his lap or over to his desktop, where it fingered what looked like a glass of iced prune juice.

I said, "Are you finished venting? May Harrisburg residents return to their homes now?"

"Of course not, no. Now then, Strachey. Last night I thoroughly examined Jack Lenihan's apartment. The place had already been tossed real good by somebody who got there first. It was you, wasn't it?"

"No."

"I thought probably it wasn't. You know why? Because in amongst Lenihan's effects I found this."

"That's my business card."

"Yeah, isn't it, though. *Your business card*—'Donald Strachey, Private Investigations'—in amongst the papers of the man who died by murder *in your car*. Now then. You are about to assist with this homicide investigation instead of obstructing it. You are going to explain to me what was your connection with John C. Lenihan. I'm all ears. Go."

I said, "When I met Lenihan last summer I must have given him my card and he kept it—for whatever reasons. And lately he's been throwing my name around without my knowledge or consent—also for reasons unknown. Lenihan apparently told somebody that I have something of his. Or theirs. But I don't."

He shifted irritably, the hand leaving the prune-juice glass and making a quick pass at the nose. "Something of whose? Who told you that?"

"I received an anonymous telephone call last night from a man with a tablecloth in his mouth who said I had something that didn't belong to me and he wanted it."

"Dope?"

"I don't know. The caller offered no specifics. He said I could see how serious he and his people were, and I took this to mean that they had killed Jack and left him in my car."

"Keep talking."

"That's it. I'm trying to figure it all out myself. Lenihan must have gotten me confused with someone else. There's been a misunderstanding apparently."

"A pack of stinking lies from beginning to end. Anonymous caller my ass."

"Not at all. Ned, do us both a favor and search my house. And my office too. Here are my keys, you won't need a warrant. Maybe I do have something of Lenihan's—some stuff that was left in my house when we bought it last year, or whatever. Send some of your guys out there and turn the place inside out—not too crudely, please—and see what you can turn up. If you can find a connection between me and Jack Lenihan, I'm the one who'd most like to hear about it. Will you do it?"

As I spoke, Bowman scratched energetically away on a legal pad, his nose substitute. He said, "You're setting me up, aren't you?"

"For what? What would the point be?"

"Maybe waste my time, buy time for yourself."

"I've got all the time in the world. I'm thirty-six years old and have most of my life ahead of me."

"You're no friggin' thirty-six. You're older."

"I meant forty-six, whatever. The point is, I want this craziness cleared up as badly as you do. If I have become inadvertently involved with criminals, I want to extricate myself. I have to, I have a license to keep. I know I've behaved pretty shittily with you on a couple of occasions, Ned, and you don't owe me a damn thing. But I also know that in spite of everything you still believe that people are basically good at heart, and I'm a person."

"Huh?"

"Help me out. Help me get out of this."

"And search your house?"

"If there's something there, I want to know what it is."

"Why don't you search it yourself?"

"Because I'm not going home for a while. I don't want to risk being spotted by the anonymous caller. Timmy and I are staying at the Americana."

"You want me to go over to your place and put on a big show, is that it?"

"Yes."

"You're scared, aren't you?"

"Yes, I am."

He tried to suppress a sneer. "When push comes to shove, you people just haven't got what it takes, have you? It looks to me like you're finally going to have to admit that, Strachey."

"If by 'you people' you mean Presbyterians, Ned, I have to warn you that it might not be a good idea to generalize from my particular situation. Eisenhower was a Presbyterian, and I think MacArthur too. I don't know about Patton. Or McGeorge Bundy."

He scratched at the pad, sniffed with his nose. "Sure, I'll search your house. Maybe I'll find more than you think I'm going to find."

"Could be. And while you're over there, would you mind picking up a few things? I'll leave you a list."

"Don't be ridiculous."

"What did the ME have to report on Lenihan?"

"That is confidential police information."

I flipped a dime onto his desk. "Here—your first bribe."

He actually laughed. And pocketed the dime. "It'll be released to the media today anyway, so what the hell. Lenihan was hit hard at least five times—most of the blows from behind—with a blunt object, probably hard metal. Whatever it was left no residue. He died soon after, in your car, between ten o'clock Tuesday night and one A.M. Wednesday. The forensic indications were that he had not put up much of a struggle, so the second or third hit probably knocked him out. He might've been snuck up on, or maybe the killer was a person he knew and trusted. Since he'd made *some* attempt to defend himself, it's hard to tell."

"So he was actually dumped in my car while it was still on Crow Street."

"Your car wasn't towed until after three. I talked to the crew who hauled it out to Faxon's and they didn't notice anything, but then they wouldn't have, because your windows were all frosted up from what are presumed to have been Lenihan's last breaths. Or maybe when you parked your car that night you let one rip. We didn't analyze the window moisture."

"When had Lenihan last eaten?"

"Dinner that night, it looked like. Some kind of creamed-chicken shit."

"Creamed chickenshit?"

"Creamed chicken."

"What about Lenihan's car? Has it turned up?"

"He didn't own one. His friends say he rode the bus."

"What about my car? Was there anything helpful in it?"

"No prints, if that's what you mean. Just yours, which the state of New York wisely keeps on file. Whoever touched anything wore gloves. These are pros we're dealing with here, Strachey, it is plainly evident."

"Everybody's wearing gloves this month. It's cold out. When can I get my car back?"

"Tomorrow maybe. We'll see."

"Lenihan wore glasses. Have they been found?"

"Nah. They must have been knocked off wherever he got conked."

"Lenihan was away from his apartment over the weekend. Have you been able to track where he went?"

"Not yet. We're talking to his family and the people he knew, but nobody's been very goddamn helpful. There are a couple of them I might have to go back and lean on a little." He wrinkled his nose as if to try to make it scratch itself.

I said, "This looks like a dopers' execution, doesn't it? Is that the angle you're pursuing?"

"You know what Lenihan's record was. Of course that's what it is. I think you know that, Strachey. I think you know a whole lot more about this than you're letting on, that's what I think."

"Well, you're going to think what you're going to think."
I passed him my spare set of house and office keys. "It's 218
Crow Street, and you know where the office is. If you want
to use searchlights and bullhorns that's okay, but once you're
inside try not to get any fingerprints on the Millie Jackson
records. That's all I ask."

He gave me his demented-dunce look. "Just keep yourself available, Strachey. I mean it. I want you at my beck and
call."

"I'm always at your beck and call, Ned. Especially your
beck. If you need me for anything, just press your lips together and—beck."

"Take care of yourself. You want protection of some
kind?"

"Nah, I'm cool."

"You're at the Sheraton?"

"Americana."

"Oh, yeah."

As I went out the door I thought I caught him out of the
corner of my eye dunking his nose in the glass of prune
juice, but that couldn't have been.

The blue Dodge with two of Bowman's junior dicks in it
stayed a block behind me up Pearl. On the snowy roadway I
fishtailed into the maze of old colonial streets downhill from
the capitol and lost them in ninety seconds. Back in my
room at the Hilton I reread Lenihan's letter, laid it and my
notes out on the desk, and studied what I had. I concluded
that the people who murdered Jack Lenihan were either
very smart or very dumb, were certainly very desperate, and
were to be avoided for as long as was necessary, but not a
split second longer than that.

SIX

I HAD TIMMY ON THE LINE.

"Is it okay to go back to the house yet? I'm bored and I need my toothbrush."

"Timothy, you're so easily entertained. No, don't go back there at all. I've arranged to confuse Hankie-mouth, and for the house not to get firebombed, but either of us showing up on Crow Street might still be risky. Come on over to the Hilton and watch the soaps, pick up a bellhop, brush your teeth, whatever amuses you. Enjoy your day of character-building winter."

"Are you going to be there?"

"I have to go out for a while."

"Maybe I'll take the bus out to Macy's and shop around for a few things. When are you getting your car back?"

"Tomorrow, I think, but I wouldn't drive either yours or mine around Albany for a few days. I'm picking up a rental and maybe you should too."

"Don, this is getting expensive. Who's going to finance all this anyway? Your sort-of-client is dead, and I'm willing to bet you're not in his will."

"US bank notes are going to turn up soon. I can feel them getting closer and closer. Money is not going to be the problem, I think."

"What is?"

"Keeping it."

"But it's not yours. This has been pointed out."

"It's Jack Lenihan's money and should be disposed of as he would have liked."

"Except he obviously stole it from God-knows-who, and anyway you don't know what he would have liked. What he would have liked died with him."

"I don't think so."

"What do you know that you're not telling me? Spit it out."

"Not much. I'll know more by the end of the day—I think."

"Well, I'm going out to charge some underwear and socks and find something to read."

"You aren't enjoying *Nanook?*" He hung up.

I reached Warren Slonski at Schenectady General Electric and set up a meeting with him. He also provided me with the name and address of Jack Lenihan's sister in the North End. I phoned my service and was informed that the three pols who had tried to reach me earlier had been calling repeatedly and were becoming a nuisance. I left instructions on when and where they could meet me that evening.

Hankie-mouth had phoned, the service operator told me, but had declined to leave a number. I said if he called again to tell him yes, okay, I'd meet him that night at midnight at Clinton and Pearl. One other message had been left for me. The Greyhound station had called to notify me that my bags had arrived from Los Angeles and I could pick them up anytime. I rented a Hertz car and drove it south just four blocks.

The Greyhound station was the usual winter wonderland of wet footprints, cold drafts, college kids with backpacks, bag ladies dozing, and garbled announcements—"Bah number ploot now boarding at gay nake for Nansimer, Bumppo, Pootiton and Garkfark"—causing travelers throughout the waiting room to crane their necks and squint at the disembodied sounds futilely.

I showed my driver's license as an ID to the clerk at the freight window, and he called for a young lackey who trundled out five good-sized suitcases. They were not chic and new but they looked sturdy enough. I signed for the bags, left three with the clerk while I carried two out and locked them in the trunk of the rental car, then made two more trips back for the remaining suitcases.

No one watched me or followed me, so far as I was aware, and I was plenty aware. As I eased the last bag into the car I noted on the waybill it had been sent from Los Angeles on Monday, January 14, the day Lenihan had mailed his letter to me. The return address was a street in West Hollywood, and the sender was J. Lenihan. I ripped the waybills off each of the bags and stuffed the papers in my coat pocket.

At the Hilton main entrance I left the bags with the bell captain—"My damn bags didn't make the connection in St. Louis"—and tipped him, with instructions to deposit the suitcases in room 1407. He barked for an underling and I drove off.

The old Irish North End of Albany is full of ghosts for the natives, but I'm from New Jersey, so the spirits kept mum as I headed up North Pearl. The snowplows were out in force now, tidying up the landscape for the electorate. Jefferson was right that compulsory free education is a bulwark of democratic civilization, ranking near the top of any list of essential institutions, not too far below snow removal. Albany city government understood this every four years.

I passed under I-90, which since the 1960s flew across the Hudson on concrete pillars and sliced up a valley separating the North End from the rest of the city. The old neighborhood of double-deckers and single-family frame houses set close together was not quite decrepit, but verging on it, despite obvious spunky efforts to patch, paint over, prop up, and adorn. The parochial school was boarded up, but Sacred Heart Church looked humbly enduring behind a little plaza of snow-covered maples and oaks. A snowman wearing a red knit cap stood at the edge of the park, though I saw few children out. The sons and daughters of the old-neighborhood Irish had made it into Super America and gone off to the suburbs, except of course for those few who hadn't, and the old people who chose to stay behind or hadn't been invited anywhere else.

The home of Corrine and Ed McConkey on Walter Street was a two-story box with flaking tan shingles and dark-green wood trim. The front walk had not been shoveled, but what looked like a considerable amount of foot traffic had cleared a narrow path. I walked up it and onto the porch, where a chain swing suspended from the ceiling was coated with blown snow.

The wooden storm door had a plastic sheet stapled into the place where the glass used to be, and the only doorbell was a brass contraption, like an old faucet handle, which I twisted, causing a bell to rattle on the other side of the door. As Timmy had pointed out, the Lenihan clan had seen palmier days.

A lace curtain was jerked aside and a male face glared out at me. The door opened.

"Are you the undertaker?" His tone was surly, abrupt.

"I'm Don Strachey, a friend of Jack's. Is Corrine here? I'd like to say hello."

"Yeah, she's here. You're one of Jack's friends, you said?"

"I hadn't known him long, but we were close."

"Oh yeah? How close?"

A voice from within: "Ed, who is it? You're letting all the cold air in, Ed."

"A friend of Jackie's."

"Well, for heaven's sakes, Ed, ask him to come on in."

He gestured for me to enter, but he didn't look happy about it.

"You must be Ed McConkey, Jack's brother-in-law."

"Yeah."

As I shut the door behind me, a woman appeared, smiling feebly.

I said, "I'm Don Strachey, a friend of Jack's. I feel very bad about what happened to him."

"How do you do, Mr. Strachey, I'm Corrine. Yes, it's awful, isn't it? And so—out of the blue. Jack had a troubled life, but I never dreamed. . . . I just never dreamed. . . ."

Both McConkeys were small thin people with a bruised look whose source seemed deeper than a recent death in the family. Corrine's eyes were red, and Ed's were dull from the kind of fatigue that comes not from exercise or passionate feeling but the lack of either. He wore khaki work clothes that were clean and freshly ironed, and Corrine had on powder-blue slacks and a white turtleneck sweater of a shiny fabric that only drew attention to the dark rings around her eyes. Her smile, though weak, was warm and natural.

I left my boots on a plastic mat in front of the leaky radiator in the front hall. Corrine took my coat and draped it over the radiator itself. The odor of frying Orlon mixed with the kitchen smells—meat loaf under a tomato sauce—as she led me into the dim, heavily knick-knacked living room. Ed remained standing in the archway, Corrine perched on a straight-backed chair next to the black-and-white TV, and I seated myself on an old brown 1930s davenport whose surface had the texture of a Nigerian's beard. I thought of a happy weekend I had once spent in Lagos and felt funny sitting on this thing.

"Could I get you a cup of hot coffee, Mr. Strachey? Ed's sister Patsy was here a little bit ago and she made enough for an army."

"No, thank you."

"People are so nice when tragedy strikes. Grace Toomey from next door made a wonderful meat loaf that's keeping warm for supper. It's big enough for ten people, and I know Grace lives on Social Security and can no more afford all that hamburg than she can afford to fly to the moon. It makes you thankful for what you've got."

"Mrs. McConkey, I'm a private investigator."

"Oh my goodness."

Ed, from the doorway: "You said you were a friend of Jackie's, I thought. Huh?"

"We knew each other, and it was my car Jack's body was left in."

"Oh, that's awful!"

"Yeah, I thought I heard that name before. What do you know about all this bull, anyway?"

"Not much. That's one reason I came here. I'm as interested in finding Jack's killer as you and your wife are. I'm assisting the police with their inquiries."

"They didn't say nothin' about that to me and Corrine."

"That nice Mr. Bowman was out," Corrine said. "He's a gentleman of the old school."

"I know Ned well," I said. "We go way back."

"He asked all these questions about who Jack's friends were, and did Jack have a lot of money and give us presents. He was nice about it, but I'm sure he thought Jack was mixed up with drugs again. But I don't believe that for a minute. Jackie learned his lesson that other time, and I know he was staying out of trouble. Didn't he seem that way to you?"

"That's my impression."

"Anyhow, I know Mom asked Jack straight out if he was selling dope and he said no, absolutely not. Jack never lied to Mom, he just never could. They've always been close. Even after Mom moved to California they'd gab on the phone all the time. Mom is so broken up over losing Jack, she doesn't even think she can come to the funeral. She's been in bed since yesterday, her friend Gail told me. It's a blow for all of us, believe me, it's a blow."

"When was it that Jack told your mother he wasn't dealing drugs?"

"Oh, I couldn't really say. He was out to see her in October, but like I say, they talked on the phone."

"Did your mother tell you what prompted her to ask Jack that question, about drugs?"

"Gosh, I don't know. Mom didn't say."

"Jackie's queer," McConkey said, glaring down at us. "Did you know that?"

"Yes, I knew that."

"Do you want my opinion? My opinion is Jackie picked up a hitchhiker and tried to get smart with him and the guy bashed his head in. That's my opinion."

"Oh, Ed, you don't know beans about Jack. You never did."

McConkey ignored this. "When I was in high school I was thumbing up 9W from Selkirk one time, and this guy gives me a lift and tries to get funny. 'You fool around?' he says. 'Hey, don't you like to fool around with the boys once in a while?' Well, hell, that guy got a split lip, that's the kind of foolin' around he got from me, I'll tell you. Big bruiser, too, he was. But I was so ticked he's lucky he didn't get worse, I'll tell you."

I said, "Couldn't you just have said, 'No, thank you'?"

McConkey looked at me as if I was a spaniel who had just peed on the rug.

"Ed, Jack didn't do that type of thing," Corrine said with an exasperated sigh. "I know, because I asked him one time, and he told me he never bothered school kids, he wasn't interested. In fact, he acted insulted that I should ask. What happened to you twenty-five years ago doesn't have anything to do with anything. Heavens, Ed!"

Shaking his head, McConkey said, "You've never been a man, Corrine, and you don't know. There's an awful lot that goes on out there that you just don't know about. You wait, the cops'll find out. It's either queers or drug pushers did it. You wait."

Her jaw tightened but she said nothing. McConkey threw up his hands and strode off toward the back of the house.

I said, "You seem to have known your brother pretty well, Mrs. McConkey. Did you see a lot of each other?"

"Oh yes, Jack and I were close in our way too. Not like Jack and Ma, but close. Last fall, now that was real nice. Jack was over this way quite a bit helping Dad around the house, so we saw a lot of him back then. We sort of got to know each other all over again."

"I'm sorry, but I thought your father was dead."

"He is. No, that's Pa. Pa died in 1967 from an ailment. No, I meant Dad Lenihan, my grandfather, who lives a block over on Pearl Street. Jack did some cleaning and painting for Dad, and sometimes he'd stop afterwards at our place for supper. Jack quit over at Dad's, though, one day in October, and we didn't see much of him after that. But it was fun for a little while."

"I'd gotten the impression that Jack and his grandfather didn't get along. Is that not so?"

She tilted her head and let loose with a strange little half-smile. "Well, let's just say they didn't see eye to eye about a lot of things. But family is important to Jack, the way it is to Dad. They argued a lot, sure they did. The nurse who's with Dad during the day told me Jack and Dad went at it tooth and nail, and she was always surprised when Jack would show up again the next day. They got along in their fashion, I guess you could say."

"What kinds of things did they argue about?"

She smiled again, almost laughed. "Politics. Jack was a Lenihan, wasn't he?"

"It seems he was, at that. Why did Jack quit working for his grandfather in October? Did he say?"

"No, I guess they'd just had enough of each other for a while. It was around then that Jack dropped out of business school too. That was a big disappointment to all of us. Just when he seemed to be finding himself. Jack said he didn't have the time, but I think that was just an excuse. What else did he have to do with his spare time? I think he just got in a mood. He was always like that."

"Jack's death must have hit Grandfather Lenihan hard. He's quite old, isn't he?"

"Ninety-six last month. When I told him—I had to tell him because he looks at the news on the TV—and when I went over and told Dad, he cried. He just looked out the window and cried like a baby. I never saw him do that before, even when Pa passed on. People think Dad's such a tough guy, but he's not such a toughie anymore, poor old thing."

"When did you last see Jack?"

"New Year's Day he dropped by. He watched the game with Ed for a while. But he was in a mood and didn't have too much to say. Jack had been kind of quiet the last couple of times we saw him, as a matter of fact. Maybe he missed his friend Warren, I don't know. He and Warren were so close, and Warren had been so good for Jack, I thought. Warren is just so settled and considerate. Whatever was on Jack's mind, he didn't mention it. You know, I'm sure going to miss Jack. After all, he was my baby brother. Ed and I were never blessed, so Jack and Ma and Dad Lenihan were the only family I had left. Family's always been important to the Lenihans."

"It must be hard for you that your mother won't be able to come home for the funeral."

She forced a smile but couldn't keep it, and her chin wobbled. "Yes, if I could just—hug her. Just put my arms around Ma and hold on. That's what I keep feeling I want to do. Ma and I don't—we haven't been together since Pa passed on and Ma moved away. Ma tried to get Ed and I to move out there, but of course Ed has his ties here. And he takes good care and he doesn't go out. Ma's paying for the funeral, thank the Lord. Ed was laid off last spring out at Green Island Ford, so this hasn't been an easy year for Ed and I. I clerk out at Feigelbaums in ladies' undergarments,

but you know how that is. You don't get rich slaving away for
Hal and Bernice."

"Uh-huh."

"They gave me the rest of the week off with pay, though.
That was real nice of them. The funeral's on Sunday."

The door bell rattled and Ed McConkey reappeared to
usher in three heavily bundled elderly women bearing cas-
serole dishes. I offered a few more lame expressions of con-
dolence, excused myself, retrieved my mountaineering outfit
from the hall radiator, and burned my fingers on the hot
zipper. I went back and asked which house on Pearl was
Dad Lenihan's and Corrine described it. "He won't let you
in though," she said. "Dad's kind of crabby with people he
doesn't know. To tell you the truth, he's kind of crabby with
everybody. I guess it's all his aches and pains makes him that
way. And now with Jack passing on, Dad's weaker than ever,
poor old thing."

Pug Lenihan's place was a small 1920s brown brick bungalow across from the deserted Immaculate Conception
School. The Lenihan homestead had a brightly painted front
porch and looked well kept up. Parked in the narrow driveway was a maroon Pontiac Firebird, which I supposed belonged to Pug's nurse. I paused for a few seconds on the
well-plowed street—Pearl was almost completely snowless
here—then drove back toward the interstate.

My visit to the North End seemed not to have been illuminating, except in a general way, and I guessed I'd visit
the neighborhood again once I figured out which questions
to ask, and which house to ask them in. I now knew for
certain only that something had happened to Jack Lenihan in
October that had changed his life and three months later had
ended it.

SEVEN

THE LANDSCAPE ALONG I-90 WAS AN EYE-
aching white under the January ice ball of a sun, but as I
drove west through gray slush, the traffic charging up and
down the roadway around me was filthy. I could sense the
road salt eating away at my axle beam and remembered a
newspaper story about a man tooling along at sixty when the
driver's seat dropped out the bottom of his '71 Honda. Eye-
witnesses were said to have screamed, then laughed, then
screamed again. I held on to the steering wheel hard.

From the Northway I headed east on Albany-Shaker Road
and made my way past the new residential developments that
catered to a mix of yuppies and retirees from the state bureau-
cracies who'd opted for the high rentals and maintenance fees
out in nature's neatly bulldozed bosom, where they hoped to
find a life of quietude and cleanliness, not that I didn't know
people who lived noisily and dirtily in the suburbs.

A mile and a half down the highway no heather was in
view in front of La Casa Heatherview, just a large wood sign
that said LA CASA HEATHERVIEW—A PLACE IN THE COUN-
TRY, and a snowy field bisected by a long drive leading up to
two twisting configurations of stucco-and-stained-wood town
houses that from the air must have looked like a set of Spanish question marks. I thought maybe it was a clue, but I
doubted it. I parked the car and walked up to 2-C.

"You can leave your boots there on the rug," the irresistible Warren Slonski said, looking me over noncommittally. I
gave him an equally noncommittal handshake and performed
as instructed. In the age of AIDS I had been making it a
practice to imagine a skull and crossbones on the forehead of
every possibly available comely gay man I found myself

alone with, but Slonski's kept fading in, fading out. I unlaced my scuffed Sears clodhoppers and placed them alongside Slonski's gleaming black Frye boots. In our stocking feet we moved into the living room, where I sank into the navy-blue velvet plush sofa while Slonski ambled on to the kitchen.

"What will you drink? Heineken? Beck's?"

"Beck's would be nice."

The white draperies covering the sliding glass doors were closed but fluttered in one corner where the wind leaked in. The magazines on the butcher-block coffee table were *Newsweek, High Fidelity,* and *Opera News.* On one wall were hung plastic-encased posters from the Met; the other was taken up by polyurethaned pine record shelves filled with what looked like every opera ever composed, from Monteverdi to *Einstein on the Beach,* and a sound system which resembled the electronic paraphernalia that accompanied the Jacksons on their Victory tour.

"Nuts? Cheese? A sandwich?" Slonski said, delivering the beer along with a chilled pewter mug.

"No, thanks, I'm meeting some people for dinner later. The Beck's will hold me for now."

He went back to the kitchen and brought out his own bottle and mug.

I said, "Nice sound system. Nice couch. That's a nice vest you've got on too. Pucci?"

"Gucci. Gucci makes vests. Pucci makes underwear."

"Ahh." I sipped my beer.

Slonski was close to flawless in appearance. In form-fitting black slacks and a loose cotton off-white shirt, over which he wore the vest, he was neat and elegantly formed. A silky black stream curved up and out of his well-toned cleavage like a fine hair undershirt. A gift from nature, or hirsucci. His clean-shaven face had the thickness of central Europe in it but with pleasing proportions and alert gray eyes under short blue-black hair with just a touch of punk in the styling. Slonski looked like an advertisement for himself. His only visible defect was a small wartlike discoloration, presumably not venereal, on the left side of his nose. And, of course, the skull and crossbones on his forehead.

He looked at me and said, "I know about you."

"What do you know?"

"That you were at Herb Brinkman's pool party last summer. With your lover. You made a big impression on Jack."

I said, "I'm very sorry about Jack."

He gazed at me levelly for a few seconds, then said, "Yes. I am too." He sipped his beer.

"You never expect someone you've been close to to be killed."

Watching me steadily, he said, "What do you have to do with this?"

"I'm not sure. I'm trying to find that out myself. That's why I've come out here to talk with you. At first I thought Jack's body being left in my car was just possibly a coincidence. But I don't believe that anymore." I thought, should I show him the letter, tell him about the suitcases? I decided no, I would spare Slonski my guilty knowledge for the time being in order to protect him—or myself—from—I didn't yet know what.

"I didn't believe for a minute that Jack's dying in your car was a coincidence," Slonski said. "In July Jack told me you were a private detective. He seemed unusually interested in that—as if he might have occasion one day to employ your services."

"Did he say why?"

"He never actually said even that much. Now that he's been killed I can see that that's what he must have meant. That he was in some kind of trouble that a private detective might help him get out of. Trouble with—I can't imagine who, if it's not dope sellers, which I am certain it is not. But that's hindsight. Last summer I was sure Jack's interest in you must have been sexual." He watched me.

"No. Not that I was aware of. And I usually pick right up on that."

"Do you?"

"Oh, sure."

More beer. "Jack was the most important person in my life for almost two years. In many ways, the *only* important person in my life. I don't see my family anymore, and before I met Jack I had always been largely self-sufficient emotionally."

"Some people manage to pull that off."

He shook his head. "I regarded my self-sufficiency as a character flaw. I worked systematically to overcome it and I succeeded. That's the way I do things, logically and systematically."

"I understand that you're a chemical engineer at GE. What kind of stuff do you work on?"

He kept studying me. He hadn't looked away once. The tension in the room was terrific and I wasn't sure where he was heading. He said, "It was very hard for me when Jack left."

"I'm sure it was."

Now he gazed down at the mug in his fist and said, "Were you sleeping with Jack?"

"No."

His face came up with a hard quizzical look. "Then what *were* you doing with him?"

"Nothing. Until Wednesday evening, when I discovered his body in my car at Faxon Towing and Storage, I hadn't seen Jack since the Fourth of July. When I first saw his body I didn't even realize who he was. Was sexual jealousy the reason you and Jack split up?"

He sighed, shook his head, and looked perplexed but a little less tense. He swigged down more beer, which he was taking in a little faster than he might have. "No, that wasn't the problem," he said. "That's just an idea I came up with at the time. It was an explanation that made sense."

"Explanation for what?"

"Jack's behavior. His brooding, his quitting school, his shutting me out. This is getting crazier and crazier. You don't know anything about this, do you? You really don't."

"Not much, no. I have my own reasons for gathering the facts about Jack's final months, some obvious, some not. You thought maybe there was another man who was affecting Jack's life?"

He took another drink and slung a shapely thigh over the arm of his chair. "Jack was so irritable and hard to get along with. Naturally I thought it was guilt. I arrived at that naive conclusion because in my other past relationships—the few brief ones I'd had—that's the way I acted when I was feeling guilty about something. Men, usually. Except, Jack swore there were no other men. He said his sex life with me was everything any man could possibly ever desire."

He spoke these words as though they comprised a mere point of information. I said, "Uh-huh."

"And then I—I shouldn't have brought it up, but I asked him if he was dealing drugs again. I suppose you know, he used to."

"I know."

"Jack went right through the roof when I mentioned drugs, because he'd promised me when we moved in together that he wouldn't do that, and Jack's word was important to him. I think I can say that Jack valued honesty above all else. It's probably because of his grandfather's shady past, but he had what I would consider an almost neurotic need to be open and direct about the most important things in his life. And when I asked about drugs—and all I did was *ask*— Jack was terribly, terribly hurt."

"And he explicitly denied it?"

"Oh, he denied it, all right. You know, I've built a career, I've worked hard for what I accomplished, and *I* value *that*. Work isn't everything—I think that's one of the valuable lessons I learned from Jack. No man on his deathbed ever said, 'I wish I'd spent more time at the office.' Jack had broader values and that's one of the things that attracted me to him, the way he could put our life together in a larger perspective. I even went to a gay-lib type of meeting with him one time. But the thing was, I just couldn't afford to become connected in any way with illegal drug activity. So, stupidly I asked Jack about the drugs. I should have known better. I knew Jack's word was good, and I shouldn't have asked. But I did."

Slonski sat there squirming in his regret. He had made a mistake of a not uncommon type in human relations and now the hurt was deepened because he knew he would never be able to undo it. I said, "And that's when you and Jack broke up?"

"It was the beginning of the end. That was midsummer, and Jack stayed with me until mid-October—October sixteenth, to be precise. But he was moody and difficult all summer and fall, and he refused to tell me what the *real* problem was. He said I was too conventional—too 'straight arrow' was how he put it—to understand. And that hurt me."

"In some circles it's a dreadful thing to accuse a person of. Anyway, if Jack prized openness and honesty as much as you say, he must have been feeling guilty himself for not confiding in you, not trusting you, and that would have accounted in part for his rotten state of mind. Maybe his conscience was bothered by the thing itself—whatever it was he was involved in."

He sipped at the beer and thought this over. "I doubt it. Jack had his own moral code. He was arrogant that way. He could break the law with no compunction if he thought the law was wrong. He was a child of the sixties in that respect. I stayed out of Vietnam by getting an essential job in a defense industry while Jack was out in the streets burning his draft card. That's how he could rationalize the drug dealing he'd done. He said as long as you didn't sell it to the kids, it was just another popular consumer item you were providing."

"Right. Like alcohol—which killed his father and must have made Jack's young life miserable."

"That's what I said," he said, and set the beer mug on the floor. "But Jack just said any habit could be abused, and then refused to discuss it any further. He didn't like talking about his father. It was just too loaded a subject for him. Though I think he thought about his family a lot. They were always a strong presence in his mind and could set off some powerful feelings."

"Right. Family has always been important to the Lenihans."

"When I look back to last summer and fall, I keep thinking there must have been some point where I *missed* something, where something happened to Jack and I didn't recognize its importance. Or that I'd closed myself up, or been preoccupied with work. We'd had such a good thing going, and I just can't understand what *I* might have done to foul it up."

"Maybe nothing. Nothing at all."

"One of the characteristics that attracted me to Jack when we met was his ambition, the way he was working so hard to put some order in his life. Enrolling in business school, planning for the future, putting his past behind him, even getting close to his family again. What happened that changed all that so suddenly? I've racked my brain, but I cannot for the life of me put my finger on what it might have been. Of course—it's all academic now. Even if somehow the misunderstanding could be cleared up—if that's what it was—Jack's not coming back. That's a fact I'm trying to face, and I'm having a very hard time with it."

"Had you thought he might come back?"

"Of course," he said with a little shrug. "No one had ever left me before. I've always been the one to do the leaving. I'm known as 'the irresistible Warren Slonski.' People call me that."

"What a nice compliment."

"So, the thing is, I wasn't used to a situation like that. Men are usually trying to get *into* my bed, not out of it."

I said, "Hell, I know exactly what you mean." If he'd looked suddenly queasy, I'd have shot him through the heart. But he didn't blanch, or laugh. He just put his hands behind his head, gazed at the ceiling tragically, and flexed his biceps.

I said, "Maybe Jack's volatile reaction to your question about drug dealing was a result of his being confronted with the awful truth. Maybe he *was* back in the business and exploded out of guilt. Isn't that a possibility?"

He shook his head. "No. I knew Jack. He would have admitted it. I was wrong to suspect him and wrong to bring it up. It had to have been something else. I knew Jack."

"You mentioned that Jack was getting close to his family again. Was he seeing a lot of them?"

"For a while he was, and they all seemed to be hitting it off fairly well. During the summer and into the fall Jack was even doing some work around the house for his grandfather in the North End. And he'd see his sister Corrine while he was out there. I went with him a couple of times and Corrine was nice to me, even though we had a hard time finding things to talk about. Her husband wasn't exactly a barrel of laughs though. 'Dreadful Ed,' Jack and I called him."

"Did you meet Jack's grandfather?"

"No, but I was curious about him. He's apparently some type of famous political figure in Albany—I'm from Watertown and don't know much about that. I know he was part of the Boyle brothers' machine here for fifty years, and it would have been fascinating to meet him. But Jack never offered and I didn't push it." He picked up his empty mug. "Say, how about a refill on the Beck's? It looks as if the well is about to run dry."

"I'll pass, but you go ahead."

He did and returned with another beer for me too. "Just in case," he said.

"Thank you."

He flopped back in his chair, throwing one leg over the arm again.

"I understand Jack was close to his mother," I said. "Did he see her often?"

"They talked on the phone once a week, and that's where Jack went when he first left me, out to LA. By the time he actually packed up and moved out, he was in bad shape, a real nervous wreck. I guess he went out to his mom's to wind down. She and Corrine were really the only people in the family who never gave Jack a hard time about being gay, and his mom had been supportive in a lot of other ways over the years. She had her own troubles, of course, raising two kids with an alcoholic husband who couldn't hold a job more than a day. I think she left Albany behind a long time ago, but she did stay close to Jack and Corrine. She kept trying to convince Corrine to move out there, or at least to visit, and offered to pay her way, but Corrine seemed unable to make any kind of break from the North End, even for a week. I never met Mrs. Lenihan, but Jack made her sound like a very strong and exceptional person."

"What about you? When did you last see Jack?"

He grimaced. "As I told that idiot Bowman from the Albany police department this morning, I've seen Jack *once* in three months. On Christmas Day we had dinner at the Quackenbush House. It was my stupid idea. The afternoon was so tense and Jack was so uncommunicative we skipped dessert and went our separate ways, and I never really expected to see him again. Of course, now I won't."

"Then I suppose Jack didn't mention—either then or last fall—a particular project he was working on?"

He frowned across his beer mug. "Project?"

"Something that might be considered immoral by some people but not by others. Something that would right a wrong."

"No, I'm sure I'd remember. Why do you ask that?"

"It's come up, but specifics are lacking. There might be a connection between this project and Jack's death."

"I can't imagine what. No, business school was Jack's only project until he quit last fall. That and learning about opera. I was helping Jack gain access to the very considerable pleasures of opera, and I think he was really beginning to love it. Opera has been important to me since I was fifteen. It's been a way to experience the passion of human life without getting my own hands too dirty, if you know what I mean. Opera has always been my chief emotional release. Along with sex, of course."

"Of course."

"But Jack never mentioned any other project, no. Could that have been what was eating away at him?"

"I think so, yes."

"Something some people might consider immoral? I suppose *I* was one of those people. Is that what you're thinking?"

"There's a good chance that that's the case. What could Jack have been involved in that you would have found immoral?" He thought this over, then shook his head. I said, "Run through the Ten Commandments. Which ones do you feel most strongly about?"

He smiled sheepishly. "This is embarrassing. I can only remember a few. It's been a while."

"Go for the hard-core stuff, the foundations of Judeo-Christian ethics."

Without hesitation he said, "Stealing."

"Thou shalt not steal."

"I've always believed strongly that people should earn anything of value they received, or be given it because they need it or deserve it. For a person to take something that doesn't belong to him disgusts me. It's the beginning of anarchy. Jack knew how deeply I feel about that. Is it possible? Do you think Jack stole something?"

"Could be," I said. "Though if he did, he didn't consider it stealing, I think. Not in the usual strict sense of the word."

"But I would have. And he knew it."

"There's a good possibility of that."

"What was it that you think he stole?"

"Money. There is evidence that it was money." Now he placed both feet on the floor and leaned forward. "But how could that be right? How could Jack consider stealing money a moral act?"

"I don't know yet. I'm curious too. Did Jack know any-one who owned a lot of money, or had access to it?"

"How much money?"

"A vast amount. A fortune."

"Not that I can think of—no one in Albany. Except drug dealers perhaps. But it wouldn't be that, I'm sure."

"Did any of Jack's former business associates ever come here, or phone?"

"Absolutely not. I was firm about that. Anyhow, I think they were all in jail."

"All of them?"

"As far as I know. According to Jack, he was the only one of that bunch who wasn't convicted. The rest of them were locked up for twenty years."

"Jack must have had a terrific lawyer."

"Oh, he did—the best. Thomas Pelligrinelli came up from New York to handle his case."

"Really? Pelligrinelli has to be one of the most expensive criminal lawyers in the state of New York. Jack must have been paying him off right up to the day he died."

"Oh no, Jack's mother paid for the lawyer. He told me that. I think it was one of the reasons he never intended to get in trouble with the law again. His acquittal had cost his mother so much."

"Is she wealthy? What does she do?"

"Mrs. Lenihan's a nurse. I don't know, maybe she took out a loan, or has rich friends. Jack never went into that. But the day after the trial ended she wired him twenty thousand dollars and he paid off Pelligrinelli."

"She didn't attend the trial?"

"No, Jack said she detested Albany and never intended to set foot in it again. Her life here was awfully unhappy. Though I got the idea she's doing much better now."

"It sounds that way."

"She must be taking Jack's death very hard."

"Corrine told me she was, yes."

"I guess I'll finally meet her at the funeral," Slonski said, and lifted his mug.

I said, "She's not coming."

"She isn't?" The mug hung in the air.

"She's gone to bed, sick with grief."

"That's terrible, just terrible. Jack told me his mother had never been sick a day in her life. She never missed a single day of work. He said she was made of iron."

"She sounds like quite an unusual lady."

"The Lenihans are an unusual family," Slonski said, and I was only just beginning to understand that that was putting it mildly.

I told him I had to leave for my dinner engagement, thanked him for his candid remarks about Jack and their relationship, and said I understood his initial skepticism about me.

"Oh, no problem. But you still haven't explained to me exactly what your connection with Jack *was*."

"It was professional on my part, which makes it confidential. I'm sorry I can't tell you more."

"You know, I miss him more than ever," Slonski said in a shaky voice. "I still can't quite believe that *he* actually left *me*. And that he's never coming back."

"I'm wondering about something, Warren. What was it

about Jack Lenihan that evoked such an emotional response in you? He was sweet-natured and had his other virtues, but he wasn't a particularly attractive man physically. You seem to have a keener than normal appreciation for that which appeals to the senses. I would have expected you to bed down with a man who was—well, more like yourself."

He flushed and looked away. "The thing is," he said after a moment, "I've always gone for men who are less attractive than I am. I guess they—make me look better. And feel better. And the chances are, they're not going to leave me. It's a way of controlling the situation, I suppose you could say, of protecting myself. For instance, you really turn me on. But I would never make a direct move with somebody like you. You might turn me down."

Now it was out in the open, a slight relief. "But if I did turn you down—and reluctantly I would—it wouldn't have anything to do with you. It would be the fact that I have a lover, my deep and entirely rational fear of AIDS, and my already-too-elastic professional ethics. It wouldn't be personal at all."

His face fell. "There. You see what I mean?"

I started to laugh, but didn't when he didn't. I would have liked to hang around and attempt first aid on Slonski's damaged soul. Five years earlier, such acts of warmhearted crisis intervention were not uncommon for me, and I always got as much as I gave, often more. But my life had its complications now, and Slonski's needed a few, none of which I was in a position to provide.

He put some Wagner on the stereo, and I went out and rubbed snow on my face before driving off. The islands beckoned again briefly, but that was not where I was headed. From a pay phone I reached a friend at the *Times Union* who provided me with background information on the three men I was about to dine with. By the time I hung up, I thought I had figured out what Jack Lenihan's morally ambiguous project was.

If I was right, then Lenihan had been correct in his prediction that I would approve of it. We had spent only ten minutes together one summer afternoon, yet he knew me that well. I would have liked to ask him how he'd done that.

EIGHT

I WAS LED TO THE LAST AVAILABLE table for four at Queequeg's, a restored art-deco diner—all streamlined aluminum glitz on the outside, goldenly glowing carved wood paneling on the inside, as in a wagon-lit—that had been turned into a kebab, salad and beer joint for the youngish trendies who lived and worked around Albany Medical Center.

The food at Queequeg's was good and cheap, and the owners had managed to conjure up an illusion of authentic fast-lane city life by packing a large number of eaters and drinkers into an area of severely constricted square footage. The music—jazz, disco, fusion—was sufficiently loud, as were frequently the customers, so that, amidst the atmosphere of boozy congestion, it was possible to converse without being overheard, or even, if your diction was sloppy or you were a little bit shy, heard at all.

Sim Kempelman was the first to arrive at five till seven. I'd never met him, but I watched for a middle-aged lawyer in the throes of mild culture shock, and I spotted him right away and signaled for him to join me.

"Mr. Strachey?"

"Attorney Kempelman, I presume."

"That's me, kiddo. And how are you today? This establishment reminds me of my student days at the University of

Pittsburgh. There was a place just like this one just off Schenley, near Forbes Field, before it went the way of the rest of my youth. Do you know Pittsburgh?"

"I've only passed through. It's somewhere near St. Louis, isn't it?"

He navigated his physical amplitude onto one of the chrome steel chairs. "It's not quite that far beyond the New Yorker's pale. I take it you're a Manhattanite, Mr. Strachey. You must find Albany to be somewhere near St. Louis too."

"I'm from New Jersey, so I'm adaptable. It's not quite a real place to most people—like saying you grew up on an offshore barge. But it was real enough for me."

"And how are you enjoying Albany? Is it real enough for you?"

"More than enough."

He had a big amiably droll face whose weight seemed to pull his head forward, and the brownest eyes I had ever seen. "I'm an attorney," Kempelman said, bending toward me, "but sometimes I think I would appreciate this city better if I were an anthropologist. In many ways Albany is like a museum display of American urban political folkways during the first half of this century. It's the powerful few snuffling at the public trough with the not-so-powerful many picking up the tab when it comes due each year. It's an outmoded system—like Havana before Castro, or Prague after Dubcek. You don't find patronage-and-payoff politics in the more prosperous, future-oriented cities—Atlanta, San Diego, Denver. It's outmoded, it's unfair, it's too expensive, and it doesn't work."

"How long is it going to take you to change it?"

"Another twenty-five years at the rate we're moving. *Two* years if my organization can find a way to tap the support we know is out there. Are you familiar with Democrats for Better Government in Albany? Or maybe you're even a dues-paying member, could that be so?"

"I'm not a member, no. But I've read about your group."

"But you are politically progressive, I take it. I received the distinct impression from a number of colleagues that you might be."

I said, "I'm an old-fashioned liberal, Mr. Kempelman. I'd be a socialist if I thought governments could be counted on always to do the right thing. But they can't, so I'm not. I am sort of fond of the social democracies. I like to think of Denmark with all those cheese fields waving in the northern sunlight. Of course, I've never been there, so that makes it easier. In this country I work for the Democrats in national elections, and in Albany I vote Republican, which makes me an anarchist. I'm gay, too, so around here that makes me pretty much of an outlaw if I do much more than leave the house, which I often do. I suppose my brazen behavior in that respect automatically confers on me 'progressive' credentials. But I don't know, you're the president of the club."

He had listened carefully to this, and now he gave me a little half-smile. He said, "You know why I wanted to speak with you, don't you?"

"Yes."

"Jack Lenihan told me that if anything happened to him, I should contact you."

"I guessed that."

"You didn't know?"

"No, but you are merely one of the legions Jack seems to have mentioned my name to."

He frowned. "I think poor Jack died horribly on account of some money he had—a great deal of money. That's my opinion."

"Jack Lenihan was murdered. Have you gone to the police with your opinion?"

"Yes. This afternoon, after much soul-searching, I spoke with Detective Lieutenant Bowman. I had no choice but to report my knowledge to him. You understand that, don't you?"

"I do. Did my name come up?"

"It had to, naturally. I believe Officer Bowman would like to speak with you, in fact. He is searching for you at this very moment."

"I'll give him a call when I get a chance. I already saw him once today, which was plenty. What did you tell him?"

"That Jack Lenihan had offered my organization two and a half million dollars to finance a campaign to elect a progressive mayor of Albany."

"Oh."

"And that you were involved in his plans in a manner which Jack did not spell out to me."

"You told Bowman all that?"

"I had to."

"Crap."

"You said the word, Mr. Strachey, Jack Lenihan was *murdered*. Under the circumstances, there is no way I could have withheld information that is clearly relevant to the police investigation. My duty as an officer of the court is both legally and morally clear."

I said, "But you hesitated, didn't you?" I watched him squirm. "You waited half a day before you went to Bowman trying to figure out a way to get hold of Lenihan's cash before you did your moral duty."

"Yes, I did take time out to mull over the ramifications of any action I might take."

"Good for you, Kempelman. I think I'll join your club." He chuckled mildly. "But first I have to tell you that Jack Lenihan used my name without permission. Before he died, I knew nothing of his money or his plans for it. That sounds like a line for the cops, and you can take it or leave it, but it's true." He shrugged. I said, "When did Jack first approach you?"

"January third."

"Was he making an offer, or was he just feeling you out?"

"It was a feeler. Jack made it plain that *other* political

organizations might possibly become the recipients of his public-spirited largesse. He said he would be in touch but that he was having unspecified problems with some people whose identities he did not reveal, and if anything happened to him I should get in touch with you."

"Jack Lenihan was a waiter on Lark Street who was not independently wealthy. Where did he say he got the money?"

Kempelman smiled and shook his head. "From his godfather. He inherited two and a half million dollars from his godfather in Los Angeles."

"No."

"That's what he said. He showed me documents—Jack was prepared for a certain skepticism on my part, you see—and he sat in my office and dumped a pile of documents on my desk. A probated will, tax-payment receipts, the whole lot of it, and all entirely on the up and up. I photocopied the papers, made some calls to attorneys of my acquaintance in Los Angeles after Jack left, and was convinced in my mind and heart that the whole business was legit."

"What was the godfather's name?"

"Albert Piatek."

"May I have copies of the documents?"

"Of course. I have already provided Lieutenant Bowman with copies, and there is no reason I shouldn't do the same favor for you. Now I have a question for you, Mr. Strachey." He looked me carefully in the eye and said, "Where's the money?"

"Good question."

"Jack left the impression that the money would be in your possesssion. For safekeeping, he seemed to be saying. Did you kill him for the money?"

"No."

"I didn't think so. I've asked around about you—discreetly, mind you—and your reputation is that of a pain in the ass but not a murderer."

"Thank you."

"Lieutenant Bowman—a man in love with the obvious if I ever met one—Officer Bowman may have other ideas about you. He is not fond of you and this interferes with his objectivity, I think."

"Oh, hell."

"So, where's the money?"

A waitress charged up to our table and rapidly recited the menu, which consisted of four items. Kempelman picked the chicken teriyaki and I ordered the beef teriyaki rare. I asked him if he'd like to split a pitcher of beer, but he said a glass of white wine would suit him better. I went ahead and ordered the pitcher.

When the waitress left, Kempelman said it again. "Where's the money?"

"It's safe," I said. "But I have no instructions as yet concerning its disposal."

"Did Jack leave a will?"

"I don't know. I thought you'd know. You're the lawyer."

"No will has been filed in Albany County. Or Los Angeles County. I've looked into that."

"Did you tell Bowman you were meeting me here tonight?"

"No, I am giving you that much. I think it's what Jack Lenihan would have wanted. So, where's the money?"

"As I said, it's safe."

"What will become of it?"

"I don't know. That's kind of a confused area."

I had been looking over Kempelman's shoulder at a man elbowing his way through the bar crowd, and when I signaled to him, Kempelman turned around. His two bushy eyebrows shot up.

Kempelman said, "Him *too*?"

"I'm afraid so. He's Creighton Prell, right?"

"That's Creighton, sure enough."

The Republican county chairman was a tall dewlapped

man in an alpaca coat with puffy hazel eyes and a wind-burned patrician nose. I guessed he was the man with the fifty-dollar haircut who'd been looking for Jack Lenihan at Annie's Quiche Quorner on Friday. When Prell saw Kempelman with me, he winced, hesitated, then moved toward us with a look of despair.

"Mr. Strachey?"

"I am he."

"And Sim—Sim, what a delightful surprise."

"You look more surprised than delighted, Creighton."

Prell eased himself onto his little seat. "I had no idea you were involved in this business, Sim. Or are you?"

"Involved in what business, Creighton?"

"May I speak frankly?" The question was for me.

I said, "I'm all for it."

Instead of speaking frankly, Prell went gray as his eye caught the eye of another man making his way into the dining area.

I said, "That must be Larry Dooley. Hey, over here, Lar!"

Dooley, a low heavily ballasted primate in a shiny blue suit and wet cigar in his paw, pummeled his way toward us and scowled down. "What is this crap? You Strachey?"

"Yeah, I Strachey. This Creighton, this Sim."

"I know these two buggers. What are they doing here?"

"Sit down, Larry," Kempelman said. "Come on, kid, take a load off your feet."

"You might as well join us," Prell said. "May I inquire, Mr. Strachey, if you have invited still other guests to this little fete? It's already awfully crowded in here, if I may offer an opinion."

I said, "This is it, gents. Otherwise I would have hired the Hilton ballroom." Dooley banged the remaining chair around, then sat on it. I looked around the table and said, "Which one of you killed Jack Lenihan for the money?"

Dooley and Prell went ashen, but Kempelman just shook his head sadly. "Not funny, Mr. Strachey. Under the circumstances, I will not permit myself to laugh."

"It was no joke, Sim. I figure Lenihan approached all three of you to find out which of you would provide a mayoral candidate who, if elected, would run Albany in a manner closest to Jack's liking. One of you picked up the impression you were about to lose out to another group, and you killed Jack so that you could grab the money or, failing that, at least keep it out of the other organizations' hands. Ned Bowman is not so dumb that this scenario won't occur to him, so you should all consider yourself police suspects in Jack's murder. Or is it possible that two of you haven't yet been in to see Ned and own up, voluntarily or involuntarily?"

Prell went neon-red. He said, "Lieutenant Bowman came to visit me, in point of fact. My name and telephone number were found by the police in Jack Lenihan's wallet."

"Mine too," Kempelman said placidly, and glanced at me. "But I didn't wait for Mr. Bowman to call on me. I went to him."

Dooley, who had sat stewing through all of this, aimed his cigar at me and said, "Bowman is after your ass, fella, you know that?"

"Did you tell him you were meeting me here tonight?" He said, "Nah."

"You want the money. You think I have it."

Two plates of teriyaki were deftly slung in front of Kempelman and me. "Would you gentlemen like to order now?"

"Scotch and soda," Prell said.

Dooley waved the waitress away. He then leaned up to my face and snarled, "Now you see here, Strachey. I thought I was dealing with a man of integrity in a confidential tone of voice and now I come down here and I find this fucking fireman's ball going on with half the politicians in the county waiting around for some broad to jump out of a birthday cake or some goddamn thing. Now you tell me, what is this, wise guy? Ya know, this is Albany, New York, not San Franpansy-town, USA, so you talk to me and you talk plain. I know all about you, Strachey, and you better not fuck with me or I'll make plenty of trouble for you and I can do it. Now, what is this shit?"

I leaned close to him and said very quietly, "Of all the foul turds floating in the cesspool of Albany political life, you, Larry, are by far the most repulsive I have met so far."

"Why, you—!"

"If you want a chance at the money, Larry, then shut your fat mouth."

He shut up and sat back big-eyed. This was fun. I was buying an Albany pol, my second—or first if I didn't count the dime I'd slipped Bowman that afternoon. Kempelman and Prell looked docile enough too.

I said, "Now here is what took place over the past two weeks. Please correct me, any of you, if I veer off the track at any point. Jack Lenihan felt each of you out on how you would spend the two and a half million he was dangling. He wanted to know what he would get in return, a time-honored tradition in Albany, though with a switch this time. It wasn't city contracts Lenihan wanted, or insurance deals, or the toilet-paper concession for city hall. He was not interested in court-clerk positions, or commissionerships, or a contract for police uniforms. Uh-uh. That wasn't Jack. He didn't go for all that business as usual. In fact, he loathed it—for his own very personal reasons. That's what this whole deal was about."

They watched me, not moving, their pulses visible at a variety of pressure points.

"Jack's plan was he wanted the opposite of business as usual. Let me guess—open bidding on all city contracts? Professionals instead of party hacks running the departments? Property tax rate equalization? More blacks on the city payroll? A police civilian review board? Maybe even a gay rights ordinance. Hey, I'll bet that's it. That's where *you* began to hem and haw, Larry, am I right? Jack naively wanted all this in writing, and his agenda was a bit on the socially enlightened side for your tastes. So you hesitated over gay rights, and Mr. Prell, you couldn't stomach the police civilian review board or any sort of quotas on minority hiring, and it was very likely the forward-looking Mr. Kempelman here who just about had it sewed up in the end.

"Except none of you *knew* where you stood. Each of you knew that Jack was bargaining with other factions, and one of you suddenly felt panicky, and you killed him to keep him from financing one of the other groups, and with the hope that you could then snatch the big money or pry it out of me. The one of you who did it then arranged for me to be threatened into turning over the money to some thugs you hired, a matter that I am giving serious consideration to, on account of my wanting to keep my skull intact. On the other hand, I might not. I'm thinking it over."

Kempelman had sat sighing and shaking his head through all this. Prell's alpaca was molting, his haircut down to $7.50. Dooley had barely contained his fury, and now he let loose. "Listen, you faggoty-maggoty sack of shit, I don't have to put up with this type of insulting treatment! In fact, I've had about as much of your lip as I'm going to take! *Screw* the money, and I'm not through with *you* either!"

I said, "Larry, your demeanor here tonight represents a breach of protocol that is beyond my capacity to endure. Some of your dandruff dropped into my beer just now, and therefore there is no chance that you will ever receive the money."

Dooley's eyes went wild. He stood up and made for the exit, flinging voters aside hither and thither as he went. I called after him, "Have a nice evening, Councilman Dooley!"

"That man is a disgrace," Prell muttered. "How he continues to be reelected is beyond my comprehension."

Kempelman waved a forkful of chicken and green pepper. "Oh, come on, kid. You know exactly how he does it, and so do I. They got the dough, they got the jobs, they got the contracts. Larry's on the outs with the machine boys this month, but after the primary he'll be back in, for the simple reason that for a man like Larry there is no place else to go. It's all he knows and all he wants to know. It was foolish of Jack Lenihan to approach Dooley, who is as much of a reform politician as I am a rock and roll singer."

"Yes, Sim, you're such an expert on firmly gripping the reins of government in Albany," Prell said. "Is it true you're planning on running a Unitarian minister for mayor this year on a nuclear-freeze platform?"

"That issue will come up," Kempelman said mildly, mouthing a chunk of chicken. "What issue could possibly be more important than the survival of the human species?"

I listened for several minutes while they went at each other in their cordially disrespectful way, each of them a martyr keeping his martyrdom beautiful through distance from the other martyrs. Then I nailed them down on precisely when and where each had last spoken with Jack Lenihan, and exactly what was said by whom. I asked Kempelman when I could pick up the documents showing the legality of Lenihan's "inheritance," and he pulled a thick envelope out of his breast pocket.

"Use them in good health."

Prell produced an identical set and handed it over. "Are you, by chance, the executor of Lenihan's will?" he asked.

"No will has turned up yet. Informally, though, it looks as if I'm it."

Prell's Scotch arrived and he went at it with a shaky hand. He said, "Mr. Strachey, you don't really believe that Sim, Larry, or I killed Jack Lenihan, do you? That's a horrible thing to suggest, you know."

"Horrible questions often suggest horrible answers. Don't be offended, Mr. Prell. It looks as if I'm in this even deeper than you are."

"Don't forget to give Officer Bowman a call," Kempelman said, wiping his mouth. "I promised him that if I ran into you I'd put you two sleuths in touch with each other."

"Sure."

"And don't lose track of that two and a half million, will you? Is it in a good safe place, I hope?"

"None safer," I said, and figured it was time to drop by the Hilton and find out how reliable the bellhops were.

NINE

I EXITED QUEEQUEG'S THROUGH THE kitchen and went up a snowy alley to the side street where I'd parked the rental car. The night air was still now, frozen in place, it seemed, and a scattering of stars hung in a remote black sky. I had to remove a glove to insert the key in the Chrysler's ignition, and when I did so the front seat did not explode, blowing my lower torso into disgusting pulpy fragments. That was a relief.

My breath froze on the windshield, so while the car warmed up I tuned in the all-news radio station and learned that Albany police had no suspect in the Tuesday slaying of a Swan Street man, but that they had developed a number of leads and were searching for the Albany private investigator in whose car the body had been found and who was now believed to be in possession of "additional information." I also was informed that a gorilla in Woodside, California, had given birth to a single gray kitten, though by that time I was headed down Madison and on the lookout for cop cars, so I might have gotten the gorilla story wrong.

I left the rental car outside the Hertz office and dropped

the keys through the night-return slot. Bowman would soon have a make on any car rented locally in my name, if he hadn't already, and I wanted to steer clear of him a while longer. Like so many people I kept running into, he would have his nosy questions concerning the whereabouts of Jack Lenihan's two and a half million, except Bowman's manner of inquiry would be ruder than that of the others and I chose to avoid it.

Up in room 1407 Timmy had the TV on and was watching a *20/20* report on a chemical animal feed factory built in 1983 next to an army base where all the soldiers soon grew breasts. The feed company's lawyers said it was a coincidence.

"We're going to where it's warm," I told him, kissing his bare ankle, which was propped atop one of Jack Lenihan's five fat suitcases.

"I don't think so. What's in these bags anyway? I just picked up a toothbrush, some underwear and a couple of shirts. You look as though you've settled in for the decade."

"The bags are Jack Lenihan's. They arrived by bus from Los Angeles and they contain two and a half million dollars."

He removed his ankle. "Did you steal them?"

"No, they were addressed to me—sent by Jack on Monday. As it said in the letter, I'm supposed to keep them safe until I hear from Jack."

He stared at the suitcases with his baby blues, which began to flutter arrhythmically.

"But you're not *going* to hear from Jack."

"No. I'm not."

I flopped onto the bed as he sat on the edge of his chair shaking his head. "It's not yours," he said. "I don't know whose it is, but it's not yours. I want no part of this."

"Part of what? Of course the money's not mine."

"You said we were going somewhere warm. You didn't mean Rio, did you, along with those five suitcases?"

"Nah."

"Then what did you mean?"

"Los Angeles. It's hardly Antigua, but it'll do for now. If I can prove that Lenihan came by this money legitimately, I can go ahead and carry out the project he was planning that was so important to him. Take the day off—you've got one coming—and we'll leave in the morning."

Timmy looked perplexed, so I described the afternoon's and evening's events.

He said, "Let me see the letter again." I fished it out and he read it. "I don't get it. Jack says right here that what he was doing was not immoral but it *was* illegal. That doesn't square at all with this wild story he told the three pols about an inheritance from a godfather."

I brought out the documents Sim Kempelman had given me. "Sim says it's all on the up-and-up. Look at these."

He perused the papers. "This stuff looks okay, but that still doesn't explain the language in the letter. It doesn't fit."

"I know."

"You know?"

"*Superficially* it doesn't fit, that's true. But there are larger forces at work here, larger truths. I'll have to sort out the details as I go along."

He gave me a strained look. "Don, please come off it and don't give me that vague stuff you always come up with when it suits your current whim. You've put aside your objectivity in this because you think you can give the Albany machine a kick in the groin. But it won't be that simple, and you know it. Maybe this so-called godfather is a Mafia godfather, a big drug dealer, or some other god-awful thing."

"A Mafia godfather named Al Piatek?"

"It's true, the name doesn't ring a bell. Maybe it's an alias."

"Sim Kempelman states unequivocally that these documents are genuine," I said, "and you can't get papers like these under an alias."

"Not unless you're powerful enough to own a few government clerks in the right places. Really, I think you should stay clear of this crowd, whoever they are. Hankie-mouth obviously doesn't work for the Department of Agriculture. Do you still plan on not meeting him tonight?"

"I'm not exactly meeting him, no. You're determined to keep me from getting away to a warm place, aren't you? But it won't work, my friend. Hang on." I picked up the phone, got an outside line, and dialed the McConkeys' number on Walter Street. Dreadful Ed answered and grudgingly called Corrine to the phone.

"Don Strachey, Corrine. How are you doing?"

"Not very well, Mr. Strachey. But some very nice people are taking good care of me, so I'm just trying to count my blessings and hang on. Oh, did you know Officer Bowman was looking for you? Maybe you better see what he wants. It sounded important."

"I'll give him a call when I get a chance. Tell me something, Corrine. Did Jack have a godfather?"

"Jack's godfather was a real sweetie—Mike Tompkins, a friend of Dad Lenihan's. He would have been just crushed by Jack's passing, so maybe it's best that Mike joined the majority himself last year."

For a second I thought she meant the Moral Majority, but then it sank in. "Mr. Tompkins died recently?"

"Oh, it's been almost a year now. Last February or March, I think. I know there was snow on the ground. Mary Tompkins dropped by earlier tonight and we talked about Mike's passing. It was merciful, she said, because the cancer had turned him into a little tiny thing not much more than a ghost. He'd been suffering quite a bit. He lived down the street from Dad, and Dad misses him too."

"Was Mr. Tompkins a wealthy man?"

"Wealthy? Oh, no, I wouldn't think so. Oh, no."

"Does the name Al Piatek mean anything to you?"

"Piatek?"

"Yes."

"I can't think of any Piateks. I've heard the name, I guess."

"Thank you. I'm sorry to have bothered you and I hope I won't have to do it again. But I might."

"Oh, that's all right. I was just having a cup of tea and a sticky bun."

When I'd hung up, Timmy said, "So."

"So? So what? This just makes it all the more imperative that I fly out there and sort this out."

"The beaches won't be any good. This time of year the water's too cold."

"You're not coming along?"

"Of course I'm coming. It's just for the weekend."

"Good. Bowman wants to haul me in and might have the security people at the airport watching for me, so we'll drive down and fly from Kennedy. Did you rent a car?"

"It's down on Lodge Street. God, an Albany Lenihan who turned into a civic reformer. Who'd ever have thought it? If Jack hadn't died, what an amazing historical event that would have been."

"Will be," I said. "An amazing historical event that *will be*."

He'd had enough of me for a while and watched the eleven-o'clock news while I phoned my airline contact at home.

"Don Strachey, Alex. What did you come up with?"

"Joe's here for a few hours and he's awake. I'm busy."

"Give him my best—or yours, if that's what he prefers—but in the meantime, go get that stuff on Lenihan I asked for, will you? I'm going to be out of touch for a couple of days and I need it before I leave."

The phone hit something with a clunk. He came back rattling papers. "John C. Lenihan flew to Los Angeles via

O'Hare on Tuesday, October sixteenth, and returned to Albany on Sunday, October twenty-first, again changing at O'Hare. If he flew anywhere on any other dates during the month of October, it wasn't with us. May I go now?"

"You may. And thanks—many thanks. You'll be rewarded for this on some distant day."

"Oh, it won't be that long."

I hung up and dialed Ned Bowman at home. "Fenton Hardy here. Is this Chief Collig of the Bayport police department?"

"You're under arrest, Strachey!"

"Nope."

"Well, you sure as hell will be if you don't haul your ass down to my office at eight A.M. sharp. And you are *not* at the Americana. You lied."

"Listen, Ned, I want to help you out, so don't make it hard for me. Our separate efforts on this one can be complementary and beneficial."

"You have it, don't you?" he hissed.

"Have what?"

"The famous two and a half million bucks everybody and his brother keeps walking in off the street and telling me about. You know, Strachey, Larry Dooley is awful mad at you. When you make a mistake, it's a pisser."

"Dooley may have killed Jack Lenihan. Are you pursuing that?"

"Dooley, Kempelman, Creighton Pell—they're all suspects until they can establish alibis, which naturally they're all busting their asses to come up with real fast."

"There's a better suspect, I think."

"What? Who do you mean?"

"Whoever killed Jack Lenihan was smart enough to dump him in my car instead of in a ditch somewhere. This served the purpose of frightening me into turning over the two and a half million—which, incidentally, I've never seen—and also of pointing a finger at me. It follows that the killer was also smart enough to go through Lenihan's pockets and remove any paper with his own name and phone number on it, but leave behind any papers with Dooley's, Prell's and Kempelman's names. I suggest you check out other reform-minded politicians whom Lenihan might have approached with his proposal. The ones who are *not* showing up are the ones who, I think, bear scrutinizing. I'd do it myself, but far be it from me to involve myself in an investigation that properly falls within your purview."

"Are you trying to tell me how the Albany police department should conduct an investigation?"

"I've been trying for years with scant success. But think it over. It makes sense, Ned. Have you traced Lenihan's movements in the days before he was killed? I've been curious about that."

"He was in Los Angeles," Bowman said. "One of my officers found it on some flight manifests, and we assume Lenihan was visiting his mother, but I haven't been able to get Joanie to come to the phone. Of course, I'm sure you already know all about that, you being my superior officer in this investigation. Am I right, huh? Am I right?"

"I did hear something about Los Angeles. Or was it Salt Lake City?"

"I might be flying out there tomorrow if the chief okays it, so you be here bright and early, no later than eight. You got that?"

My heart sank. "Why are you going to LA? To question Lenihan's mother?"

"That, and to find out who this Al Piatek character is who's supposed to have left Lenihan a lot of money. Hell, I'm beginning to have my doubts about whether these famous millions even exist."

I glanced at the suitcases, which Timmy had an ankle propped up on again. I said, "Have a nice flight."

"And I'll see *you* at eight."

"Sure you will." I hung up.

"That's an interesting idea," Timmy said. "But I don't think it holds up."

I said, "Crap. Bowman might be going to LA tomorrow. We'll have to leave tonight and get there first, or he'll just send everybody running for cover. What's an interesting idea?"

"About some other pol Lenihan might have approached whose name was removed from Jack's belongings. Except, who would it be? There's nobody else running a mayoral candidate who's even vaguely reformist."

"What about the Liberal party?"

"They're not putting anybody up in local elections. Anyway, who ever heard of a liberal beating somebody over the head with a tire iron? We're more subtly insidious than that."

"True, Lenihan wasn't mollycoddled to death."

"What did you mean when you said you were 'not exactly' meeting Hankie-mouth tonight?"

"I'll show you if you feel like accompanying me out into the winter air which you find so bracing. It's eleven-twenty, time to get going."

"You're going out now?"

"Just down the hill. I want to watch something happen."

"The weather twinkie on Channel 12 just said it was three below out. I'm not going out into *that*."

"And you're the one who finds this arctic purity so invigorating," I said, and dropped an ice cube down his back.

Using the deserted side streets north of the Hilton, I walked down the hill toward the river, the snow underfoot grabbing my boot soles with its tiny fangs. I scraped it away at each curb I came to. At 11:40 I fiddled the lock of a rear door on an old four-story business building at Clinton and

Pearl. Inside the darkened top-floor front office of Nardia Prosthetic Technicians I found a quietly sighing radiator beneath a clean-enough window overlooking the intersection. I pulled up a wheelchair, applied the brakes, and waited.

Traffic below was light and sporadic. From time to time a car cruised down the I-787 exit ramp and turned onto Pearl or ground on up Clinton on the hard-packed snow. A few lights burned in the Federal Building, catty-corner from where I sat. Across Clinton the old Palace Theater was dark; the marquee said GIV NOW TO THE UN TED AY.

At 11:56 a large station wagon rolled down from the expressway in the left-turn lane and paused. It made an illegal left through a red light and moved slowly south on Pearl. The wagon left my field of vision but reappeared a minute later heading north. This time it made a U-turn in the intersection and pulled into the no-parking zone in front of the Palace. The wagon was a black late '70s model Ford with New York plates, possibly number ATX-947, though the numbers and letters were partially covered with winter road grime, so I wasn't certain.

The station wagon waited in front of the theater, its lights off but engine idling, for just under half an hour. The front seat was occupied only by the driver, whose face was obscured by the glare of a streetlight on the car's windshield. When the wagon had been maneuvering earlier, no passengers had been visible in it.

Eight other cars, including an Albany PD black-and-white, passed through the intersection during the period the wagon stayed there. None stopped or slowed down in any way not dictated by the changing traffic signals. At 12:26 the wagon's lights went on. The driver waited for another thirty seconds before suddenly sending up a shower of sand and snow, then roaring through a red light and on up to the interstate, where it turned north toward either Troy or the I-90 east-west interchange.

No other cars appeared below, and I sat for a time warming my hands over the friendly radiator. I wheeled over and used Nardia Prosthetics' telephone to wake up an acquaintance who worked for the Department of Motor Vehicles. He agreed to track down the ownership of the station wagon the next day and leave the information with my answering service. I called the service—which reported no messages other than many urgent requests to contact Lieutenant Ned Bowman—and told them I would continue to be out of touch over the weekend but that I would check in periodically.

For a while longer I sat in the wheelchair warming my hands and watching the traffic signals change. At one o'clock I pulled my cap down over my ears and went back out into the cold, locking several doors behind me, and wondering why Hankie-mouth had been so certain that I would not show up for our rendezvous with the cops on my side and accompanying me.

"I'm packed," Timmy said. "Will they let us on the plane with just a Macy's shopping bag?"

"You're really coming? I'm glad. I like to travel with you. Except for your psychopathic insistence on clean sheets wherever you sleep, you travel well. You're open to the vicissitudes."

"I woke up the boss and told him I wouldn't be in tomorrow. But I'm counting on you to keep the vicissitudes to a minimum on this trip."

"That's always my firm intention."

"You have cash, I hope. I've only got about twelve dollars."

"Do I have cash? Do I have *cash?*" I took out the five small numbered keys Jack Lenihan had sent me, flopped a suitcase onto the bed, and unlocked it. I undid the latches and raised the lid. We stared silently at the contents.

After a moment, Timmy said, "That's one."

"One what?"

"Vicissitude."

The suitcase was full of newspapers.

"Let's try another one."

With my pulse rumba-ing in my ears, I opened the second bag.

"That's two."

"Oy."

We opened the three remaining bags and sorted through the contents. All five contained copies of the Los Angeles *Times* dating back over the past nine months. The most recent was the previous Saturday's, January 12.

"You have been diddled," Timmy said.

"Somebody has. Bloody hell."

"Are we still going?"

"Hell, yes, we're going. We'll pick up some cash from a machine at Kennedy. Hell."

"That's not what I meant. Maybe Lenihan was *nuts*, and he created this furor out of *nothing*. This is insane."

I took out Lenihan's letter and reread it carefully. I said, "No. I don't think so, no. Lenihan had a history of erratic behavior but not of mental illness. This letter is not only sincere, it shows every sign of his having a firm grip on a quixotic but plausible reality. No, Lenihan shipped these suitcases believing the money was inside them—the two and a half million legally passed on to him by Al Piatek. The money was removed from the bags between the time Lenihan locked them and the time we opened them. Now it's just a matter of following the track backwards. Look, I know you think I've lost my marbles on this one. That I've been bewitched by the possibility of defanging the municipal werewolves of Albany. I admit that I am salivating at the thought. But there *is* something genuine going on here.

Something so real to somebody that Jack Lenihan was killed over it. And that's real enough for me."

He sighed resignedly, one of his sighs that originate down around his knees and work their way up through his thighs, groin, midsection, chest, trachea, and out his mouth, nose, ears and hair follicles. "Maybe you're right. I've got to try to open my mind and keep it that way a while longer. My own objectivity has been clouded somewhat by the fact that what I really want right now is to go home and set the electric mattress pad on high. Maybe I'm getting too old for vicissitudes this messy. But I have to admit that now I'm almost as curious as you are, so let's go. Let's get it over with."

"Now you're talking—showing the trust and generosity of spirit that I've come to expect of you, and which you've hardly ever regretted. Could I borrow some of the underwear and socks you bought? I'll take a quick shower and then we'll hit the road. Is your new toothbrush in the bathroom?"

"You didn't pick one up? God, you know I hate it when you use my toothbrush."

"I can put your cock in my mouth, but not your toothbrush."

"I don't brush my teeth with my cock."

"That's not what they say about you in Poughkeepsie."

TEN

TWO HUNDRED TWELVE PEOPLE WITH bloodshot eyes and winter coats over their arms hiked down a series of long pastel corridors punctuated by ramps, belts, moving stairways, and tombstone-like inscriptions of welcome from Thomas C. Bradley, mayor.

Timmy said, "I accept the airline's word that this place is

Los Angeles, but it feels like a subway station in Philadelphia."

"You'll like LA a little better once we're outside. Think of New Jersey with palm trees."

"I'll bet it's not as simple as that."

"You're right, it isn't."

Luggage-less except for Timmy's shopping bag, we moved directly to the car-rental agency and picked up a Ford Escort identical to the one we'd left at JFK.

Timmy said, "I thought everybody out here drove a Rolls. Or is there a thirty-day waiting period?"

"You're thinking of Beverly Hills. We're going to West Hollywood, where people still ride buses, or even walk on their feet. Another popular mode of transportation there is the skateboard with silver sparkles on the wheels."

"I saw one of those in Albany once, last summer in Washington park."

"What you saw in Albany was an individualist. In Los Angeles you'll witness the future of us all."

"What if I don't like it?"

"I guess you can always emigrate to Belgium."

"I don't believe it. Back east, people will *shop* in shopping malls, but in the end they'll refuse to live in them."

"Poughkeepsie will be under a big plastic dome, like the lid from a can of underarm deodorant, and underneath it'll look and feel just like this. Take it or leave it. It's this or Belgium."

"Well, I've always enjoyed powdered waffles."

A breeze from the mountains had shoved out to sea the gaseous tumor that often hangs over the LA basin, and the air was clean and pleasingly warm in the bleached winter sunlight. We drove north, then east on the San Diego and Santa Monica freeways, then over to Sunset Boulevard and checked into a motel in a neighborhood where the economy appeared to be based on service industries.

"How long will you be staying?" asked the desk clerk, a middle-aged man with sea-green hair growing out of both ears and all three nostrils.

"Two, three days."

"Want a woman?"

"No, thank you."

"A man?"

"We're here for the Moral Majority convention," Timmy said, "so watch your tongue, mister."

"I can get you a nice religious boy who likes to be hit with a palm frond."

I said, "What about a pair of secular humanist twins who'll recite Rousseau in our ears while they bang it at home? Can you get us that?"

"I'd have to make some calls."

"We've only got a few days, so get to work. We'll make it worth your while."

"I can get you Mormons in ten minutes. You don't want a nice clean Mormon?"

"Secular humanists, pops. You send over a couple of Augustinian friars, and we take our business elsewhere, got it?"

"Sure, but I'll have to make some calls."

Out back in our room, Timmy said, "I know the Beverly Hills Hotel is expensive, but do we have to cut corners this closely?"

"It's not that Michelin recommends this particular motel, but this is the neighborhood we'll be operating from. It's convenient. Al Piatek's address, as listed on his probated will, is not far from here, and so is the address on the Greyhound waybills for the five suitcases. My guess is, that's Joan Lenihan's address." I hauled out the five-pound LA phone book and found J. Lenihan at the address on the way-bills. "That's it. We're here. We're getting close to finding out a few things."

"We're getting close to people who *know* a few things, but how can you be sure they'll tell you what they know?"

"I'm not. But it sure is great to be out of Albany, isn't it?"

He gave me a look, then went about emptying his shopping bag and neatly placing its meager contents in a drawer. He had removed his thermal underwear in the airliner's lavatory—when I'd knocked on the door and asked if I could come in and watch how he went about this, he refused me—but we were both overdressed for the seventy-degree temperature, so we walked several blocks up to a slightly tonier neighborhood closer to Beverly Hills, found a men's store and bought chinos and polo shirts. All the shirts had the manufacturer's little logos on the front—small mammals, reptiles, amphibians. I asked for one with an invertebrate, but the clerk said he'd never heard of that company.

Timmy took the car, studied the rental agency's map of Greater Los Angeles, and headed downtown toward the LA County courthouse to further verify the authenticity of Al Piatek's will. Just before noon I walked up into the hills east of Sunset Boulevard to call on the woman I had been told was made of iron but was now prostrate with grief.

The apartment building was a well-preserved relic of ancient Los Angeles, about 1927. It was gray stucco with Spanish colonial grillwork, but it had Elizabethan exposed crossbeams and tile-roofed gables, like some bastard offspring of Queen Isabella and the Duke of Kent. The place was weird but imposing, a sturdy eccentric survivor that said patronize me if you want, but I am beyond the reach of your niggling aesthetic purity. A walkway of small raspberry-colored concrete squares led past a narrow expanse of shadowy green lawn that was clipped nearly to the roots, like a gay haircut in 1978, and up to a high arched entryway with mailboxes and door buzzers. I pressed the button for 5-H, under which the nameplate read *Lenihan—Tesney*. She was a nurse, so she might be home. If she worked eight to four, I'd come back at four-thirty.

"Yes?"

"Mrs. Lenihan?"

"No, Mrs. Lenihan is—to whom am I speaking, please?"

"I'm Don Strachey, a friend of Jack's, and I'd like to talk to Mrs. Lenihan about him."

Her mike remained open, but no sound came forth.

I said, "Before he died Jack asked me to help him with a project that was important to him. I'm now attempting to complete the project, but I need help. I'd just like to sit down with her for a few minutes, if I may. I've flown all the way out here from Albany."

More empty static. Then: "Just a minute, please." The tone was hesitant but not hostile. The static clicked off. I checked my watch and it was nearly three minutes before the voice returned. "Joan says it's all right for you to come up. Just for a few minutes." The door buzzed open.

I took the elevator to the fifth floor and followed a carpeted high-ceilinged corridor to 5-H, where the door stood open and a woman too young to be Jack Lenihan's mother extended her hand and said, "I'm Gail Tesney, a friend of Joan's. Please come in."

I guessed her age to be forty-one or -two. She was tall and slender in white shorts and a red halter, with small breasts and the type of lithe but firm musculature that suggested her tan came from regular tennis and not from lying by the pool with the latest *Cosmo*. Her black hair was lustrous even in the half-light and I felt a faint stirring, a kind of nostalgia for something that had never been more than an enforced experiment in social conditioning with me, a vestigial twitch. She had a wide mouth, lively and slightly asymmetrical black eyes, and she looked relieved to see me, as if a burden she had been under finally was going to be shared.

"Sit down, please. Joan worked eleven to seven last night, but she hasn't been sleeping well lately and she's been up for half an hour. This past week has been very hard on her. I'm sure you understand that."

"You mean the past three days, don't you? Mrs. Lenihan learned of Jack's death on Wednesday and today is Friday. Or had there been other bad news too?"

A good bit of the warmth went out of her smile. She said, "Perhaps you and Joan should talk this out."

The room was bright and comfortable in the California way, with white walls and a low orange-and-blue couch, bamboo shades on the ceramic lamps, an assortment of current Book-of-the-Month Club fiction on rosewood shelving and a good stereo setup with an Oscar Peterson LP propped in front of one speaker. An archway on the right led into a formal dining room with a glass-topped steel-tube table and a blond wood sideboard, beside which were stacked five suitcases of identical size, color and design, and which looked new.

Gail Tesney saw me catch sight of the suitcases as she turned toward a doorway leading to the other end of the apartment. She did a quick double take but said nothing and passed out of sight as I seated myself on the couch. The *American Journal of Nursing* on the end table was addressed to Ms. Gail Tesney, Apartment 5-H, 714 North Scotsmont, which was the apartment I was in.

Muffled voices came from behind a closed door. After several minutes of this I heard a door open—but not close—and Gail Tesney returned. She sat looking tense on a chair facing me and said, "Joan is lying down. She's really not feeling up to talking to anyone about Jack. I'm sorry. I really am. I appreciate that you've come all the way from Albany, and you're disappointed. But—what can I say? I hope you'll understand. Is there some message I can give Joan?"

I said, "Where's the money?"

Her mouth snapped shut and her black eyes flashed, but it wasn't all anger. She seemed frustrated and unable to make up her mind about something. It was also evident that

I was not the sole cause of Gail Tesney's unsettled conflicting emotions.

Working hard not to glance in the direction of the dining room, she said, "What money are you referring to, Mr. Strachey?"

I laid it all out for her—them. How Jack's body had been left in my car; the menacing calls from Hankie-mouth and his assumption that I had the money; my tracing Jack's visits to Joan Lenihan in October and again the weekend before he died; Jack's negotiations with the Albany pols; the letter from Jack asking my help and the arrival of five suitcases full of newspapers with Joan Lenihan's return address on them.

I said, "My aim is to recover the two and a half million, deduct a relatively modest sum to cover my fee and expenses as per Jack's instructions, and then carry out his project—provided, of course, that I can verify to my satisfaction that the money was legitimately obtained in the first place. Who is this Al Piatek anyway?"

Tesney sat poised on the edge of her chair looking stricken throughout my monologue. When I'd finished, she just stared at me. Finally, she said, "I am going to tell you something in confidence."

"All right."

"This is not to be repeated in Albany."

"Is it illegal?"

"Not in California anymore. Texas, I think."

"Then as far as I'm concerned, mum's the word."

"You're gay, aren't you? Jack mentioned that."

"Yes."

"Then you'll understand. Joan and I are lovers."

"I thought you might be. But why the secrecy? This is West Hollywood, where the city hall probably has a statue of Sappho on the roof. Sappho and Montgomery Clift with raised fists."

She wanted to smile but couldn't quite. "Joan and I are

in the medical profession, which is not as consistently enlightened as you might think it is, even in California. There
are certain administrators—closeted dykes themselves in
two cases—who would make our lives a lot more difficult if
we were as open as we'd like to be. Nothing we could sue
over, but a lot of petty meannesses we would prefer to
avoid. We saw it happen to another couple once who were
so brazen as to kiss each other good-bye one morning in the
hospital parking lot."

"I understand that."

"But I am mainly talking about Albany. Joan has her own
reasons for not wanting it known that she's a lesbian, and
although I don't agree with her that it should matter anymore, I do respect her wishes absolutely. I am asking—
insisting—that you do the same."

"I will. But what has that got to do with the problem
we're all facing here?"

"You just said it, Mr. Strachey. The problem we're *all*
dealing with here. I want you to understand that any problem of Joan's is *my* problem too. In fact, Joan wanted to keep
me out of this. And I agree that there are some things that
each of us has to handle on our own. But this is not one of
them. It's too big."

"I agree. Murder is an event that has to command everybody's full attention."

She blanched, then opened her mouth to speak. No
words came out and her chin trembled.

I said, "Who do you and Joan think killed Jack?"

"Why—why, one of those politicians. Isn't that obvious?
Joan has told me all about what Albany politicians are like.
And the horror of it is, they'll probably get away with it. The
police will cover it up. It's sickening."

"And Joan is prepared to let that happen by not telling
them what she knows?"

With a puzzled shake of the head, she said, "I really

don't understand her thinking about that. I just can't get it into my head. She says she simply doesn't want to have *anything* to do with Albany—that nothing but disaster could ever come of it. Yet—oh, I don't know. I *wish* I could understand. I'm *trying* to understand."

Here was some serious strain on a relationship that I guessed was unaccustomed to it. I said, "Please tell me about Al Piatek."

A sound came from the hallway and we both looked up as Joan Lenihan entered the room. She calmly leaned down and kissed Gail on the cheek, squeezed her hand, then sat on the other end of the couch and gazed at me with pained, resentful eyes.

"You did not have to do this," she said. "None of it. I read the letter Jack wrote to you. You could have turned it over to the police and left Albany until the whole thing blew over. But here you are, aren't you? Big as life and twice as persistent." She slipped a cigarette from the pack on the end table and lit it. "Jack was a true Lenihan in some ways—a brooder, sometimes vindictive, often a little too footloose and fancy-free for his own good. But he was always a superb judge of character."

"Not always," I said. "Someone he trusted killed him."

She didn't flinch, just stared at me with eyes full of suppressed rage, the cigarette poised in the air, smoke curling around the feathery close-cropped hair, which was the color of the smoke. She was sixtyish, small-boned but full-breasted, with a long worn face and a slight overbite. She wore jeans and a brown UCLA sweatshirt and was not so tanned as Gail Tesney, though her slight body gave off an aura of tensile strength. She came across as a woman capable of remarkable feats of work or pleasure, and a woman not to be messed with.

She said, "I'll pay your expenses. But there is no fee, Mr. Strachey. I'm sorry, but your client is dead."

"Who killed him?"

"I don't know. Nothing anyone in Albany does surprises me."

"You think it was one of the politicians he was bargaining with?"

"I suppose."

"But not dope dealers?"

"Jack wasn't doing that anymore. He told me. And he never lied to me. He didn't have to. We were like that."

"His death must be very hard for you to accept."

She blew smoke out the side of her mouth, turned to watch it trail away, and said, "Yes. It is."

"Did Jack know he was in danger? Did you?"

A faint shiver passed through her. "No. No, not that kind of danger."

"In his letter to me, Jack said someone was very angry with him. You said you read the letter before he mailed it. Who was he referring to?"

She sat there seeming to work at manufacturing a careful response in her mind. "Perhaps he meant me," she said.

"Why you?"

"Because I was against this whole business from the very beginning. Jack was like a giddy child with it, and I was the mother telling him it was foolish and irresponsible. There *is* no way to save Albany. I told him that. The place is rotten to the core, and Jack was wasting his time. There are people in Albany who can kill you just by touching you. The only thing you can do is stay away from them. I *know* this."

"I take it your own experience there was not a happy one."

A hard look. "Not happy? Don't trivialize what I am telling you, Mr. Strachey. Yes, I was a young Catholic lesbian on Walter Street married to a drunk, and there was not a day that passed from my twenty-third year to my forty-first year when I did not consider sticking my head in the oven and letting the Lenihans try to explain it to the neighborhood. If it hadn't been for Jack and Corrine—for their needing me, and for the love they gave to me—I would have done it. Except for my children, I detested my life in Albany, and until my husband died I was too weak a person to change it. But my own experience was my own doing. It was all I knew at the time, and I would have done the same thing in any town. Albany's rottenness is bigger than that."

Tesney was sitting with her chin in hands, listening hard, trying to make sense of what we were hearing, as was I.

I said, "I think I get the drift of what you're saying, but I'm not sure. Can you elaborate?"

She said, "No. I can't. It's not worth it."

"All right. For now, then, who is Al Piatek?"

She blew smoke toward a half-open window where the breeze made the smoke shudder suddenly and vanish. "Albert Piatek was a very sad young man. He should not have died. But he's gone now, and it's better that you let him rest. Can you understand that?"

"That can't be. You know it."

Her look was bitter. "*Do* I know that? I didn't know I knew that."

"An Albany police detective by the name of Bowman is on his way out here. He'll want to question you, and he'll be checking on Piatek. It's better that I discover first whatever there is to know. I think *you* understand *that*."

Her face reddened and she abruptly stubbed out the cigarette. She stood, her whole body working, uncertain about whether to leave the room or smash a lamp over my head. She left the room suddenly and a door slammed down the hallway.

Gail Tesney sat gazing fiercely at the ceiling, tears streaming down her face. She looked over at me after a moment and said, "Please leave now. Would you mind?"

"I'll have to come back. I'm sorry you're caught in the middle of this."

"It's all right. I choose to be where I am. I'm sick of it, but it's all right."

"The money is in those bags in the dining room, isn't it?" She quickly shook her head. "No. No, those bags are empty."

"Joan said Jack showed her his letter to me. Five keys were taped to the bottom of it. It is my belief that just before Jack shipped the bags, his mother removed the keys from the letter, opened the bags, took the money, filled the bags with newspapers, locked them, and replaced the keys in the letter. Why?"

"I don't know! I don't know! I don't know! Please—" She snatched a Kleenex out of a box with one hand and gestured toward the door with the other. As I moved toward it, Tesney turned toward me and blurted, "I can only take so much of this. Wait." She went to the bookshelf, pulled down a copy of Michener's *Space*, and removed a newspaper clipping that had been stuck inside the jacket. This she handed to me and said, "If you can put an end to this damned confusion, please do it. I know I can't. I've tried and I just can't get through to her. *You* try. I've had just about as much of this insanity as I can take."

I said, "I guess you know that you might have to take some more," and her look said she knew it.

Outside, I studied the newsclip, an obituary for Albert R. Piatek, Funston Lane, West Hollywood, who had died the previous October 28 "after a long illness."

ELEVEN

BACK AT THE MOTEL I PHONED AN LA IN- vestigator who'd done some work for me, as I had for him, in times gone by. I asked him to use his phone-company contacts to get a list of calls made from Joan Lenihan's number to Albany, New York, over the previous weekend when Jack had been there. It was 2:25 when I called and he said he'd have the list by five o'clock.

I phoned my service in Albany, which had two messages. One was from an unnamed caller with a muffled voice who asked the operator to inform Mr. Strachey that "you are dead." The other was from my contact at the Department of Motor Vehicles notifying me that the license plate number I'd asked him to track down belonged to a Mrs. Bella Kunkle of North Greenbush, New York, and that she had reported her station wagon stolen from a supermarket parking lot Thursday evening. The theft appeared to have been professionally done.

I consulted a West Hollywood street map in the motel office, then trekked the eight blocks down Sunset to Funston Lane, where I turned right along a narrow residential street lined with small wooden beige bungalows set close together. The tiny houses looked as if they should have had a Lionel train whooshing this way and that way among them. Here and there a lawn sprinkler exhaled a misty spray over a six-foot square of green-bearded earth, though most of the water, having nearly completed its circuitous journey from the Rockies to the Pacific, ran into the gutter and down a grate.

Number 937 Funston Lane had a walkway leading up to a three-by-four-foot side porch with some bougainvillea clinging to a sagging trellis. I rapped on the door, which had a square of window in it with the view inward blocked by a curtain the color of the house. The curtain was shoved aside and a male face peered out at me. The door opened.

"Hi. I already have a set of encyclopedias, you'd have to talk to the owner about aluminum siding, and I already have Jesus in my heart. But thanks anyway."

I said, "How much are you paying for your long-distance calls?"

"I don't make any. Everybody I know lives in West Hollywood."

"But perhaps one of them will move to Fresno and you'll want to stay in touch. Micky's Phone Company will enable you to do that for just pennies a day."

"Anybody who moved to Fresno voluntarily would not be a person who'd want to hear from me. I wish you all the luck in the world with your phone company, Micky, but right now I'm kind of busy."

He tried to shut the door, but I stuck my foot in it. "I'm Don Strachey, a private investigator from Albany, New York, and I'd like to talk with you about Al Piatek."

Slightly built and a little stoop-shouldered, he wore jeans and a lavender T-shirt with printing across the front that said BORN TO RAISE ORCHIDS. He had a sweetly comic oblong face and droll blue eyes that were just right for the sly chirpiness of his manner, but now his face fell. He blinked a couple of times and recited, "The sky was black with chickens coming home to roost."

"What's that from, *Macbeth*?"

"*Camille*, I think. I guess you'd better come in. I'm Kyle Toot."

I entered the miniature house, or houselet.

"Sit wherever you can find a place. No, let's go out to the kitchen."

"Is it nearby?"

We passed through the living roomette, where stacks of paper with printing on them were arranged on the floor, coffee table, couch seat and arms.

"Did Jack Lenihan send you out here, or is he in trouble himself?"

"Both."

"Could I get you anything?"

"Information."

"I'd better have a drink."

I wedged myself into a seat between the Formica table and the south and east walls. Toot brought out a jug labeled "Grackle Valley Pure Spring Water—no additives, no faddatives." He poured from the container into a glass, then replaced the jug in the refrigerator, which had a canister motor atop it, circa 1934. Los Angeles, land of antiquities.

"Do you keep gin in there?"

"No, I keep water in there. It's obvious you're from Albany." He squeezed into the seat across from me.

"Why do you say that?"

"It's a town where the consumption of gin from a jug in midafternoon is probably a commonplace."

"It's endemic but not epidemic. And now you're going to tell me that in Los Angeles the ingestion of mind-altering substances is practically unknown."

"It's known, but not by me. People who want to work can't stay stoned all the time. Unless they're already under contract. I'm not."

"You're an actor?"

"Sometimes. I also cut and staple raffle tickets for a printer. That's the mess in the living room. I get a penny a book, and it's a rich and rewarding life."

"I've heard that acting is chancy."

"Last month it was *Uncle Vanya* at the Harriet and Raymond P. Rathgeber Pavilion, and this month it's raffle tickets. I auditioned for the fool to Charlton Heston's *Lear*, which is opening in May, but Chuck thought I was too tall. Fools in Elizabethan times were never more than four feet tall, he told me, and he wants to keep it authentic. I'm up for the part of Ticky, a new character they're introducing on *Love Boat* next season, but it'll all depend on how my eye-rolling test came out. You have to be able to roll your eyes up into your skull, down the inside of the back of your head, up your jawbone, and into the sockets again. That's how the writers wrote the character, and the producers have too much integrity to alter the conception. I had sinus problems the day I auditioned, so I don't know how well I did."

"Well, I'll watch for you in case you make it. It's my favorite show except for reruns of *Love That Bob*."

He laughed and said, "How's crazy Jack Lenihan doing? Has the law caught up with him yet? Now *there's* an actor."

"He's dead."

Toot went white. "No."

"Yeah."

"What *happened* to him? Jack was fine in October. He's *dead?*"

"Jack died on Tuesday. He was murdered." Toot had been nursing his glass of spring water, but now he set it down and stared at me. I said, "How did you know Jack? Are you from Albany?"

"No, I'm from Encino. Who killed him? *Why?*"

"Those are two things I'm trying to find out. So are the police. An Albany cop by the name of Bowman will probably come by here. It's known that Jack had a connection of some kind with Al Piatek. Everybody wants to know what it was. Did you live with Al here?"

"For a year and a half."

"Lovers?"

He shook his head and shuddered. "No. Thank God, no. We'd tricked once a long time ago, but that was years ago, when he first came out here from Albany. No, Al and I were *not* lovers. I want to make that clear. As it is, a lot of people won't get within ten feet of me. I seem to run into two types these days, guys who think nothing's changed, that we're still back in '77 and Donna Summer's in her heaven and all's right with the world, and guys who think the plague's waiting for them on the rim of every drinking glass. But you don't get AIDS from sharing the rent. There's just no known instance of it."

I said, "I didn't know."

"Know what?"

"How Al Piatek died."

"Oh well, it lasted eight months, and it was inhuman, grotesque."

"He was here with you?"

"Of course. This was his home."

"You two must have been close."

He shrugged. "No. To tell you the truth, I didn't even like Al very much. His interests were in rock music—he was a recording engineer at Zimmer Studios—and was into the musicians and their dope. I like baroque music and I'm indifferent to most pop stuff, except to dance to. In fact, Al wasn't even here very much until he got sick. Mostly, Al went his way and I went mine."

"But you took care of him through the illness?"

"About half the time he was in the hospital. When he was here, I did what I could. People from the AIDS support group came by, and I helped out. I was able to do it because—well, because I knew it wasn't going to last. That Al wasn't going to last. That's cynical, I know, but it was better I did that than cutting out, don't you think?" I nodded. "I did what I could. Al went back to the church toward the end. I took him to Mass the few times he could get out of bed and walk, and I know it helped. I even pretended to regain my own faith. He seemed to want me to. It was phony as all get-out, but I'm a good actor. I sometimes feel guilty about that—that I demeaned Al by pretending. But the alternatives seemed even worse. I think I did the right thing."

"It's complicated, but I think you did too."

"It's a horrible way to die. You're gay, right?"

"How did you know?"

"Oh, puh-*leez*, Mary!"

Twenty years earlier my indignation would have known no bounds, but I'd been carried gasping for air along with the times, so I smiled sweetly. I wasn't wearing an earring or hot hankie, however, so I wondered what the devil he meant. I supposed he had some uncanny sixth sense. Or maybe it was the fact that I hadn't flinched when, as he was speaking, he leaned across the table and placed his hand on mine.

I said, "Your palm is sweating."

He withdrew the hand. "I wanted to see if you were who you said you were."

"Are all private investigators from Albany supposed to be gay? So far as I know, I'm it."

"Al told me Jack Lenihan used to deal dope. And the people he was involved with in that were straight. I thought you might be one of them."

"Why?"

"The money. They'd want their money back. They probably killed Jack trying to get it."

"What money is that?"

"The two and a half million Jack Lenihan gave to Al in October and then asked Al to leave to Jack in his will. Jack was laundering his own money. The story they cooked up was, Janis Joplin had given it to Al when she was stoned one time, and then Al—who was afraid to spend the money and kept it in the trunk of his car—left it to Jack. You didn't know that? I thought that's why you were here."

"I knew Al had left Jack the money. But I didn't know Jack had given it to Al first. That's what I came out here to find out. Where Al had gotten the two and a half million. Jack told Al it was doper's money?"

"No, that was Al's theory. Where else would Jack have gotten it? Jack asked Al to take it and then leave it to him, and Al agreed. Originally it was closer to three and a quarter million, but the estate tax and Al's back income tax plus penalties were something terrific. Jack said he knew he'd lose a lot of it to the tax guys, but that was the price he was willing to pay, he said, to make the cash legitimate. Naturally Al asked Jack where he got the money, but Jack couldn't say. He just kept insisting that what he was doing was not at all immoral, and Al took his word for it. He knew Jack well enough to understand that Jack was sincere, that his word on that score was good. By then, Al had accepted the fact that he was going to die soon, so it gave him something useful to do for an old friend."

"They'd known each other in Albany?"

Toot smiled sadly. "You are in the dark, aren't you? Haven't you spoken with Joan Lenihan? She's here in LA. If you found me, you must have found her."

"Mrs. Lenihan was not overly forthcoming. She's upset about Jack and she's got problems of her own."

Toot looked at me and said, "Al and Jack were lovers in high school. Each was the other's first. The two families didn't know about it—they thought Al and Jack were assembling model airplanes up in the Piateks' attic. What they were really doing was sniffing the glue and fucking each other silly. Al once told me he would remember and fantasize about those hours up there on an old mattress until the day he died. Which I'm sure he did.

"Al said it was never quite as good after those first attic trysts with Jack Lenihan. But it didn't last. One day, while Al was up 'working on his airplanes' with Jack, the senior Piateks and Al's two younger sisters were killed in a car crash outside Albany. Al was brought to LA to live with his grandparents—who died a couple of years ago—and Al and Jack never saw each other again until Joan Lenihan reunited them last October. Some years ago, Jack had told his mother about his first love, so when she met Al out here she arranged a reunion. She thought it might be therapeutic for Al. You see, when Al first went into the hospital and got the news of a positive diagnosis, Joan Lenihan was his nurse."

"She's obviously a kind and sensitive woman."

"She is, and that's not all she is."

"I know."

"Her humanitarianism is not entirely disinterested. She's protecting the tribe. She's lesbian and her son was gay. She's as aware as anybody that under the best of circumstances it ain't easy being puce, and the present circumstances are far from the best. When the AIDS unit opened up at the hospital, Joan Lenihan was the first nurse to volunteer."

I said, "I think I will have a glass of that stuff. Have you got a beer?"

Toot brought me a Bud from the Frigidaire and said, "I keep it around for tricks."

"Tricks? No."

"Sure. Haven't you heard of safe sex? The AIDS council put out a pornographic pamphlet on minimum-risk sex. It's a real turn-on, and I've got one."

"A pamphlet, eh? Well, here I am in kinky LA."

"Wanna see it? It's in Spanish too, if your English is not too good."

"I'll pass. I loathe safe sex. Safe sex is to erotic communion what the Salisbury steak in a restaurant on the New Jersey Turnpike is to food. I do it because it's what there is, but I don't want to think about it any more that I have to." I slugged down some of the beer. Toot's house was cool and the cold beer warmed me up.

With a little smile he said, "I wasn't trying to seduce you. I'm sure you have your professional ethics."

"And my lover in a motel over on Sunset. Whether you were trying to seduce me or not, two or three years ago I would have loved a quick tumble in the sack with you and probably would have initiated it. But that's over. That life has gone the way of cheap gas and free air for your tires. If the two alternatives to monogamy are death and Salisbury steak, I choose monogamy, even though as I speak the words aloud the sound of them makes me a little dizzy."

"Actually there's a third alternative," Toot said with a grin. "If you're rich, that is. I have an actor friend who made a lot of money several years ago and now he spends every third month in Patagonia."

"Patagonia? Patagonia in southern Argentina?"

"There is no AIDS in all of Patagonia, and he found some hotel down there where gay cowboys hang out. He says it's terrific, just like in the olden days—'78, back then. Last summer he spent eleven thousand dollars on airfare. He hasn't had sex with anybody in North America since 1981. He saves it all for the gauchos. Or in Patagonia is it penguins?"

"My God."

"Ernie has Patagonia, but I've at least got my pamphlet. I do what works. I guess you're more of a purist. Like Ernie, except without the cash to act on it."

"I certainly do envy your wealthy and highly imaginative friend," I said. "And I guess I envy you the apparently satisfying erotic existence that your pamphlet has provided you. But I've never been able to do anything halfway. Like Jack Lenihan. Once Jack decided what he wanted to do, he went all the way with it." While Toot watched me bug-eyed, I described Jack's two-and-a-half-million-dollar political project in Albany. "Did he tell you about this?" I asked.

Toot's mouth hung open. "No. No, he didn't. Jesus!"

"Did he tell Al?"

"Not that I know of. No, Al would have told me. Where's the money now?"

"I don't know. Joan Lenihan may have it, I'm not sure. Jack was about to ship the money to me in Albany for safe-keeping, but Joan kept him from doing that. She was against the project for reasons that are not at all clear to me. My plan is to find the money, take it and carry out Jack's project for him. Will you help me?"

He swallowed hard. "Well—maybe. But Jack was killed,

you said. Doesn't that probably mean the owners of the money are trying to reclaim it? Maybe they already have."

"I don't think so. I think it's here in Los Angeles. How well do you know Joan Lenihan? Somebody has to reach her, but it looks as if it's not going to be me."

"I've met her a few times, but that's all. She wouldn't trust me any more than she'd trust you."

"Who *does* she trust?"

"Gail Tesney, her lover."

"She's been shut out too. She doesn't like it, but she can't seem to do anything about it."

"Then forget it. If Gail can't get Joan to open up, nobody can."

"Then Gail will have to do it. She has no choice."

He peered at me, looking a little queasy. "You'd interfere in Gail and Joan's relationship just so you might influence an election in some fur-trading outpost in upstate New York?"

I thought about this, then said lamely, evasively, "It's what Jack Lenihan wanted. It's what he would have wanted me to do."

Eyeing me evenly, Toot said, "Maybe in that respect Jack Lenihan was a heartless creep. Did you ever consider that?"

I had to admit that I hadn't. I had been careful not to. Where was Timmy? *He* was my moral guardian, not this raffle-ticket-stapling Uncle Vanya. I said, "Why don't you come over to the motel and meet Timmy? Maybe he can make this whole business clearer than I've been able to. Bring your raffle tickets along and a couple of extra staplers. This evening we can have a wild threesome—click-shoosh, click-shoosh. The motel we're staying in can probably even come up with a couple of extra stapling artists. Though I don't know that they'd necessarily be the safe-stapling type."

"What's the name of the place?"

"The Golden Grapefruit."

"Oh, that guy can get safe-staplers. He can get you anything you want."

"He can? Uh-oh."

Toot followed me into my room at the motel.

"Hi, sake-zy."

"Who are you?"

"I'm Ramon, and this is my friend Juan. Hey, your friend is very cute too, but *I* wan *chu*."

. They were propped up on pillows on the bed watching *Sale of the Century*. Ramon was in red briefs, Juan in tiger stripes. Their clothes were heaped on a chair. Toot tried to look bemused.

I said, "Who let you in here? This is my room."

Ramon winked. "We the sexular human boys. We gonna have a good time, sweetheart, you will see. Hey, you want me go out and pick up some booze? We gonna get thirsty, I'm thinking."

I said, "Out," and pointed to the open door.

Juan looked worried, but Ramon stood up, slithered out of his briefs, walked over and placed my hand on his unexceptional erection. "I gone fuck you till you blow up, man. I gone fuck you till you the happiest man in LA. I gone . . ."

I led him away. He resisted when we came to the doorsill, but I had a firm grip and he yielded soon enough. As we emerged into the parking lot Timmy pulled up in the rental car, got out, and said, "My little horse must think it queer to stop without a farmhouse near."

"I found him and his friend in the room. They're just on their way out. They claim to be secular humanists, but I know a couple of Alexandrian Copts when I see them. I *told* that guy."

Juan sidled out the door wearing pants now and carrying a distressed bundle of clothing and shoes. I released Ramon, who dressed rapidly, muttering and hurling imprecations at

me in two languages. "I gonna talk to Teddy, man! I don'
like getting fucked over, and somebody gonna pay for this,
man!"

I introduced Timmy to Kyle Toot, then went in and rang
the desk. "Is this Teddy?"

"Speaking."

"This is Donald Strachey in one-oh-six. I said secular humanist twins and you sent me a couple of Aztec Jehovah's
Witnesses. Now if you can't even come up with a pair of
certified Unitarians, just *forget it*. I'm warning you, I'll want
to see their ACLU membership cards. Do you understand
what I'm saying? My friend and I have very specific tastes."

"I'll have to make some more calls."

"If we have to go back to Lynchburg horny, it'll be *your
fault*." I slammed down the receiver.

Timmy was shaking his head. "Don, really."

"You're making a big mistake," Toot said. "He'll have a
set of hot Unitarians in here inside of an hour. This is LA."

I said, "No. It isn't possible."

"You'll see."

I rang Teddy back and said, "This is Strachey in one-oh-
six again. Cancel the Unitarians. We just heard about a Triv-
ial Pursuit tournament at a bar in Westwood, and it's first
things first."

"Fuckin' eastern kooks!" Teddy said, and hung up on me.

TWELVE

WE SAT IN THE MOTEL STAPLING RAFFLE
tickets for an American Legion post in Pomona that was selling chances on a VCR, two cases of Johnnie Walker, and
eighteen frozen turkeys. I brought Timmy up-to-date on the
day's events, and he described his visit to the LA County

courthouse, where he verified the legitimacy of Al Piatek's will. Kyle Toot told us more about Piatek's last days, including his dipping into Lenihan's millions—with Jack's permission—to throw a good-bye party for himself. He invited twenty-three friends in the recording business; five showed up. They consumed thirty-seven ounces of Beluga caviar spread on Nabisco saltines and six bottles of *Clos Vougeot* '64. At two in the morning Piatek passed out in his chair by the stereo, where he had been selecting the tapes to be played. He never regained consciousness and died in a hospital bed three days later. His last words, as far as anyone could recall, had been, "My feet are cold."

At 4:45 my contact at the investigating agency downtown phoned with the news that two toll calls had been placed from Joan Lenihan's phone the previous weekend. One, on Saturday, at 5:43 P.M., was to Jack Lenihan's Albany number, and the conversation had lasted for just three minutes. The other call, on Monday, at 9:12 A.M. was to a number in Troy, New York, listed under the name Florence Trenky. That call lasted twenty-two minutes. I thanked my friend and told him to bill me at my Albany address, thinking he'd say forget it, but he didn't.

I told Timmy and Kyle Toot what I had learned, and asked Toot, "Did Jack ever mention a Florence Trenky?"

"No, I'd remember that one. Though Jack didn't talk much about his current life in Albany. He and Al mostly talked about the old days there, growing up and their secret life in the Piateks' attic. When he came here in October to bring the money out to Al, Jack did tell me about his recent separation from his lover, Warren something-or-other."

"Slonski."

"He didn't really want to leave Slonski, he said, but there was something important he said he had to do that Slonski wouldn't approve of and wouldn't want to be mixed up in. I guess that was the big money and the political wheeling and dealing, right?"

"Right. And he never gave you any clue about where he'd gotten the two and a half million?"

"He joked about being afraid the suitcases containing the money might break open in the plane's baggage compartment, though that hadn't happened. Otherwise, all he said was that what he was doing was completely moral. He kept repeating that to both me and Al, trying to reassure us."

"Maybe he was trying to reassure himself too. Did you ever get that impression?"

Toot put down his stapler and considered this. After a moment, he said, "No. I don't think there was any doubt in Jack's mind at all about the ethical correctness of what he was doing. In fact, he once said, 'Two wrongs *can* make a right.' He seemed to be certain of this, and very determined to right some kind of wrong. Whatever it was. Maybe Joan Lenihan knows all about it. I got the impression that they were quite close, that they confided in each other. Do you think she knows the whole story?"

"I think so, yes. The essentials, anyway. The question is, will she ever tell a living soul?"

"If she does," Toot said, "it will be Gail Tesney, not any of us."

"We're back to Gail. I'd like to talk with her alone. Does she work on the AIDS unit too?"

"No, on the next floor up, cardiac care."

"Can you find out when she's on today?"

Toot phoned the hospital where Lenihan and Tesney worked and learned that Gail had come on duty at four o'clock. "She'll probably have her dinner break at seven or seven-thirty. If you go out there, I'd like to come along—to keep you from asking too much of Gail, or pressuring her into something that'll make trouble between her and Joan."

"She can say no to anything I ask her to do. She's a grown-up."

"Yeah, she's a grown-up, but you're an arrogant, conniving son of a bitch. I think I'm going to have to keep a close eye on you."

Timmy, never happier than when playing the task-oriented monk, was sitting cross-legged on the floor stapling maniacally, complaining from time to time of lower back pains but not letting up in raffle-book production. Now he set his stapler down and said, "He's not always like that, Kyle. But when he thinks he can put one over on Albany municipal government, his brain sputters and shorts out. He turns into this one-man vigilante mob out to pour hot lead—metaphorically speaking, of course—into the corrupt guts of the Albany city fathers. If an innocent bystander or two gets in the way, tough luck."

I said, "I'm being ganged up on. I don't like that."

"Rather than turning this whole business over to the police," Timmy went on blithely, "where a murder investigation properly belongs, he's got the both of us flying back and forth across North America—on *my* MasterCard, mind you; he's over his limit, as usual—trying to get hold of five suitcases full of money that belongs to God-knows-who. And it's all because I refused to run away to the Caribbean with him on a whim."

"Not entirely true."

"And," he went on, as Toot listened gravely, "this whole deal is predicated on the assumption that Jack Lenihan's two and a half million was legitimately obtained. Now that we know that Al Piatek was just a friendly conduit and not a wealthy philanthropist, we *have* to be highly suspicious of the money's origins. I think we're back to dopers' money, and that scares the hell out of me. People like that are not to be diddled with, as it appears Jack Lenihan learned too late."

He was relentless. He went on in this sententious vein for some minutes, as Toot sat there nodding and occasionally blanching at particularly breathtaking examples of my lunatic behavior. "On the other hand," Timmy sweetly concluded, "Don is a loyal friend, a stimulating social companion, and a great fuck. It's just that he's sloppy around the house and unable to abide sloppiness outside it. As you can see, this makes life complicated for him—and for just about everybody who crosses his path."

I winked at Toot and said, "Timmy likes to think of himself as my Boswell, but what he is is the *National Enquirer* of my soul. In his reporting on me, zany exaggerations and lurid distortions abound."

Toot shrugged and said, "I've only known you for half a day, but it all sounded pretty accurate to me. Of course, I wouldn't know about the 'great fuck' part," he added and lowered his eyes shyly.

These two were meant for each other. I left them, borrowed a bathing suit from Teddy, and went out for a swim in the small pool, which at the Golden Grapefruit was gonococcus-shaped.

The three of us descended on Gail Tesney at her table in the hospital employees' cafeteria. She was seated alone, and if she wanted company, her look suggested we were not it. She greeted Toot with what warmth she could muster and offered me a faint hello. I introduced Timmy, who immediately said, "Don here means well, but don't let him push you around." I wanted to pick up Tesney's plate of chicken tetrazzini and push it in Timmy's face.

Gail said coolly, "I can take care of myself, Mr. Callahan. I've been doing it for many years." He seated himself, chastened for the moment.

I sat across from her and said, "Jack Lenihan is not coming back and I can't do anything about that. But what I can do is finish the admirable job Jack started." For ten minutes I described in what seemed to me irresistibly gut-wrenching detail the horrors of Albany city government and how two and a half million dollars in the right hands might change all that. Throughout my dissertation, Timmy and Kyle sat stiffly, gazing at the walls. When I concluded my remarks, Timmy's stomach rumbled loudly and he said, "Sorry."

Gail peered at me solemnly across her tetrazzini and said, "You want me to get information from Joan, is that it? Sneak around, perhaps read her mail, browbeat her, threaten to leave her—do whatever it takes to find out what happened to all that money—and then pass the information on to you. Do I understand you correctly, Mr. Strachey?"

"No, not exactly. I just thought if you happened to break through the wall of secrecy Joan has built up around herself, you would be happier, she would be happier, and it could only strengthen your relationship and clear the tension out of it. And if in the process you managed to convince Joan to share her knowledge of the history of Jack's money with a trustworthy, well-meaning third-party—that would be me—then so much the better."

She looked at me as if her tetrazzini were not agreeing with her. She said, "You are the most arrogant and smugly presumptuous man I have ever met."

"People have been saying that about me lately."

"Well, I'm not surprised." She tilted her head and gave it a quick shake, as if she'd been swimming and wanted to dislodge some water from her ear. "You are something out of—I don't know what."

"Joseph Conrad? I sometimes fancy myself that way."

"No, Judith Krantz, I think."

"Oh."

"In any case, you won't be needing my help in your quest to alter history in the Hudson Valley."

"I won't?"

"No, you won't. Joan has agreed to speak with you."

"Well now—good for her!"

"Joan phoned me a while ago. She called in sick for her

shift, and while she was at home some obnoxious policeman from Albany came to the apartment. She couldn't stand him. He reminded her of the type of man who had made her life miserable twenty years ago. She didn't tell him anything, but she realizes that someone has got to clear up the confusion and find Jack's killer if she is ever to have any peace of mind again, and she has decided to take a chance on you. Jack trusted you, she said, so Joan is going to risk trusting you too. I'm beginning to wonder, though, if Jack was in his right mind when he got mixed up with you."

On the way out of the hospital, Timmy said, "Mr. Charm strikes again."

Toot added, "Back east you must be considered the David Susskind of your profession."

I insisted on going off to see Joan Lenihan alone and dropped Timmy and Kyle off at the motel. But I was beginning to suspect that they might be on to something. Inept attempts at psychological torture were not among my usual bag of tricks. But then this situation was special, wasn't it? I had to drive the beasts from the city. I had a quest, a mission. Everybody thought I was nuts, but what I was was inspired.

Aflame, I drove over to Scotsmont Avenue, where I was certain Joan Lenihan would add fuel to the holy fire. But that is not what she did at all.

THIRTEEN

"I HAVE RETURNED THE MONEY TO ITS rightful owners, Mr. Strachey. I hate to disappoint you, but I really had no choice in the matter."

I glanced into the dining room, where the five suitcases

were no longer stacked up. "It was in those bags that were in there when I was here earlier, right?"

"No. The cash was in trash bags in our storage area in the basement of this building. Now it's in the suitcases and on its way back to the people it belongs to. I just returned from the Air Freight office a few minutes ago."

Air Freight. I briefly considered a grand heist but figured pantywaist Timmy would consider armed robbery going too far. I said, "Why?"

She lit a cigarette and stuck it up under her overbite. She was wearing a Yucatecan huapili white shift with fancy blue and green embroidery and she was barefooted. Her toenails were cracked and painted fuchsia. She said, "My son took something that didn't belong to him. He was killed because of it. I don't want anyone else to be hurt—you, or your friend—or Gail, or me. Or Corrine. Poor Corrine, she's so unsophisticated and innocent, and who knows what people might suspect. No, it's not worth it. What Jack wanted to do—what you want to do with the money—I admire it. Truly, I do. When Jack first told me about it, I had to laugh. I admit it, I laughed." Her eyes brightened at the thought of it, then went gray again. "But you cannot—cannot—get away with something like that. Not when the people you are dealing with are savages."

"And who are these savages?"

"I think you must know."

"No."

She looked at me carefully and said, "Dope pushers. Surely in your line of work you must have heard the type of people they are."

"Which dope pushers?"

"The ones Jack was arrested with. Robert Milius and—I've forgotten the names of the others. Jake something, I think."

"They're still in prison, aren't they?"

"But they have friends on the outside. People who were protecting the money for them until their release. Jack somehow got hold of the money and came up with this crazy pipe dream of his. And they found out he had taken it."

"Precisely who was keeping the money in what place, and how did Jack manage to take possession of it?"

She coughed out some smoke and said, "Oh, I wouldn't know that. Jack never went into the details. He just said they could never prove he'd taken it, and he had all these alibis worked out, he said, and—I just don't know all the details."

"And you urged him to return the money?"

"Of course I did. Anyone who sees the six-o'clock news knows that you simply cannot cheat people of that type and expect to get away with it."

"Jack must have watched the six-o'clock news too, and he had firsthand knowledge of dealers and their ways as well. Why didn't he listen to you?"

A wan smile. "I'm his mother. When your mother offers you advice, do you accept it for what it's worth, or do you just think, oh, crazy old Ma, there she goes again?"

"My mother hasn't offered me advice for a number of years. She's a little confused about my life and how to approach it. Gail told me Ned Bowman had been here. I'm sure he had some motherly advice. What did you tell him?"

"Nothing."

"Why?"

"Because I don't want Jack's name brought up again in connection with drugs. I'm thinking of Corrine, and of Jack's memory. I told Officer Bowman I knew nothing. He didn't take it well, but that's his problem."

"He knows about Al Piatek. He'll learn soon enough that Piatek had no money to speak of and couldn't have left Jack the two and a half million in Piatek's will. He'll lean on you and on Kyle Toot, and possibly Gail. He won't let up. I think you should tell him everything you told me. Tomorrow, I mean—tell him tomorrow. Don't you want Jack's killer punished?"

A look of profound sadness settled across her face. "Yes," she said. "Yes, I do. So much, I do. But maybe that isn't possible without ruining other people's lives. Good lives that people have made out of—of nothing at all."

"I don't follow. Whose lives?"

She said nothing, just stubbed out the half-smoked cigarette in an ashtray full of half-smoked butts.

I said, "Who did you ship the money to? Not Milius, if he's in prison. How did you know who to send it to? Jack didn't provide details, you said. Have these 'friends' of Milius been in touch? How did they know you even *had* the money? Back in Albany word is going around that *I've* got it. Mrs. Lenihan, you're not making sense."

She looked away and thought hard about something. She said, "I can't tell you any more. I'm sorry, but I can't." She faced me again. "The important thing is Jack is dead, and nothing anyone says or does is going to change that. So forget the money, Mr. Strachey. Just go on as you did before. I've written a check that should cover your trip out here, but that's as far as I'm able to help you. I'm still paying off a loan I took out to underwrite Jack's legal fees when he was arrested. I have eight more years to go on that loan and I only hope I live that long, because Gail has agreed to inherit my debts as well as my meager assets.

"Gail has been—except for Jack and Corrine, Gail has been *everything* to me. I met her three days after I arrived in California eighteen years ago next Sunday, and in many respects that was the day my real life began. I told Jack I would do almost anything to keep that life from falling apart and—if he had only known—" Her face trembled and she looked away, suddenly slapping the side of her head as if she had misbehaved and was striking out at herself in anger and confusion.

I said, "I won't bother you anymore. But if you would just tell me who—"

She shook her head once vehemently.

"I know you don't deserve any of this," I said. "You've obviously paid heavily in advance for your life here. I hope it lasts a long time."

"It will," she said, in tears. "I've been happy—a happy person. I never used to believe there was such a thing. And Jack was—he was happy for me."

She wept.

Timmy and Kyle Toot were sitting on the motel-room floor stapling raffle tickets and discussing my character flaws.

"Pack your shopping bag. We've got to get back to Albany fast."

"Now? I thought we could find a good Mexican restaurant, see some sights, and then sack out for twelve hours. Come on, we've earned it."

I described my visit with Joan Lenihan. "I've got to see who picks up the five suitcases that were in Joan's dining room. They were a kind of maroon plastic with a black band around them. I'll stake out the Albany Air Freight office tomorrow, and when somebody shows and claims those bags I'll be back in the ball game."

"Doesn't Air Freight deliver a lot of its arriving cargo by truck? It's not like shipping by bus, where you have to pick up your own packages."

"Crap. That's right. Do we know anybody at Air Freight in Albany?"

"I don't think so."

"Well, I'll find somebody. I've got to make a couple of phone calls, and then let's get going."

The two of them sat there clutching their staplers and looking irritated. "I thought you two might like to see some LA gay nightlife," Toot said. "It's Friday night in West Hollywood. You can see some of your favorite TV stars with their hair down. Down around their ankles in some cases. For instance, Bonkie Dimpleton of *Undertaker Uggams* usually shows up at the Compost Heap around two in the morning with his slave Raoul, who wears a T-shirt with a picture of the Colombian flag on the front made out of sewn-on diamonds. Do you want to miss out on that?"

"It sounds like an eye-opening way to spend an evening, but I'm afraid Timmy would become disillusioned and never watch *Undertaker Uggams* again. There's nobody from *Masterpiece Theatre* out here acting like that, I hope."

"Oh, sure. Even *Wall Street Week in Review*. Especially *Wall Street Week in Review*."

"Don't tell me, I don't want to know."

"Travel is sometimes unavoidably broadening," Toot said.

Timmy looked glum. "I'd really like to get a glimpse of it. Just once. My life in Albany is so glitzless."

"I thought you *preferred* it that way. Quiet evenings by the picture of the fire, building snowmen in the park on a Sunday afternoon."

"I just want to see it, that's all. So I can go home feeling morally superior."

"You can't manage that on your own? You live in *Albany*, for chrissakes. And, of course, you've got *me* for that too."

"Would you mind a whole lot if I stayed over until Sunday? I could be back home early Sunday night. You won't need me for anything, will you?"

"Well, naturally I'll need you for something. I always need you for something."

"You're envious. You want to stay too."

"There is that, yes."

"Kyle was telling me about this good production he heard about of *Krapp's Last Tape* at a storefront Chicano Theater in East LA. I'd like to go with him to see it."

"Hispanic Beckett? You once told me you didn't even

like it when Pearl Bailey went into *Hello, Dolly!* You said there wouldn't have been any black Jews in Yonkers in 1912. You're the most neurotically purist theatergoer I've ever known."

"Well, I'm in LA now, where the biggest service industry after movie-making, drug pushing and prostitution is the human-potential movement. Come on, Don, give me a break. It's no big deal for us to be out of each other's company for a couple of days. We've done it before. We're friends and lovers, not Siamese twins."

"He can stay at my place," Toot said, "and I'll be careful to keep him out of harm's way. I'll keep him on the sidelines as it boogies by."

I was a little worried about Timmy showing up in the barrio in the company of a man wearing a lavender T-shirt that said BORN TO RAISE ORCHIDS, but if that's what he wanted to do, who was I to keep him from widening his cultural horizons? The main truth was, I just wanted him with me for the next few days back in Albany. The more I thought about it, the more Joan Lenihan's story of unnamed dope dealers losing two and a half million in cash—actually three and a quarter million—to Jack Lenihan, and then fumbling and bumbling around trying to get it back, sounded screwy. There were too many holes in it, too much that was only shakily and superficially plausible. Still, I didn't know who or what I would run into back in Albany, and I was apprehensive—scared—and would have liked Timmy nearby. If I had told him that, he would have come with me without a second thought. Out of habit and dumb pride, I didn't say it.

I said, "I'm deeply envious, but it's up to you. You'd just better have some good stories to dine out on when you get back."

He grinned. "You mean I can relax and have fun without worrying that you're being a pain in the neck about it?"

"I'm not your mother, am I? And you're well past four-teen. God knows."

"Look, be careful back there. If you get the urge to do anything foolhardy, call me first."

"Right. Dial-a-Jesuit."

"And don't mess with any dopers, okay? When you find out what the story is—and I don't doubt that you will—pass the damned information on to the cops, will you? The two and a half million is lost now anyway. It's evidence in a crim-inal proceeding. It properly belongs to the state of New York."

"Sure. If that's the way it works out, sure. You know me, Timothy. I may use poor judgment from time to time, but I am not a crook."

Time was running out, so I got him packing his shopping bag while I placed my calls. I tracked down my LA in-vestigator friend at home and asked him to come up with a list of toll calls made from Joan Lenihan's number from Tuesday, the day my earlier list ended, up to the present time. He said he couldn't do it that night at all, that it would be tough on a Saturday, that it would cost me, but he'd see what he could do in the morning. I said I'd check back with him at noon on Saturday LA time.

I phoned my service in Albany and was told that there had been no calls for me from Hankie-mouth or anyone else. That could have meant that Joan Lenihan had quieted Han-kie-mouth by assuring him of the money's imminent safe re-turn to him, or it could have meant something else. I was unable to figure out what.

Finally I phoned the airline and made reservations for Timmy, LA to Albany, on Sunday afternoon, and for me, LA to JFK, where we'd left a rental car, at 10:15 that night.

Ten minutes later I bade farewell to the Golden Grape-fruit. Timmy and Kyle watched me stuff my face at a taco joint on Wilshire before I drove them over to Funston Lane.

A big Buick with a rental agency insignia was parked in front of Toot's little house, and Ned Bowman was standing on the lawnlet peering in a front window.

I cruised on by, parked down the block, and explained to Toot who was waiting for him. "Tell Bowman about Jack's using Al as a conduit to launder the two and a half million. He'll check up on Piatek's financial situation and figure it out anyway. But don't tell him more than that—Joan Lenihan's story about dopers, or anything else that came from her. She wants it that way for her own reasons, which are still unclear to me, but she doesn't need Bowman going at her with a rubber hose right now. He'll probably recognize Timmy and deduce that I'm in LA, but don't tell him I've gone back to Albany. Tell him—tell him I've driven down to check out a lead in the mountains of central Mexico."

Timmy said, "He'll never believe that."

Toot had a better idea. "I'll tell him you'll be showing up later at the Compost Heap and maybe he'd like to meet us there."

I said I thought that was a lovely idea and I was almost tempted to hang around just to watch Bowman's face when he walked in and realized there were places that made Albany's Central Avenue look like an evening in—Patagonia? Not that, I guessed.

FOURTEEN

THE DC-10 TOURED THE STORM-CLOUD layer above Long Island for an hour and twenty minutes before we banged down an electronic chute and onto the snowy runway. The Kennedy terminal buildings were not visible through the blizzard, though after a while the pilot found them. I had hoped to be back in Albany by ten Saturday morning, but by the time I'd crawled up the snow-clogged Thruway and fishtailed down the exit ramp, it was after noon. I drove directly to the Air Freight office at Albany County Airport.

"I have some bags coming in from LA. They were shipped from there late yesterday afternoon. Any idea when they might arrive?"

"They should have gone out first thing this morning, but they'd be coming through O'Hare, and it's closed. Chicago's completely socked in, so I don't know what to tell you. Tonight, tomorrow morning—it's hard to say. It's touch and go anyway. We might be shutting down ourselves. Why don't you leave your name and somebody can give you a call when the stuff comes in?"

"No, that's okay, I won't be near a phone, but I'll check back later."

"Were the bags for delivery or pickup here?"

Mumble, mumble.

"I beg your pardon, sir?" He was squinting so he could hear me better, but by then I had turned and sped off. So, now what?

I drove toward my office on Central. The odd snowplow was to be seen here and there, but the wind kept whipping snow back onto the roads, which were slick in the eight-degree wet air. An old Ford Fairlane turned out too fast from the Westgate shopping plaza, hula-hula-ed into a new Mazda in the lane next to mine, and the Mazda's front end tinkled to the pavement. When both drivers emerged intact from their crumpled machines, I drove on.

The door to my office was off its hinges and leaned against the wall. Before I surveyed the mess beyond, I re-hung the door. The damage in the office was slight; the intruders were after five good-sized suitcases, not a microdot. So when they hadn't found them readily they'd given up and left. The pie tin under the leaky radiator valve had been kicked aside, and the puddle of rusty water on the floor looked like about forty-eight hours' worth, which meant Thursday afternoon or thereabouts, back when Hankie-mouth still thought I had the money. I wanted to move about Albany freely now and was counting on Hankie-mouth's having been in touch with Joan Lenihan and lost interest in me—provided, of course, that that part (or any part) of her story *had* been true and that she hadn't kept the money, if she'd ever had possession of it in the first place. I, among many, had never actually set eyes on the cash.

I parked up the street from the house on Crow Street and slogged homeward for the first time in three days. The front door was ajar. Home is the place where, when you have to go there, the door occasionally falls in. It did. The hinge bolts were on the floor nearby, so I completed my second door-hanging job of the afternoon. I brushed the blown snow off the hall table and toured the untidiness beyond. Timmy surely would reprimand me for carelessly leaving an overstuffed chair atop the couch, so I lifted it off.

Actual breakage was minimal but the disorder was spectacular, and I spent half an hour setting pieces of furniture upright, returning drawers to their chests and cabinets, and putting books back on their shelves in an order probably not recommended by the Library of Congress. With the front door shut now the place was starting to warm up. I gave the picture of the fire a poke and sat by it for a time.

I thought about the meaning of the housebreaking. Bowman had agreed to have his cops search the place on Thursday. This was a charade to discourage Hankie-mouth from a fruitless-to-him but aggravating-to-me break-in, and to leave the impression that I'd brought in the authorities and the law was on my side. Bowman perhaps had failed to carry out his duties. Or, it occurred to me, the cops themselves had made this mess, though I doubted that; their sensitivity to property was higher than it was to people.

The other possibilities were: Hankie-mouth had simply gotten there before Bowman did; or Hankie-mouth was utterly unimpressed by the presence of the Albany police department and went in after the cops had left, believing— or perhaps knowing from experience—that the cops' skills as searchers were imperfect and they were likely to miss something. Or Hankie-mouth had been privy to inside police information and knew full well how meaningless and perfunctory the cops' visit had been. That one bothered me.

I showered, got into clothing appropriate for tramping around on the face of a glacier, fixed a plate of eggs, ate them, and made some phone calls. The first was to Los Angeles, where I learned from my investigative contact there that three toll calls had been placed from Joan Lenihan's number during the period Tuesday through Friday night. Two of them—Thursday at 9:11 A.M. and again Thursday at 11:55 P.M.—had been lengthy calls placed to a number listed under the name Edward McConkey in Albany. I guessed that was Joan speaking to Corrine and reacting to the news of Jack's death. I'd find out. The third call had been placed on Friday at 4:36 P.M., Pacific time, to the same number in Troy, New York, to which a call had been placed on Monday, when Jack had been alive and still in LA. The phone company subscriber at that number was Florence Trenky. More and more, Flo seemed like a person worth getting to know.

I dialed the Troy number.

"Yes?"

"This is Air Freight calling. Did one of our employees call you a short while ago? There's a lot of confusion down here, what with the snowstorm."

"No, but Mackie's upstairs waiting for you guys to call, been down here every five minutes. Did his delivery come in?"

"To whom am I speaking?"

"Flo Trenky. You the fella Mackie talked to this morning?"

"No, that must have been Bill."

"You want me to get him? Mackie's delivery come from LA?"

"I'm sorry, it hasn't. I just wanted to let him know that there are delays through Chicago, but we're doing everything we can under extremely difficult circumstances. Mr. Mackie is planning to pick up his parcels, have I got that right?"

"That's what he told me. It's Fay—Mack Fay's his right name."

"Oh, yeah, I see it here now. Well, if we haven't called yet, I suggest Mr. Fay check back with us early this evening. Could you relay that message, please?"

"Yeah, I'll tell 'im."

"Thank you, ma'am."

"Okay, sure."

I wrote the name in my notebook, *Mack Fay,* dug out my Troy phone directory, and copied down Flo Trenky's street address. I checked, but no Mack Fay was listed in the Troy, Albany or Schenectedy phone books.

When I called the Federal Building I was told by the duty officer in the drug-enforcement office that my friend the narc wouldn't be in until Monday morning but that I might reach him at home in Clifton Park. When I called there a tiny voice said to try again around six. I said I would and left my name.

I called American Airlines and was informed that O'Hare was expected to reopen in midafternoon and the first flight into Albany would arrive around 7:30 P.M., provided that Albany Airport itself didn't shut down. This was good. I had a few hours, at least, to get organized.

*   *   *

Except for the occasional lunatic, traffic crept along at a realistically fainthearted thirty-five in the fast lane of the interstate going north along the river. Near Menands a car had slid off the roadway into the median gulley and the tow truck trying to pull it out looked stuck in a drift. I eased in behind a plow and sand truck and followed it to the Green Island bridge. The snow was still coming down in flakes the size of pages from the Farmers' Almanac.

Florence Trenky's place on Third Avenue was an old three-story row house with white aluminum siding on the flat front wall and a sign in the window that said ROOMS. I cruised four houses up to the end of the block and parked across the street at a Cumberland Farms convenience store. I bought eight dollars' worth of gas, a sodium-nitrite sub made with a stale bun, a foam cup of black vinegar the clerk casually referred to as coffee, and dined in the car with the engine idling, the lights off and the heater humming. The snow had begun to let up a bit by then, and I had a clear view of Florence Trenky's front door and the vehicle parked in front of it—the green pickup truck that had followed me from Crow Street to the Albany main post office on Thursday.

I watched the lighted windows of the Trenky house, ate, drank, and listened to Garrison Keillor's good jokes about the weather in Minnesota. Whenever anybody began to play a dulcimer, I switched over to the six-o'clock jazz show on WMHT. At 6:40 I phoned my DEA contact from the pay phone in front of the store.

"Mack Fay. Name ring a bell?"

"Not offhand. I can check. Give me twenty minutes. I'll have to call in."

"Also, Robert Milius and the other entrepreneurs who were busted along with Jack Lenihan in '82. Present place of incarceration and known associates who might still be in the Albany area."

"Twenty minutes."

Back in the store I bought a pint of grapefruit juice and sloshed it around inside my head to mask the taste of the cold cuts, which in fact had been cold and cut off something. With a pocket full of quarters for the pay phone, I went back to the car and watched the Trenky house until a little after seven, when I made my call.

"Robert Milius, Jacob Farnum, Alton 'Boo' Waggoner, and Leonard 'Ringo' Romeo will remain in Sing Sing State Correctional Facility until the year 2002 at the earliest. Mack Fay, born Albany, 1931, convicted of felony auto theft in 1976, paroled from Sing Sing November seven of last year, currently residing Troy, New York. No previous convictions." He gave me Fay's address on Third Avenue while I watched its front door. "No known associates of Milius and company remain in the area. The rest of them took off for parts unknown in '82, and of course Jack Lenihan is dead. Anything else?"

"Can you find out if Fay knew Milius or any of the others at Sing Sing?"

"That'll take a little longer. Why do you ask? It's time I found out what you were mixed up in, Strachey."

"No, it's not time, yet. Soon."

"Uh-huh. I think you owe me, however. I've been more than generous. Give me a simple explanation and we'll call it even."

"A simple explanation is too much to ask. How about if I sent you four dollars?"

"Are you in trouble?"

"Sure."

"I hope whatever you expect to get out of this is worth it?"

I said, "You can't put a price tag on good government," and, before he could call me a pompous fool, hung up. I had no time for cynics.

I'd missed Keillor's monologue but got back in the car in

time for some good stride piano playing, to which I tapped my sweating feet. I tapped them off and on for another forty minutes, at the end of which time the front door opened at the Trenky residence and a man emerged.

Stocky, fiftyish, wrapped in a heavy green parka, the man quickly wiped the snow from the roof and windshield of the pickup truck, started it, waited half a minute for it to begin to warm up, and pulled out onto the avenue. He made a U-turn in the intersection in front of me and headed south. I followed.

Traffic was light on account of the storm, and I stayed well behind the truck through Troy, across the river, out Route 7, down the Northway, and into the Albany County Airport access road. When the pickup slowed and turned right by the AIR FREIGHT sign, I went on by, circled past the main terminal, and parked on the verge along the exit road. Ten minutes later the pickup passed me, moving back east again, and I followed.

When the pickup stopped for a red light on Route 7, I pulled up close behind it. Its bed appeared to be empty except for two feet of snow, but through the rear window I could make out what looked like suitcases stacked on the seat beside the driver. So much for any attempts at sleight of hand from the truck bed.

I let the truck move ahead of me again, pulled into a McDonald's, drove around the building to an exit, then followed the taillights of the pickup through the light snow back into Troy. I turned up First Avenue, went three miles an hour faster than I should have, and was parked in the Cumberland Farms lot when Mack Fay came up Third and pulled up in front of the Trenky house. He got out and hollered something in the front door and, one by one, handed the five bags up to a middle-aged blond woman who stood in the entryway in a pink housecoat. Fay followed the woman into the house then and shut the door.

I sat. I thought about calling APD and spilling it all to whoever Bowman had left in charge of the murder investigation during his trip west. Fay's possession of the five suitcases, presumably from Joan Lenihan and presumably containing the two and a half million, would be circumstantial but powerfully so. As a parolee, Fay could be asked to account for his sudden vast wealth, and other relevant information might be made to shake loose.

On the other hand, if Fay was in fact Jack Lenihan's killer, anything short of an immediate arrest and incarceration without bail might set him running—in the company of the suitcases—and the DA might consider the circumstantial evidence too flimsy to justify holding Fay. I had seen that happen.

What I needed was more evidence connecting Fay to Jack Lenihan. There had been the phone call from LA to Flo Trenky's number on Monday, when Jack was alive—this, I thought, was Jack notifying Fay of his flight number and arrival time on Tuesday. And there had been the call from LA to Flo Trenky's number Friday afternoon—this presumably was Joan notifying Fay that she was returning the cash via Air Freight. But it was all so circumstantial that it seemed possible Fay might cook up an explanation and a set of alibis that would get him off the hook just long enough for him to bolt with the five suitcases, whose contents I intended to possess.

Two questions nagged. Why had Jack Lenihan trusted Mack Fay to the extent that Lenihan could phone Fay from LA and ask him to meet his plane? And why, if she knew that Fay could well have been the man who killed her son— and she must have suspected him—did Joan Lenihan turn over the money to Fay instead of notifying the police? She had been vague and unconvincing on that topic, giving me opinions about the wickedness of Albany that lacked illuminating specifics.

I decided there was a lot more I had to find out before I went to Bowman. He might conceivably identify and even arrest, charge, and convict Jack Lenihan's killer, but the two and a half million might end up in the state's coffers and get spent on bridge repairs and new hats for fish wardens, both worthy expenditures, but Jack Lenihan had a better idea and I was high with the fever to carry it out. I was going to change history, make improvements on it.

I made a plan of action and set out. First, I went back to the pay phone. It was just after six in Los Angeles and I caught Timmy at Kyle Toot's place. They had just come in from taking the Universal Studios tour, where Timmy said he had witnessed Hump Finkley of *Chompin' Choppers* drinking from a carton of chocolate milk. I said I was sorry I'd had to leave early and miss it. It took me twenty minutes to convince the two of them to drive to the LA airport and get on the first flight with an O'Hare connection to Albany. But after I described my own plans for the night and promised to cover all expenses from a special account I planned to open soon, they took mild grudging pity and agreed to do it.

I shut off the car, locked it, and explored the neighborhood, which was quiet except for the plop of wet snow plummeting from utility lines. I glanced up at Flo Trenky's heavily curtained front windows, then went around the block and down an alley, counting houses as I went. The snow in the alley was heavy and deep. My feet were cold. I kept wiping my nose and wished Timmy were there to produce a hanky from his sleeve, stitched with the seal of the New York state legislature.

The Trenky property, like its neighbors, had a crumbling board fence walling off the alley from a narrow yard. The gate of the Trenky fence was ajar, lodged in a snowdrift, which I was glad to take note of. I entered the yard, slogged through the drifts, and crouched below the decrepit three-story back porch, which clung to the rear wall of the house feebly, as if it would soon lose its benumbed grip and tumble away. Stairs ran up to the second floor of the porch and on to the third.

I now knew how I could distract Fay and get inside the house. It seemed to me he was making it too easy for me, but I had to admit to myself that I did not know what kind of awful security devices Fay might have arranged for the two and a half million inside the house.

For just an instant it went through my mind that maybe the five suitcases contained no millions at all, but actually held Fay's summer wardrobe or his leather-bound indexed complete set of *Hustler* magazine, or fifty stolen car stereos, or—could it be?—three hundred copies of Friday's edition of the *Los Angeles Times*. I tried hard to push these pessimistic and additionally confusing thoughts out of my head.

I moved rapidly back to the Cumberland Farms store, bought another cup of black vinegar along with four plain yogurts and a packet of plastic spoons, and climbed back into the car. I set the heater on medium and tuned in *The Jazz Decades* on WAMC. I watched Flo Trenky's front door. If Mack Fay went any place, I wanted to know what he was taking along. If he had the bags, I'd follow. If he didn't, I'd stay put. I cranked my seatback down a couple of notches and sat there watching, waiting for help to arrive from across the continent.

FIFTEEN

FAY CAME OUT THE DOOR AND DOWN the front steps at 1:12 Sunday afternoon. The sky had cleared again, and despite my blurred vision resulting from lack of sleep, I got my first good look at him. The hood of his parka was down and he wore a black watch cap in its place.

He had on dark-blue dress pants and what looked like the bulk of a suit jacket or sport coat under the parka. Clean-shaven now, his face was wide and incipiently jowly with a set, turned-down mouth and hard dark eyes. He glanced at the bright sky, then up and down the street. The five bags were nowhere in sight.

Muttering, Fay kicked at the snow heaped up alongside his truck. He climbed into the pickup, started it up, and rocked it around until it bounced clear of the frozen ruts. I slid down in my seat as he made another U-turn in the inter-section and drove south on Third Avenue. I edged up and watched him go. This time I did not follow.

Instead I drove over to a gas station on First Avenue, filled the gas tank, used the men's room, and went back to Cumberland Farms, where I purchased a hearty breakfast of the store's famous dark brew, a Frooty-Tooty pie—baked with the fresh-picked produce of the frooty-tooty tree—and a side of six Twinkies. Civic reform is not for finicky eaters.

At 11:55 another Ford, a sibling of the one I was sitting in, moved slowly up Third Avenue, then swung in beside me. They both climbed into my car and I said, "Howdy."

"Have you really been sitting here since you called yes-terday?" Timmy leaned toward me for a greeting but caught a whiff of my frooty-tooty breath and gave me a gentlemanly handshake.

Toot said, "How come you didn't freeze to death? This place is some kind of no-man's land!" He was wearing an old heavy topcoat of Timmy's and had a red knit scarf wrapped around his neck and lower face. His rubber galoshes, mine, were three sizes too big.

"Hasn't Timmy explained to you how the climate here enriches character and hones intelligence? For instance, you might have noticed how Reagan, since he moved east, seems to have grown wiser and wiser. He used to be a real bub-blehead in California. But back here—hell."

Timmy said, "We got here as fast as we could. We made it to Chicago, then had to sleep on the floor at O'Hare until the Albany plane left at ten this morning. We stopped at the house to pick up some warm clothes for Kyle along with the other things you said we should bring. Incidentally, our house—"

"Your face is the color of iceberg lettuce. I've never seen you do that before."

"It's probably gangrene," Toot said, and peered in awe at the landscape around him.

"Who did it?" Timmy asked gravely. "Who was the person who entered my home and did that?"

"Hankie-mouth. His name is Mack Fay, the guy I told you about on the phone. He lives over there. Are you two ready to make his life miserable?"

Timmy, his jaw tight, nodded.

Toot said, "Will we have to get out of the car and walk around outside?"

Timmy sat beside me and watched as Toot drove the other rental car over to Flo Trenky's house, parked, went up the front steps, and rang the bell. The door was soon opened and after a moment Toot went in, shutting the door behind him. Five minutes later he emerged, glanced our way, opened the car's hatch, and took out five gray canvas suitcases that belonged to Timmy and carried them into Mrs. Trenky's rooming house.

"How long are we going to sit here?" Timmy said.

"However long it takes. If Toot locates Fay's room in ten minutes, I'm all for it. But it might take longer. Hours, days, weeks. I hope you brought your toothbrush."

"I wish you'd brought yours. God."

"How was the Chicano *Krapp's Last Tape?*"

"We never got there. We came here instead."

"Well, you missed out on another day of warm sunshine, but you still get the theater of the absurd."

"You're telling me. Kyle's a little nervous about this, so I hope you know what you're doing."

"I'm sure he's done improvisational theater before. He'll shine in the part. I can tell."

"He says he prefers the classics. Molière, Ibsen, Chekhov."

"How about Willy Loman? That would stand him in good stead."

"This feels more like the Ritz brothers. The Ritz brothers with a social conscience, of course."

"I see that you remain skeptical of my efforts toward civic improvement. You think I'm a loony, a deranged visionary, a crackpot."

He shook his head. "No. As much as anybody could, I admire your intentions. And I have to admit I admire Jack Lenihan for getting it all started. It's just that it won't have been worth it if you—or all of us—are hacked to bits by crazed dope fiends. Martyrdom interests me only when it's somebody else's, preferably having taken place in the fourteenth century. The pain is eased by chronological distance, and if you haven't slept with the person."

"I think I can work it out so that you won't become Poughkeepsie's first saint. Not that Aunt Moira wouldn't be real proud of you if you did."

"How? How will you work that out?"

"I'm giving it a lot of thought."

He said, "I'll be right back. They'd have toothbrushes in there, wouldn't they? And Saratoga water?"

"Probably."

"In this diocese there is no canonization for the orally unkempt."

*   *   *

At 5:25 P.M., under a frozen black sky, Mack Fay returned. He parked the pickup behind the Ford Toot had left in front of the Trenky house and let himself in the front door with a key. Twenty minutes later Toot came out and walked toward the convenience store. I pulled around the corner and out of sight of the house, and Toot climbed in the back seat.

"Fay is in 2-C, second floor rear, next to the bathroom. I'm in 2-A, and I think somebody is in 2-B—I can hear a radio in there playing Jerry Falwell's top hits. If anybody's on the third floor they don't talk or walk. It looks as if the third floor is empty. There's a locked door at the entrance to the stairwell leading up to it."

"Where is Fay now?"

"He came upstairs and went into his room. As soon as I heard footsteps outside my door, I made for the bathroom and passed him while he unlocked the door. I got one quick glimpse of his room but I didn't see any suitcases. After I peed, I went back to my room and listened. A couple of minutes later Fay left his room and went down the stairs. He didn't come outside, did he?"

"No."

"Then he must be in Mrs. Trenky's apartment. Both doorways from the front hallway lead into it. I wish you could meet her. She's a sweetheart—Pert Kelton doing Carole Lombard."

"She bought your 'salesman' story?"

"I'm Jim O'Connor the Third and I sell designer fan belts to fashion-conscious yuppies who might have to open the hoods of their Volvos in front of strangers."

"No. Tell me you didn't tell her that."

Toot grinned. "No, just ordinary fan belts. I picked something I figured she wouldn't want one of."

"Does Flo serve meals?"

"Not to tenants like me. To Fay maybe. They appear to be good friends, at least."

"Why don't you grab a sandwich and a Sunday paper inside the store, then go back and relax? If Fay goes out without the bags, we'll move in right away while you distract Mrs. Trenky. If he stays put, it's Plan B at nine-thirty tonight." I explained Plan B.

Timmy sat goggle-eyed and Toot looked a little queasy too. We tried to synchronize Toot's watch with mine, but we couldn't figure out which of the tiny holes to push a pin into—and we had no pin—so I synchronized my watch—which had a stem, a big hand, and a little hand—with Toot's and we agreed that Plan B would go into effect precisely at 6:30 P.M., Pacific Standard Time.

Through the evening and into the night Mack Fay did not leave the Trenky rooming house. At 6:30 PST, right on schedule, Toot emerged from the house, got into his rental car, and pulled around the corner. Timmy climbed in with him and they drove off. I waited and watched. Lights burned in the Trenky front windows, but none were lighted on the second or third floors.

An hour and fifteen minutes later Kyle and Timmy returned. They had traded in the little Ford Escort for a Thunderbird, whose trunk contained objects I had instructed them to pick up from the basement of our house. Kyle walked back to Trenky's, and Timmy and I went to work. It took half an hour to get the snow chains on the T-bird's big wheels, and as soon as we had finished that job I drove the car over to the alley behind Mrs. Trenky's house and backed down it. The alley had been plowed earlier in the day and maybe the chains wouldn't have been necessary, but better safe than sorry, and sorry in this case could have been sorrier than I had ever been.

While Timmy slid behind the wheel of the T-bird, I removed the two hundred feet of nylon rope from the trunk, looped one end around the car's bumper, and tied it in a sheep shank. The other end I dragged through the snowy darkness of Flo's backyard and ran it around the two main supporting posts of Flo's old three-story back porch. I pulled the rope taut, tied it, and trudged back to Timmy.

"Three minutes."

"What if somebody drives up the alley? There are garages back here."

"Then don't wait. Go."

"He bent down and rested his head against the steering wheel. "This is a crime and probably a mortal sin. I can't believe I am doing this." He was genuinely distressed.

"Do you want me to do it? I'm Presbyterian. I could do it myself and still get out to the front door in time."

He stared glumly at the windshield and thought this over. "No. Go ahead. The worst that can happen is I'll burn in hellfire for eternity."

"If that's what happens, thanks for the favor. I guess I'll owe you one."

His shoulders shook with a little laugh, or sob, and he said, "Okay. Three minutes." We checked our watches.

I had taken the Thunderbird's tire iron out earlier and now I stuck it up my sleeve. I ambled around the corner onto the side street and then down Third. I passed the Trenky house, where a raised shade on the second floor was quickly lowered and raised again, a signal from Toot that he had seen me pass by. The street was quiet in the frigid night. I heard only the muffled gabble of TV sets inside the houses I crunched past. At the end of the block I turned and moved back north, pacing myself so that I would arrive in front of the Trenky house at exactly 8:27 P.M., Pacific time, 11:27 Eastern.

The roar was impressive, like Alec Guinness' bridge dropping into the river Kwai. My heart hopped twice in my rib cage. A loud yelp came from inside the Trenky living room and I pressed hard against the wall as a curtain was yanked aside. Then a raised voice, male, and pounding footsteps moved away from me. I dashed up the wooden steps and as I went caught a quick sideways glimpse of the T-bird clanking across the intersection and past the convenience store, the car trailing odds and ends of nylon and splintered lumber behind it.

Toot yanked open the front door and gestured toward the stairs. I went up them as he headed toward the door to Flo's kitchen. It took me ninety seconds to fiddle the lock on 2-C—too long, I was afraid, but there I was—and another ninety seconds to ascertain that the suitcases were not in Fay's room. Not in the closet, not under the unmade bed, not amidst the paperback novels on the floor by the bedside with titles like *The Sultan of Twat*.

The door to the third-floor stairway was secured by a padlock. I used the tire iron to rip off the U-bolt. The stairwell was dark and I hadn't brought a flashlight, so I risked the wall switch, which illuminated a ceiling fixture in the third-floor hall. I sped upward.

Groping through the three third-floor rooms and their closets, I found nothing but old odds and ends of furniture. Below me were sounds of increasing commotion, and other excited voices came from Third Avenue. I checked the third-floor bathroom. Nothing.

I had just about concluded that the five suitcases were either in Flo Trenky's apartment or in the basement and that I would somehow have to come up with a Plan C, when I spotted the attic entry hatch panel on the ceiling. An old wooden kitchen chair rested nearby—not for sitting on, it appeared. Standing on the chair, I unlatched the hook and eye that held the panel in place and lowered the unhinged side. I reached up, groped, and found them.

I chinned myself up into the black hole, memorized the approximate location of each bag, then—being unable to hand them down to myself—dropped them to the floor below one by one. The sound of the falling bags was lost, I hoped, among the noise of a rapidly gathering crowd outside and the approaching police and fire sirens.

The bags were maroon with black bands around them, the ones I'd seen in Joan Lenihan's dining room. I dashed down the stairs with two of them, flung them into 2-A, Toot's room, then ran up and brought two more, then finally the fifth and last. When I came down the stairs the third time, the door to 2-B was wide open and a man stood staring at me.

The man was somewhere between thirty and seventy, potbellied, and wore a flannel bathrobe over his pajamas. His slippers had bunny faces on the toes. In flattened tones but with great fervor, he said to me, "I am Dover Clover. I know Dover Clover. I know all eternity in hell. Satan is a fool, but I know fate gave me power over parable. I am Doctor Who."

I said, "The back porch fell down. It will be repaired. The appropriate behavior is, please go back in your room."

The man turned away instantly and shut the door in my face. Inside Toot's room, with the door shut and bolted, I used my lobster pick on the lock of the first of the five suitcases. I lifted the lid and gazed down. No newspapers this time, or dirty socks, just US currency. The old bills—twenties, fifties, hundreds—were stacked but not bound. I stuffed a bundle of fifties into my coat pocket, then opened the other four bags. Toot had left Timmy's five canvas bags open on the bed, as instructed, and I dumped the cash into them and zipped them shut. Kyle had also left a bundle of old *Times Unions* on the floor nearby. These I placed in the maroon bags, shut and locked them, and carried them in three swift trips up to the attic. I placed the bags where I had found them and closed the hatch.

From down below came the sound of raised voices and other signs of frantic coming and going. I went back to Toot's room, shut the door, and waited inside. Out on Third Avenue a crowd had gathered, as well as a fire engine, red lights turning and flashing and radios barking, and a Troy PD patrol car.

Footsteps thudded up the stairs, and my heart played an interesting short piece by Poulenc. Two sharp raps on the door. "It's me."

I let him in. Toot had on jeans and Timmy's old Georgetown sweatshirt and was dripping like Lear on the moors. I said, "Nice performance. Would you autograph my program?" and held out a stack of fifties.

"You gotta get out of here now! The building inspector's on his way and they'll be coming up here."

"Where are they?"

"Mack and Flo are both out back with two policemen and some firemen. You gotta move *now*."

I followed him quickly down the stairs and out the front door. We walked casually past the fire engine and cop car on the corner. "Did you tell her you were moving out?"

"Yeah, I said I was afraid the whole place was unsafe, and she said oh, no, honey, why don't you wait for the building inspector, but I was shaking like crazy—from the cold, mostly—and she thinks I'm really scared. Of course, I am that, too."

"Do they know how it happened?"

"Snow on the roof, they think."

"Good. They might figure out otherwise in daylight, but that's okay. I'll send Mrs. Trenky four or five grand for a new porch if her insurance doesn't cover the damage. See you in a little while."

"I hope so."

Timmy and the T-bird were long gone, so I stood inside the convenience store drinking coffee and chatting with the clerk about the neighborhood excitement for twenty minutes until I saw Toot load the Ford with Timmy's gray bags. He asked the firemen to move their pumper six feet so that he could get his car out, and after some jawing and milling about, they did. Toot pulled onto the avenue, cruised over to the convenience store, then moved over to the passenger seat. I climbed in and drove directly to the Green Island bridge, then south to Albany, where we rendezvoused in Room 1407 at the Hilton just after one.

"First thing in the morning," Timmy said, "I am going to confession for the first time in eighteen years. And then I am going to work. Right now I am going to sleep. If I scream in the night, rush me over to the Albany Med burn unit."

Toot said, "I'm taking a hot bath before I do anything. I think I've got gangrene of the prostate."

"Timmy will sleep, but you can't," I told him. "I'm driving you to JFK, where you'll get on the first flight for LA. Fay is going to draw some conclusions very fast, and if you hang around here you might be recognized. The cops won't be a problem—I don't think Fay will report his loss to the authorities—but it's better if you are three thousand miles away when Fay puts one and one and a half together and comes up with Jim O'Connor the Third, the fan-belt sales-man."

Timmy said, "Fay's not dumb. Won't he also realize that you're somehow involved? Hell, we're *never* going to be able to go home."

"I've been thinking about that too. I also have been start-ing to miss evenings by the picture of the fire. I think I know how I can work it all out. There are just a couple of things I have to check on tomorrow."

"It's practically tomorrow already. Kyle, good night and good luck. And, Donald, congratulations on your civic-minded grand larceny. You're Legs Diamond with a heart of gold."

"Thank you," I said, and gazed at the five suitcases full of money. It occurred to me that I could probably spend the two and a half million on the purchase of a small island in the Bahamas. St. Don's. I reluctantly shoved that thought aside, although suddenly it became brilliantly clear to me that now, finally, I did have real choices to make.

At the airport I asked Toot, "What will you tell people who ask where you disappeared to for thirty-six hours?"

He grinned. "I'll say I was in Troy, New York, helping a private eye and his boyfriend demolish Carole Lombard's back porch in order to steal two and a half million dollars."

"That's a wonderful story. Nobody will believe it."

"That's right."

"You learn fast." I tried to stuff a roll of fifties in Toot's pocket, but he wouldn't have it. "You're a business expense," I said. "Jack Lenihan wrote that I should take what I needed for my expenses. It's legitimate, believe me."

He looked a little hurt. "I'll take twenty for cab fare back to West Hollywood, but otherwise forget it. I'm not supposed to take non-union acting jobs anyway. Not that I could ever include this one on my résumé. This performance was for Al Piatek—and for the memory of Al and Jack Lenihan back in the Piateks' attic. Who knows, maybe they're together now."

"It would be nice to believe that."

Having gone without sleep for nearly forty-eight hours, I drove directly to the airport Sheraton, bought a room with six twenties, lay down, and conked out. I wanted to be wide awake and in full possession of my faculties when I got back to Albany, because the tricky part was coming next: disbursing the two and a half million, handing Jack Lenihan's murderer to Ned Bowman, and staying alive while I was at it.

SIXTEEN

I PHONED SIM KEMPELMAN FROM A thruway rest stop and met him at six Monday evening at Queequeg's. He ordered the scampi and a glass of white wine, and I had two bowls of cream of broccoli soup, two spinach salads and a Beck's.

I said, "I've got it."

"Oh, my."

"Two and a half million."

He whistled, impressed.

"It's all in US currency, in a safe place. The cash's arrival was delayed for a variety of reasons, but before he died, Jack prepared to send it to me and now I've got it."

"That's a lot of money, kid. You're rich."

"Not me. You and your slate of candidates are rich. The citizenry of Albany is rich."

He gazed at me solemnly. He asked, "Has a will been located?"

"I don't know. What difference does it make? Lenihan sent me the money before he died, with instructions to—"

"To what?"

"To—to hold it for him. To keep it safe."

"Ahhh."

"But Jack's intentions were clear from the context of his letter. It was plainly his wish that if anything happened to him, I should carry out the project. There is no arguing with that. None."

Kempelman sighed and shook his head. "I don't know about you, kid, but I'm too old to go to jail. I like my cup of tea when I crawl out from under the covers in the morning, and I like a little smootz from Mrs. Freda Kempelman when

I get back underneath the covers at night. No, I think I'll steer clear of jail houses and any of the multitudes of sets of circumstances that might land me in one.

"Now don't get me wrong, Mr. Strachey, I *do* want that money. But it has to be on the up-and-up, with all the legal niceties attended to—which is in no way an impossibility. In fact, that is the way I earn my living, and nine times out of ten I can find a way to get what my client wants—or what I want—and still meet the requirements of the law. I'm an old hand at that.

"The question is, where do we go from here? How do we get that two and a half million dollars from your bank account into my organization's bank account without my walking out the side door of Judge Feeney's courtroom a year from today with his Honor's dentures locked on my neck? What we need is a will. Kid, I think you should look into that. Find a will. As I see it, that's your next move."

"What about a letter?"

"A letter?"

"Say Jack wrote a letter before he died, turning the money over to me for a specific purpose which he described. Would that do it?"

"Does such a letter exist?"

"It might."

"This is the first time you have talked about such a letter."

"There was no need previously to have mentioned it."

A sad shake of the head. "No forgeries," he said. "I believe you have in mind an act of forgery, and that, Mr. Strachey, it strictly no-go."

I saw it all falling away. I said, "Do you want the money, or don't you? Do you want to clean the crooks and phonies out of city hall, or don't you? Which is it, Sim? Whose side are you on, anyway?"

"Yours," he said. "I *think* I am. Except, I was told that you are a rational man. One of the few in this town. But now I am beginning to wonder."

"Rational? What *is* rational? It seems to me rational is people running their own lives without extortionist goons reaching into their wallets twice a year. Rational is—"

He waved a hairy finger. "Whoa—wait a minute. Wait one minute. Let me tell you about rational. Rational is getting what you want without offering your own head on a platter in return for it. Suicide will get you some ugly sympathy, but it is not rational. Martyrdom will get your name in the papers, but it is not rational. Irrationality has its uses in public life, that I concede, but a price must be paid, and I, for one, am not prepared to pay it. If you think about it, I doubt that you will want to pay the price either. You know, I think you've gone a little cuckoo on me since I saw you last week. That two and a half million has softened your brain, is that it? Relax a little, and let's think this thing through. Maybe there's a way."

I felt myself redden. I said, "I'll see Creighton Prell. He'll deal."

"No, he won't. Republicans hate going to jail. They think the jails are full of Democrats who'll laugh at them mopping up the lavatories. No, Republicans are proud. They only go to jail at the national level, and Creighton is not that ambitious. You can try Creighton, of course, that's up to you. But it will be a waste of your valuable time, believe me."

I slugged down some Beck's. "Larry Dooley will be interested," I said, and then had to laugh.

Kempelman smiled. "Sure. That's Larry's style. Play now, pay later. He might even get away with it. He has friends in the courts. But I think that is not what you want, kiddo. In fact, that is the very opposite of what you want."

He had me and he knew it, and I wanted to throttle him because I knew that everything he told me was the bare, unadorned, rock-bottom truth. Fucking liberals.

I said, "Has Ned Bowman been in touch? Maybe you'll go to prison anyway, for the murder of Jack Lenihan. Of course, you wouldn't have used a tire iron. You'd have lectured him to death. Or jumped on him from your high moral plain."

"Oh, I'm clean enough, but I hear Larry Dooley's in a bit of a pickle. The word is, Larry spent Tuesday night with the young missus of a certain up-and-coming young council member who was off in Rochester on a business trip. All Larry will tell Bowman is, he was attending to personal business at the time of Jack Lenihan's death, but he says he can't go into detail and then he winks, but Bowman keeps missing the point. Bowman is leaning on Larry real hard and is threatening him with the DA. What Larry and Bowman both don't know is that two—I said two—assistant DAs have been dipping their wicks in the misguided doxy as well—simultaneously, according to one possibly misinformed distant observer. So you see how complicated life can become for those caught in the grip of irrational impulses."

I said, "Maybe in the interest of fairness the *Times Union* will run a smug, finger-pointing editorial on the health risks of heterosexual promiscuity, but I doubt it. Is Bowman back in town? I heard he was away for a few days."

"I wouldn't know. But I did hear that *you* were out of town for a couple of days. I was planning on mentioning this earlier, but we got sidetracked."

"Where did you hear that?"

"At Jack Lenihan's funeral yesterday."

"I missed it. I feel bad about that, but it was unavoidable and he would have understood. Who told you I was out of town?"

"Pug Lenihan."

At last, here it came. I didn't need this, didn't want it. I said, "Not old Pug, no. What does he know about all this? About me?"

"Beats me. I was wondering about that myself. On account of the snow and cold weather, they didn't take him out to the cemetery, but they carried him into the funeral home and propped him on a lounge chair for half an hour, and I noticed he was watching me, and after a while he sent Corrine over to relay the message that he would like a few words."

"What were you doing there in the first place? The Lenihans didn't even know you'd had a connection with Jack. Your presence wouldn't have made any sense to them."

Kempelman took a sip of wine and smacked his lips. "This is quite an adequate chablis. Of course, that is the extent of my sophistication as a wine connoisseur. For me, there are two grades of wine, adequate and inadequate. Nearly all of them I find adequate."

"You can tip the sommelier on the way out. Why did you attend Lenihan's funeral?"

"I was invited."

"By whom?"

"Corrine McConkey. She phoned me Sunday morning and told me that her grandfather—Dad Lenihan, she called him—wanted me to be present. She said it would mean a lot to him, and I respectfully went along. She did not elaborate."

"This is just terribly, terribly interesting. So you went, and then Pug called you over. Do you two know each other?"

"I had never set eyes on the man. It was all very strange and discombobulating for me. I have to tell you, Mr. Strachey, that I was just a little bit frightened. Pug Lenihan is not a powerful man anymore, but I presume that he remains influential in some circles. Additionally, it entered my mind that somehow he'd gotten wind of my conversations with his late grandson and about Jack's project."

"Right. That could make you jittery. So he called you over."

"He beckoned for me to bend down—no mean feat for a man with a herniated-disk operation behind him—and I painfully obliged. He said—Pug Lenihan said to me—'You're in on this, aren't you, Kempelman?' I said, 'In on what, Mr. Lenihan?' 'Oh, don't you bullshit me!' this doddering ninety-six-year-old croaked in my ear. 'I know you'd be the one,' he said. 'Now I don't know this Strachey from a peck of potatoes, but you tell him I want to talk to him. You hear what I'm saying to you?' I stood there for a few seconds looking at the hardest, iciest set of blue eyes I'd ever seen in my life, and then do you know what I said?"

"You said, 'Yes, sir.'"

"'Yes, sir.' You got it, kid. I said, 'Mr. Lenihan, yes, sir.'"

"So he told you he wants to talk to me. Well, hell. Did he say what about?"

"Nope. He said he heard you were out of town, and when you got back to give Corrine a call and she would take you over to his house. So. I have now carried out my instructions. Sim the message-delivery boy."

"Or Sim the something-else-less-innocent." I glanced around at the other drinkers and diners but saw no familiar faces. "I just hope I'm not being set up for—what?"

"No." He got his hurt Saint Bernard look on again. "Not by me, at any rate. But I do advise that you take care. Avoid irrational outbursts."

Again I considered bolting with the two and a half million and picking up a pleasant small island somewhere. Then the almost-obvious hit me, and I said to Kempelman, "If Pug Lenihan knows about Jack's project, then maybe the machine knows. Pug surely is in touch from time to time with his political progeny."

Kempelman didn't move, except to elevate grandly two eyebrows the size of field mice.

I said, "Naturally they will not want the project carried out. They will want it stopped."

"Yes, that would be my guess too. Definitely they would."

"Is that why you suddenly have cold feet, Sim? Is that it?"

Wearily shaking his head, he said, "No, I explained plainly the reasons for my 'cold feet,' as you choose to term it. But don't let's get into that again. Fisticuffs might be the end result this time, and that could have serious repercussions for my spinal column."

I said, "Oh, hell."

"You're looking a little sickly, kid. It's those rich soups. Stay away from soups that go sour on your intestinal wall."

"Maybe the machine has known all along," I said. "Maybe Larry Dooley tipped them off right at the beginning, as soon as poor naive Jack contacted Dooley with his proposal. Maybe it was some of *them* who got Jack killed. They figured out that Jack had the doper's boodle, tipped the convicted dealers down at Sing Sing, who arranged for friends on the outside to recover the two and a half million and do away with Jack. That way the machine, using a chain of non-criminal and criminal intermediaries, could eliminate a threat and still hide behind a wall of deniability. They'd get the result they wanted, but they could rest certain that the means to that end would never reach back to them."

Kempelman screwed up his face. After a moment of pained thought, he said, "I don't think so. They would never go that far. They are crude, but they are not evil. No—no, they would never go that far. Listen, kid, they don't have to."

But he sat there awhile longer silently mulling over the possibility, as did I.

SEVENTEEN

I PHONED TIMMY, HOLED UP AT THE Hilton, and said, "Did you go to work today?"

"Yeah, I was pretty worn out, but I managed a couple of reasonably productive hours."

"Could you have been followed back to the hotel?"

A silence. "What are you saying?"

"Maybe you should make a discreet move. Is the money safe?"

"The bags are in the closet."

"Have you gone out since you got back there from work?"

"No, I just came in a couple of minutes ago. I worked late, then ate at the Larkin with Moe Dietz. Spit it out, Don. What are you trying to tell me? Is Mack Fay on to us?"

I described the meeting with Sim Kempelman. I could hear Timmy swallowing repeatedly as I spoke. I said, "If you still have the rope from the porch-wrecking episode, I suggest you rappel down the side of the Hilton with the five suitcases attached to your belt and meet me in East Timor later in the week." He said nothing. "Timmy?"

"I've got the door locked and I am not leaving this room until you get over here and explain to me how you're going to get both of us out of this endless chamber of horrors. Do you hear what I'm saying to you?"

"I thought all the early Peace Corps groups learned rappeling at a remote camp in the mountains of western Puerto Rico, and now that you finally have some use for this arcane skill, you're going to crap out. I just hope Sargent Shriver never hears about this. But have it your way. I'll be over there in another hour or two. First I want to drop in on Corrine McConkey. When I get to the hotel I'll call you from the lobby to let you know it's me coming up. Just hang on, okay?"

"I'd rather you came now."

"I can't."

"You won't."

"Look, it's seven-thirty. I'll be there by nine-thirty."

"Eight-thirty."

"Nine. Nine sharp."

"If you're not here at exactly nine o'clock, I'm taking the bloody two and a half million out of the suitcases, tossing it out into the corridor, and locking the door again. Do you understand that?"

"Before you do, pocket three grand for my fee and expenses, and another three thousand for our trip to Martinique next week. We've gotta come out of this with something."

"One minute you're a messiah and the next minute you're a petty thief. I think you're losing your grip. You used to be so rational. Well, no, not exactly rational. I didn't mean that."

"Thank you."

"Just be here at nine."

"Or close to it."

Dreadful Ed answered the door. "Corrine's laying down. I can give her the message."

"No, it's she who has the message for me. I'm sorry to bother her, but this won't take long. Her grandfather Lenihan asked that she arrange a visit for me with him."

McConkey frowned. "You go over to Dad Lenihan's? What's he want with you?"

"That's right. What's he want with me?"

He didn't like the sound of this. "Just a minute." He shut the door in my face. I stood in the cold night air shifting my feet and listening to the porch swing creaking under its load of blown snow. McConkey returned. "You can come in for a minute, but don't get Corrine all upset, you understand? Her nerves are all shot to hell."

"I suppose they would be."

I left my coat to fry on the hall radiator. Corrine was lying on the brown couch with a pink blanket up to her chin, her head propped on a pillow. She sat up as I entered the room and patted her hair. "I'm a real mess, Mr. Strachey, I hope you don't mind. How are you this evening?"

"I'm cold, tired and a little curious. I'm sorry I missed the funeral yesterday afternoon, but I want you to know that

I've been thinking about your brother a lot for the past several days. And I saw your mother in Los Angeles."

Her pale eyes brightened. "You went all the way to California and saw Ma? Well, how did she look? Was she out of bed yet? She sounded so down on the phone. She's taking this pretty hard."

"She was up and around, but she was emotionally a wreck, yes. She seemed determined, though, to get on with her life."

A faint smile. "That's Ma, all right—determined. She has more spunk than any ten people. She told me on the phone—Ma said—Ed! *Ed, will you turn that thing down?*"

Ed, sulking by the TV set, climbed over his feet, which were propped on a footstool, and reduced the volume by half a decibel.

"When Ma called yesterday, before the funeral," Corrine went on, raising her voice in order to be heard over the helicopter explosions, "do you know what she asked me? She said why don't I come out and see her next month? And you know what? I just might do it."

"That sounds as if it would be good for both of you."

"I'm really thinking about it this time. Mrs. Clert could make Ed's sandwich at noon and he could drive over to McDonald's at suppertime. Ed could drive me out to the airport and help me carry my suitcases in if I took two along. I'd rather take along a lot of clean outfits so Ma wouldn't have to do any laundry. And then I could call Ed long distance from Ma's apartment in California and tell him what time to pick me up when I came back. You know, this time I really think I'm going to do it. I just want to hug Ma so bad. I've been thinking about that ever since she called."

"You must miss her a lot. When did you last see your mother?"

"When she left, after Pa died. That's been—oh, I don't know how many years. Eighteen? Why, yes, eighteen years ago this month. Isn't that something? Eighteen years after Pa died, Jack died. They both died in the wintertime. Maybe that's why I always feel so low every January. Ma's always asking me to come and see her, even pay my way, but—well, Ed doesn't really like other people's cooking. He says it tastes funny. Ed really appreciates my cooking, even though I don't really think it's that great. But Mrs. Clert could make his sandwich. Or—maybe I could make some sandwiches and just stick them in the freezer. Can you freeze cold meat sandwiches? I don't see why not. Or would the mayonnaise go bad?"

"It might. But perhaps Ed could lift the top slice of bread and apply his own mayonnaise."

She glanced Ed's way apprehensively but he was caught up in other matters.

I said, "I think you might enjoy getting away from Albany for a while. Is this the house you grew up in?"

"From when I was one and a half. Then, when I married Ed, we moved in with his mom, but then she got hit by the number 6 bus on Pearl Street, and we moved back over here with Ma and Pa. Then soon after that, Pa died and Ma gave us the house and we've been here ever since."

I thought maybe she meant literally, but then remembered that she worked as a salesclerk. "Your mother strikes me as a generous woman who has looked after her children in the best way she's been able to. I got the impression that you and Jack were the only people she cared about back in Albany, though. She seemed otherwise to dislike the city and its people intensely, passionately even."

She looked away. "I know. Ma's life with Pa was hard on her—on account of his ailment. But after he was gone she seemed to not like Albany even more than before. Really, though, it's always seemed like a pretty nice town to me. People around here are friendly, and they're always there to lend a hand when tragedy strikes. But Ma's stubborn that way. She gets something in her head and there it sticks. Oh, well. Ma has her ways. Like Jack did. Like we all do." She shrugged philosophically.

I said, "Did Jack leave a will?"

"I wouldn't think so. Why would he? Jack was like the rest of the Lenihans. We scrape by, and that's about it. Ma's done well for herself. Went out west without a dime to her name, went to college, and got a good job that pays. I guess Ma's the only one of us that has stick-to-it-ive-ness. She applied herself and she was rewarded for it. And you hit the nail on the head when you said she's not stingy with her money. Ma helps Ed and I out when we need it, and she even helps Dad with his bills. Having a nurse all the time costs an arm and a leg, and Medicare hardly pays to empty the bedpan unless you go to the hospital. Many a time we've invited Dad to sell the house and move over here, but he likes his independence and you can't blame him for that. But we all get by and we help each other out when times get tough, and that's the important thing."

"Did your mother mention to you that I stopped in to see her?"

"Gosh—no, I guess she forgot to say. Just because she's distraught, I'm sure."

"I understand your grandfather wants to speak with me."

"Oh, did the Jewish gentleman tell you that? You know, I've had so many things on my mind that that one just went right out the window."

"Do you know why he wants to see me? I've never met your grandfather before. I only know him by reputation."

"Gee, he didn't really say. But I suppose he heard you were a friend of Jack's and wants to talk about Jack. He was real broken up by Jack's passing. I felt so sorry for the poor old fella. His only male grandson gone."

"I don't know, but I doubt that Jack would have mentioned my name to his grandfather. Who might have?"

She blushed. "Do you mean because you're—that way? Like Jack? Dad's old-fashioned and never had the time of day for—perverts, he called them. He always thought Jack being like that was just Jack trying to get back at him."

"Back at him for what?"

"Oh, for being a big-shot Democrat. Jack always said the Albany Democrats were just a bunch of crooks, and that got Dad's dandruff up every time. Dad says the party got jobs for people so they could have a roof over their head and they could put food on the table, and the party helped people when they were down and out. But Jack always said the party stole more than it gave away. Jack criticized the Democrats right in front of Dad, and sometimes Jack could get obnoxious—have these tantrums and say really mean things. And then Dad would start in on the perverts and Jack would stomp out and slam the door. But I will say that Jack always came back, and I think in his heart Dad was always glad to see him. Like last fall, until they had another falling out. Blood is thicker than water, as the saying goes."

"When could I visit your grandfather? Is tonight a possibility?"

"Oh no, not this late. Dad Lenihan goes to bed after his programs. He watches the news report and then *Wheel of Fortune* and *Hundred Thousand Dollar Name That Tune*, and he's all tucked in by eight-thirty. Dad's an early riser, so maybe in the morning would be a good idea."

"What time?"

"Ed drives me out to the store at twenty of nine, but I could call Dad first and see if it was okay for you to drop in. Mrs. Clert could get Dad ready and then Ed could take you over after he got back. Maybe about ten-thirty in the morning would be a good time. Would that suit you?"

"It would. I'll phone you at eight-thirty to confirm the time."

She smiled. "Just don't talk politics if you don't want to

get an earful. And don't"—she blushed again—"maybe you shouldn't let on you're one of Jack's gay friends. I mean, if you are."

"Don't worry, I'll come across as an Olympic gold medalist. Though not one of the gymnasts, of course. Is your grandfather in good health?"

"Strong as an ox. I mean an ox that's ninety-six, ha ha. No, seriously, Dad is showing his age lately. His hearing and eyesight are going, and he tires out. He can't walk across the room without sitting down for a minute. That's the emphysema. But when he wants to be, he can be a real hellion. We weren't going to take him to the funeral yesterday, but he wasn't about to put up with that, oh no. Dad never misses a funeral, especially family. So Mr. Fay carried him out to the car and into the funeral parlor, and you'd've thought Dad was a kid again. He always liked being around people. It really perks him up and I was glad to see it, even on such a tragic occasion."

I glanced at Ed, saw that he was absorbed in an electric-shaver commercial, and said, "Who is Mr. Fay?"

"Mack Fay is Howie Fay's boy. Howie Fay lived over by the Hainses when he was alive, and he and Dad were friends from way back. Thick as thieves, those two were. Howie Fay dropped in on Dad every day until he slipped on the ice in front of Evelyn Collins' and broke his backbone. Howie Fay passed away last March, but old lady Fay—she's kind of a sourpuss—she's still over there but she never goes out. Their boy Mack Fay was working out of town for many years, but he's back now and he and Dad seem to have hit it off. Mack visits him and they shoot the breeze just like Dad and Howie Fay did, and if Dad has to go out to the doctor or something, Mr. Fay drives him wherever he has to go. Mack Fay is not the friendliest man you'll ever meet with Ed and I, but I have to say he's been a godsend for Dad. Maybe you'll see him tomorrow if you stick around long enough. He usually drops in around noontime and they have their sandwich together. The two of them and Mrs. Clert."

"Mrs. Clert is Mr. Lenihan's nurse?"

"Days she is. Nighttime there's just an aide, Kevin, Mrs. Clert's boy. He'd be over there now. Mrs. Clert is strictly no-nonsense, but she knows how to keep Dad contented. He's a man, so he can be fussy. But she handles him. You'll see."

When I left the McConkeys, I drove over to Pearl and past Pug Lenihan's bungalow. It was ten till nine and a single light burned in a downstairs window. An old brown Olds Cutlass was parked in the driveway. I slowed briefly, then sped up and drove straight south toward the center of the city.

EIGHTEEN

"YOU'RE LATE. YOU'RE TEN MINUTES late, but you're here. I was worried about you."

"No need to worry. Everything's under control."

"It is?"

"Not my control, but somebody's. We do not live in a coldly mindless and anarchic universe. There is a plan to all of this."

"Whose?"

"I don't know. But I'm more certain than ever that it's not Adlai Stevenson's. Is the money still in the closet?"

"Sure, I checked when I came back this evening."

"Did anyone phone or knock at the door?"

"No, it looks as if I wasn't followed here. Or if I was, maybe they were waiting for you to show up. Now we're both here along with the money, so I suppose that means the end is near. Couldn't we just go home now and die in our own bed? I'm so sick of restaurant food."

"Not yet. Soon." I sprawled on the bed and dragged the phone onto the pillow beside me.

"Did you find out what Pug Lenihan wants with you?"

"I'll know in the morning when I meet him. Just a second." I dialed the number of my friend at New York Telephone, reached him at home, and asked for a list of toll calls made from Pug Lenihan's number during the previous week. He said he'd have them by noon the next day.

"What's that all about?" Timmy asked. "If Pug Lenihan's mixed up in this, it's only the machine using him to warn you away from turning the money over to Kempelman. Isn't that the way you figure it?"

"That was three hours ago. My perspective has since broadened." I explained to him Pug Lenihan's connections with Mack Fay as Corrine McConkey had described them to me.

As I told it, Timmy's face went through its wide repertoire of pale pastels. He said, "So Pug might actually have been involved in his own grandson's murder? Jesus!"

"I don't want to believe that. But it's possible. Maybe I'll ask him about it tomorrow."

"Or maybe you won't show up."

"I'm considering that."

Shakily, he said, "Call Bowman. Or the state police, or the FBI. Don, this is no longer just you against some half-assed dope fiends. It's you against—history."

As the words came out, I knew I shouldn't have spoken them in front of him. I said, "Maybe history is about to change. And I am its agent." He shut his eyes tightly and actually clutched his head: "I take it you continue to find my hopes and dreams wackily presumptuous."

"Yeah. I'm sorry. I do."

"Well, as I see it, I can either bring about the dawn of a

golden age in Albany, or I can take the money and run. I can't honestly see any middle ground at this point."

"You can give the money back, and we can go home and resume our good lives. *That* is one alternative."

I looked at him carefully. "You can't mean that. Just quit, just like that? With Jack Lenihan still warm in his grave, and after all we've gone through? You'd hate yourself. I'd hate myself. And I wouldn't be too crazy about you for a while."

He twitched with ambivalence, a state of mind that always got his juices flowing. "You're turning it into a moral dilemma when in fact what we are talking about here is the highly practical question of surviving or not surviving. Yes, of course I'd like to see the machine zapped. And yes, Jack's killer should be identified, tried and convicted. The last part you might be able to accomplish with the help of Ned Bowman and maybe the feds. But *not* singlehandedly."

"You mean, you can't fight city hall. That does not sound at all like the Tim Callahan I know."

"You can *fight* city hall but you can't bulldoze it. Not by yourself if you hope to live to see what replaces it."

I took this all in, considered it, and gave his thigh a squeeze. "This is getting too theoretical for me. Let's take our clothes off and get practical. It's been awhile. Shrieking with ecstasy always restores your perspective."

He had an argument for that too, but he only belabored his thesis for about twenty minutes. We sometimes went our separate emotional and philosophical ways, but we always remembered one place where the twain met, and this handy and inherently satisfying way of connecting served to remind us of all the other lovely ways we had of connecting, usually.

At seven Tuesday morning I checked my answering service, which had six messages. Three were social and could wait, and one was from Timmy's mother in Poughkeepsie, inquiring as to why we were not answering our home telephone. She asked that I relay the message to Timmy that Father Frank Merrill had been injured by a Molotov cocktail tossed from the St. Vincent's school roof by a fourth grader, and it would be nice if Timmy sent Father Frank a get-well card.

The fifth message was from Ned Bowman, instructing me to report to his office promptly at 3 P.M. Monday—too late for that—and the sixth message was from an anonymous caller with a muffled voice. The voice had said: "Tell Strachey, 'You are dead.'"

I gave Timmy the message from his mother and suggested that he call in sick at the office, then drive down and pay a personal call on the ailing Father Frank. He thought that would be unnecessary until I told him about "You are dead," and then he agreed. He said he would spend a night in Poughkeepsie, maybe two.

Room service brought Timmy his porridge and me my pitcher of orange juice and two eggs, which were not raw, as I had requested, but fried. To Timmy's relief, I did not stir them into the juice. Timmy left for Poughkeepsie, saying he would first stop by the house to pick up a clean shirt—Mom would be surreptitiously checking his collar—and would either meet me or phone me at the hotel that night. I said sure, I figured I'd be back at the Hilton that night, and he looked at me a little funnily.

Before I went out, I checked the money. It was intact, undisturbed, unspent. It was beginning to look restless, though, as if it wanted spending soon on a good deed. I told it, maybe today.

When I walked into Ned Bowman's office just after eight, he was already at his desk looking miserable and besieged, though the room was empty except for the two of us. His nose was heavily bandaged, with a large dirty gauze pad housing the appendage itself and six long strips of adhesive tape holding the gauze in place, as if he were under attack by a panicked sea animal.

"It looks worse, Ned. I hope amputation is not the next step."

"When did you get back from LA? You never showed up at that den of Sodom Friday night—not that I stuck around to wait for your appearance. So, where *have* you been? Tell me *now*. This *minute*."

"Seriously, I'm worried about your physical condition. I'd be happy to see you retire to a hot, cramped trailer in Sarasota, but I wouldn't want to lose you by watching you slowly rot from the top down."

He shook his head glumly. "It's a hereditary skin condition, Slotz-Planckton's disease. The cold weather aggravates it. It started to clear up in LA, but when I got back here it took a turn for the worse. It is aggravated by severe weather and by stress, my doctor tells me. *Stress*, Strachey. I am experiencing *stress*. Do you know why?"

"Financial problems? Worrisome moisture on your basement walls?"

"You know goddamn well it's you and this goddamn Lenihan thing. It's as plain as can be that everybody and his Uncle Eddie is holding out on me in this thing, and the time is close at hand when I'm going to have to start playing hardball with the likes of you. Do you catch my meaning or do I have to draw you a picture?"

"You can skip the lurid visual effects, but you can tell me who else has been holding out. I'm not admitting that I have, but who else?"

He gave me his fish eye. "You know as well as I do who else. The woman you visited in LA Friday night, before I could get there first, Mrs. Danny Lenihan. The broad went all weepy on me, which is understandable, I guess, considering, but in a full two hours of blubber and boo-hoo she didn't tell me diddly-shit about what her son was doing out there last weekend and how come this Piatek had left her boy two and a half million, and where was the two and a half million now? So, what'd she tell you? Plenty, I'll wager. You people all stick together, don't you?"

"We people?"

"I've always figured Joanie for a lez. Or maybe I heard it somewhere. You can't tell me she and that Tesney woman aren't playing doctor with the shades pulled down. So, what'd she confide in you? Come on, Strachey, make this easy for the both of us, huh?"

"'Playing doctor with the blinds pulled down.' Ned, you're the consummate romantic. No, she did not confide in me either. She just let loose with a lot of confused ill will toward Albany and its citizenry. She detests this place so much, she wouldn't even set foot in it to attend her son's funeral. It sounds as if you'd met Joan Lenihan before or know quite a lot about her."

He looked thoughtful and said, "I was the investigating officer when Dan died. It was me who took Joanie's statement back in—fifteen, sixteen years ago, it must be. Joanie wasn't a bad-looking cookie back then. Great knockers, a real pretty woman even with her buck teeth. Out in LA, Jesus, she looked like she'd been through the wringer. Or maybe she's just getting old. Hell, Joanie's older than I am, must be closing in on sixty.

"That was a sad time for the old man, let me tell you. Danny was Pug's only son, and while I can't say that Dan ever did his pop proud, even so he was all Pug had left in the world—Pug's missus passed away back in the fifties— and it was just like the bottom fell out when Dan bought the farm. I think the North End must have been draped in black for a month after that one."

Again, I was confused. "Why were the police involved in Dan Lenihan's death? I had the impression he'd died as a result of his alcoholism."

Bowman shrugged mildly, as if to recite a commonplace. "Indirectly, yeah, it was the booze. What happened was, Danny froze to death on the street. At two or three in the morning in January he passed out on the way home from Mike Shea's tavern down on Broadway. A paper boy found him at six in the morning on Second Street across from Sacred Heart, stiff as a board.

"Of course, I think Dan was stiff as a board from the time he was about eleven. How Joan put up with him all those years, I'll never know. They say she married him because Joanie was a drinker herself when she was a kid, and the two of them tied one on one night and ended up in Dan's bed, and old Pug caught 'em and made 'em make it legal. The story was, Pug had pretty much given up on Danny by then, and he wanted grandchildren.

"Well, he got 'em. Corrine's barren and Jack was a faggot, if you'll pardon the expression, which I know you won't, you being one yourself. I don't know what went wrong in that family. Pug Lenihan was one of the finest men this town ever produced, and then it all just went to hell for him. How does that happen? You tell me."

I did not offer an opinion, which would have been uselessly inflammatory. I said, "It's a sad history, but I'm more interested in the present state of the Lenihans. Jack in particular, who's been bludgeoned to death. Where does the investigation stand?"

He gave me his incredulous imbecile look, which was unusually imbecilic owing to the albino squid clinging to his face. "I can't tell you *that*. That is official police information. It is you, Strachey, who are in possession of information that could wrap this thing up in two days. I can smell it all over you. You *reek* of withheld evidence. The question is, do you give it to me voluntarily, or do I turn this simple process into something ugly and complicated for both of us? Which is it, huh?" He glared at me across his little friend.

I said, "You're up against it, Ned, am I right? You spent seven hundred dollars of the department's two-grand travel budget and you came up empty-handed. You've got nothing to show for your junket and little to go on otherwise. You're frustrated and you think your frustration will be relieved if you beat up on me. Well, forget it. I'm not interested. I can spend my time more profitably elsewhere, and so can you."

He remained calm, maybe at the urging of his physician. "Do you want to be dragged down to the lockup? Right now?"

"You could arrange that, I guess, but you won't. You're only guessing that I've got information pertinent to your investigation, and your guess is no legal basis for an arrest. Lock me up and I'll be on the streets in forty-five minutes, and you'll end up with egg on your face. I mean, if there's room for it on there."

He flinched, but remained seated, not moving, tight-lipped.

I said, "There is, however, a way we might be able to get together on this thing. Pool our resources in the interests of justice, civic improvement, and a nice commendation for you from the chief. As you have figured out, my aims in this case are broader than yours. I want Jack Lenihan's killer locked up and punished, yes, but I also want Sim Kempelman's outfit to have the two and a half million so they can run the thieves and knuckleheads out of city hall and replace them with save-the-whales, anti-nuke, ACLU goo-goos."

Bowman gripped his desk tightly, but still he said nothing. He seemed to be losing strength.

"As it happens," I said, "there is a way for both of us to accomplish everything we want to accomplish. With your assistance, I think I can hand you Jack Lenihan's killer. Notice I said 'assistance.' What I'm saying is, I'll take the risks and do most of the real work, and you'll get the credit."

After a moment, he stood calmly, walked to the door,

and closed it. Seated again, he said, "I can listen. I want Lenihan's killer tried and convicted. What do you want from me? What does this so-called assistance entail?"

"First, Ned, one thing. If we work together on this, are you willing to follow the trail wherever it leads? No matter who's involved?"

He leaned back in his swivel chair and clutched the arms. "What the fuck are you talking about, Strachey? What's a remark like *that* supposed to mean?"

"I'm not sure yet myself. Just answer the question. I know you're a blowhard and a narrow-minded jackass, but I've always thought that despite your obvious limitations you were also an honest cop. Correct me if I'm wrong."

"My entire career has been devoted to enforcing the law. You break the laws of the state of New York or the city of Albany and you reckon with Ned Bowman, whoever you are, period."

I knew that it got more complicated than that with Bowman, a man of his time and place. Yet he did have his own warped but sturdy personal integrity. Lacking alternatives at the time, I decided to place my trust in it. I said, "I want you to put a tail on me. A reliable, experienced team of plainclothes guys who will grab Jack Lenihan's killer when he tries to kill me. There is reason to believe he is going to do that, probably this morning. Just prior to that, I think, his intention is to force me to lead him to the two and a half million. He's under the impression that I've got it, though I don't want to comment on that.

"My informed opinion is that this man will make his move against me in the presence of, or more likely the close proximity of, the man he's working for, who, by the way, is a considerable personage in this town who might—I emphasize *might*—be dealing dope in a big way, though that would be out of character for him and I have deep doubts about that part.

"It's possible that when this man's employee, an ex-con, makes his attempt on me and you nail him, you will not find direct evidence linking him to the Lenihan homicide. Once you've got him on the attempted-murder charge, however, it is highly probable that he'll deal—there's a parole violation involved as well—and he'll implicate his employer, truly or falsely, in return for a reduced charge. The employer will then try to stick his employee with the Lenihan murder—offering, I hope, solid evidence—in order to save what's left of his own neck. That's all slightly chancy, but I think we can make it work. In any event, as you can see it's me who's taking all the real risks in this, and all you and your guys have to do is tag along and pick up the pieces, one of which will be me. Will you do it?"

He squinted across his septopus at me and drummed his fingers on the desktop. "I don't know enough," he said after a moment. "Tell me more. I want to hear names, places, dates."

"Can't."

"Why?"

I knew that if I mentioned Pug Lenihan's name, Bowman would choke on his own incredulity and send me back out into the cold—and possibly phone city hall the second I was out the door. The question of how much or little city hall knew was already problematic, and I wasn't about to erase all doubt by presenting myself quite so boldly. I wanted the confusion and unanswered questions that were working to my disadvantage to work to theirs too for a little while longer.

I said, "If I told you why I can't tell you, then you'd know what it was I couldn't tell you. You'd understand why I couldn't tell you it in the first place, but then it would be too late. See my problem?"

He waved that away disgustedly and thought about it some more. Beads of sweat broke out around his adhesive tape. More finger drumming and shifting about. "Twelve hours," he said then. "I'll cover you for twelve hours and not a minute more. You come up with a goose egg on this, Strachey, and you are a nonperson in this department. Except, of course, if you are caught committing a crime, like passing around two and a half million dollars that doesn't belong to you. In that case, you'll become a person again. A person in the lockup on the way to Sing Sing for so many years, you'll only be fit for the county nursing home by the time you hobble out of there."

I told him I appreciated his warm confidence in me, and we worked out the details. From a pay phone downstairs I called Corrine McConkey and confirmed my ten-thirty appointment with Pug Lenihan. Corrine said her grandfather sounded very eager to meet me but had stipulated that I arrive at his house alone.

NINETEEN

UNDER A BLEACHED-OUT SUN A SOUTH-erly breeze had dragged the temperature up to three degrees above freezing and the city was beginning to soften and melt. Fat crescents of filthy ice dropped out of motorists' wheel wells. Acids from midwestern power plants dripped off trees. The main roads were drying up, leaving a film of gray salt, but the side streets were ankle-deep in frigid slush. To step off a curb, or to breathe the air, was to risk pneumonia.

I didn't want to live in it anymore and imagined half the population of the Hudson Valley arriving simultaneously at the same sensible conclusion and suddenly making a break for it, the Thruway clogged from Selkirk to the Tappan Zee Bridge with an unbroken southward stream of sullen refugees yearning for a place in the Sunbelt where they could dry out their socks.

It didn't happen though. All the others must have had their own reasons for staying, and for the moment I had mine, which seemed to me quite grand. "Quite grandiose," Timmy would have corrected me. To make it even grander, all I had to do was stay alive.

Bowman had refused to lend me a firearm, so I drove up Washington, waded through a couple of backyards, and climbed the rear stairs to my office. The door was off its hinges again and the general disorder more general than normal. Mack Fay had been looking for his wayward luggage. I removed the loose brick from the wall where the plaster had fallen off, took my Smith & Wesson out of the bread bag that kept it dry and dustless, and stuck the gun in my coat pocket.

The telephone was working, so I called my friend the narc. "This is Strachey again. What else have you come up with on Mack Fay?"

"Are you about ready to let me in on this, my friend? That would be a reasonable condition for my passing on privileged information to you."

"No, that would be an unreasonable condition. Look, don't be offended, but I'm working with the Albany cops on this one on account of how incompetent they are. When this thing is over and the smoke clears, there's something I want to come out of this with. You guys might be smart enough to take it away from me, but Bowman's crew isn't and won't. I thought of calling you first but decided that my worthy ultimate goals in this would be jeopardized by your competence, so I went to Bowman. You understand that, don't you?"

"I appreciate what you're saying, but you understand that if you violate a federal statute I'll have to do what I'll have to do."

"No, you won't. You could, but you won't have to. You've told me yourself—discretionary blindness is a major federal crime-fighting tool. The smelliest sleazebags in North America get a pat on the back and a trip to the Bahamas if they help you convict a major doper. So don't give me a hard time on this. Next to most of the people you do business with, I'm Mother Theresa."

"Strachey, you are missing the point entirely. The point is, what have you done for me lately?"

"Nothing yet, that's true. But soon. I can't elaborate. Trust me."

He didn't hesitate. His organization had a $290 billion annual budget and a trillion-dollar deficit, so he felt confident making decisions. He said he'd give me another day or two, and then he reeled off the information I had asked him for. "Mack Fay, I am reliably informed, was not close to Robert Milius and the rest of the Albany narcotics crowd at Sing Sing. They may have known each other, but they were in no way tight."

"They weren't?"

"Fay's best buddy was a Terry Clert, paroled in October after doing seven years of a twelve-to-fifteen for armed robbery and assault with intent to kill. He held up a liquor store in Syracuse in '77 and shot the manager who, lucky for Clert, lived. Clert now resides in this area." He gave me the address on Third Street in the North End of Albany. "It's interesting that Fay and Clert are both in the area. Clert's originally from Gloversville and never lived in Albany before."

More confusion. "Are you telling me there aren't any narcotics in either Clert's or Fay's background? And they weren't hooked up in any way with the Albany dopers in Sing Sing?"

"That's the information I have. I'm willing to bet that it's good."

I thanked him and said I'd be in touch, though now I wasn't so sure anymore. The only thing I was certain of was that I was about to call on a man up to his aged neck in criminally minded Fays and Clerts, whose connection with him was unlikely to turn out to be a funny coincidence.

At 10:10 I passed through the intersection of State and Pearl and turned north. A blue Dodge parked in a bus stop edged in behind me and tagged along. Two blocks later a second Dodge joined the procession, and I thought about skimming off a small bundle of the money in the suitcases to pick up a block of Chrysler stock. At 10:25 I turned up Walter Street and parked. The two unmarked cop cars drove on by.

Dreadful Ed answered the door at the McConkeys. I could hear *The $25,000 Pyramid* squealing in the background, and McConkey seemed put out that I had interrupted his morning leisure. He had beer on his breath. He testily informed me that I was to proceed to Dad Lenihan's house on my own, that Mrs. Clert was expecting me. I drove around the block to Pug Lenihan's cottage on Pearl and parked. The two Dodges maneuvered this way and that, one of them ending up thirty yards down the block, the other one around the corner on Second Street.

The Pontiac I'd seen in Lenihan's driveway a week earlier was back. I walked up to the front porch, stamped the slush off my feet, and rang the bell. The door was opened almost immediately by a plump round-faced woman in a pale pink pants suit. She studied me with cool gray eyes and flashed a practiced institutional smile.

"Are you Mr. Strachey?"

"Yes, I am."

"I'm Miriam Clert. It's nice of you to drop by and see Dad. Come right in, please."

"Thank you."

I wiped my feet on the worn welcome mat and followed her through the bare front hall into a small, low-ceilinged living room with lace curtains and a threadbare brown rug. The furnishings consisted of what used to be called a "living room suit"—squat tan easy chair and couch to match, with shiny acrylic pillows, their manufacturer's tags unremoved under penalty of law. Arranged atop a table by the front window was an assortment of framed photographs showing various members of the Lenihan family in formal poses and tinted to the point of herpes zoster. In the one non-studio shot, Jack, Corrine, Joan, and a puffy-faced man I took to be Dan Lenihan were standing on a lawn in what must have been their Easter finery, circa 1963. Their smiles were forced and wan, and no one was touching anyone else. Except for the daffodils in the background, it could have been a police lineup.

I seated myself on the couch while Mrs. Clert went to bring Dad Lenihan to the room. In this quiet plain house, with the winter sunlight filtering through the gauzy curtains, I began to feel a little silly checking out entrances and exits and rearranging my Smith & Wesson, which was stuffed in my coat pocket on the couch beside me. The house shuddered briefly as somewhere beneath me the oil burner clicked on. A radiator sighed and I sighed back.

An accordion door leading to the room on the other side of the front hall was jerked aside. Standing in the entrance to what once must have been a dining room—a hospital bed now occupied its far wall—was the most enormous infant I had ever seen. Pug Lenihan was as shiny and pink and hairless as a Florida tomato. Though slumped and bent, he was a good six-two, and formidable even in a faded cotton bathrobe and Naugahyde slippers. His mouth was set hard, his ice-blue eyes wary under a broad, smooth forehead. My first thought was, here is Rosemary's baby at ninety-six. I checked the exits again.

Miriam Clert led Lenihan by the elbow to a chair across from me. When he was seated he shook her hand away and snapped, "Now you go on out. Go on out back." It was a once-forceful voice that came out soft and cracked, like a recording of a 1930s radio show.

"You might need something, Dad. You might have to make wee-wee."

"Go on out back and shut the door! You heard me."

Her face tightened and she turned away. "I'll be in the kitchen if you need me," she said to me. "If Dad has to go potty, come fetch me. I'll be having my cup of tea." She disappeared down the hall, though I did not hear a door close.

Lenihan arranged his bathrobe over his skinny legs. "You Strachey?"

"Yes, Mr. Lenihan, I am. Sim Kempelman said you wanted to talk to me."

With sarcasm he said, "Ohhh, Kempelman, yes-s-s, Kempelman. That man doesn't know a turd from a toadstool! Do you?"

"Sure. Early on a summer morning, toadstools have little sprites sitting on them. Turds don't."

He glared at me with disgust. Everything seemed to disgust him. "You're a wiseacre, aren't you?" I shrugged. "Well, don't you wise-guy me, mister!"

I said, "What was it you wanted to see me about, Mr. Lenihan?"

His little mouth bent down and the blue eyes narrowed. One fist clenched and unclenched repeatedly. After a moment, he said, "You gimme my money back! You know what I want. I want my money back. You got it with you?"

"What money are you referring to?"

The fist hit the arm of the chair. "Don't you play games with me, mister! You bring it along? You better've."

I watched him watching me. The oil burner quit running

and the house was quiet. Mrs. Clert was not drinking her tea noisily. I said, "Are you referring to the five suitcases stuffed with US currency? If so, I was under the impression that that money belonged to your late grandson Jack. That it had been left to him by a wealthy friend in Los Angeles. Or did Jack leave a will naming you as beneficiary?"

His look of intense disgust intensified. "What the hell are you talkin' about, you god damn chiseler? Jackie *stole* that money. He took it right out of my house last October from right under my nose. Know how I know it was him? Because he *told* me he took it, just like he was proud of it. That's where that money came from, and anything else you hear is a lotta bull. Now I want that money back, mister, do you *understand me*?"

"That's hard to believe," I said. "You don't look like a man with several million dollars to his name. If it's yours, where did you get it?"

A blue vein slithered up the inside of his pink head and throbbed. I was afraid he would keel over dead, and I didn't want that to happen while I was there. Trembling, he said, "Who—in—the—*hell*—do you think you *are*?"

I waited and listened for other sounds in the house. I heard none. "What makes you think I've got the money?" I said.

"My daughter-in-law told me you were the one who was after it. And Joanie don't lie to me, oh no, she don't. She sent the money back to me on a plane, and Howie's boy told me you took it. Mack Fay said he went out to the airport to get it for me, and he saw you take it out there. Howie's boy wouldn't lie to me, and don't *you* lie to me either. Where's my money?"

"What if I have it and I refuse to turn it over to you, Mr. Lenihan? Will you have me arrested? Why haven't you called in the police?"

Another vein ran up his skull, like a line of blue air moving inside a pink beach ball. He leaned toward me, his fist clenching and unclenching, and said, "You aren't from around here, are you?"

"I live on Crow Street."

"Ward six!" He turned his head and spat, though nothing came out.

I said, "You haven't answered my question. Why don't you pick up the phone, call the police, and have me arrested for grand larceny?"

He stuck out his chin and smirked. "Don't have to."

"Why?" I glanced toward the hallway to see if Mack Fay and Terry Clert were bounding toward me wielding tire irons. They were not.

"You were a friend of Jack's," Lenihan said. "The word I hear is, you were a friend of my grandson's."

"He was a client of mine. I'm a private investigator and Jack hired me for a particular job. We were not friends while he was alive, but I feel that I know him well. I admire a lot of things I've heard about him, his ideals especially. I didn't have the chance to be his friend, but I would like to have been."

The fist still opening and closing, he said, "Joanie your friend too?" Now a tense sly grin had formed across his face.

"I've met Jack's mother. Yes, I liked her too and wish that she wasn't so full of bitterness about so many things."

"She's a cheap slut!" His look was smug as he said it. "You want to know why I'm not gonna call the cops, and you're still gonna give me my money back, and you're not gonna ask me any more nosy questions, and then you're gonna keep your mouth shut? You know why? *Huh?*"

"No. You tell me, Mr. Lehihan."

"You ask Joanie. You go home and you call her up, and then *you bring me my money.* You'll do it. Oh yes, you will. You'll do as I say, all right." His eyes got big and he sat smirking and making fists. My impulse was to walk over and pull his plug, but his vital malevolence was fueled only from within, so that was not possible.

I said, "Who killed Jack? Who bludgeoned your grandson and placed his dying body in my car?"

The clenched fists opened and stayed open. He stared at me blankly for a moment, and then his face collapsed and trembled violently. A surge of rage went through him, and he bleated, "Perverts! Pansies and perverts! Jack laid down with perverts and one of those filthy animals killed him. Wipe 'em out! That's the only way our boys are gonna be safe! Castrate 'em! Gas 'em! Lock 'em up and fry 'em!" His whole body shook.

I said, "Is that what you wanted to happen to Jack? Jack was gay. Is that what you wanted? For Jack to be wiped out?"

Suddenly deflating, Lenihan slumped in his seat and looked confused. "No," he said after a moment. "No, not Jackie. Jackie was a good, strong boy. Jackie had spunk. Jackie had a head on his shoulders. Jackie could have amounted to something. Jack was—oh, my Jesus, how I miss that boy!" Tears flowed. With a sudden jerk, he wiped them away with his sleeve and said, "G'wan, get outta here. And gimme my goddamn money back!" He covered his eyes with one hand and waved me away with the other.

"Jack had good plans for that money," I said. "I think he would have wanted me to carry them out."

In a split second, the woe and tenderness vanished and the harsh anger came back. Giving me the evil eye again, he said, "You talk to Joanie, mister. And then you bring me my money. *Today*. You hear what I'm telling you?"

I stood up. "Is city hall in on this with you? Do they know what you're doing?"

He grunted. "City hall knows what city hall knows, and I know what I know. Now get outta here and get me my money."

Unsummoned, Mrs. Clert promptly appeared. "It looks like you've ruffled Dad's feathers, Mr. Strachey. Is that right, Dad, did the gentleman get your feathers mussed?"

"Don't *you* start in on me," he snapped, as she led me to the front door.

"Maybe we'll see you again sometime," Mrs. Clert said with her blank smile. "I think Dad would like that."

"That's the impression I have," I said, zipping up my coat in the doorway. "In fact, he mentioned specifically that he'd like me to visit again soon."

"Oh, did he? Well, that would be nice. Oh, it's so cold and damp out there. Don't catch your death now."

She shut the door and I stood looking at the abandoned Immaculate Conception School across the street. The chain-link fence around it had been ripped from its steel posts in three places and most of the windowpanes had been smashed. One of the fading graffiti on the red brick wall of the building read simply IMAGINE. I gazed at the word for a minute or so, and I began to imagine. As I did so, I knew that I had to speak with Joan Lenihan fast.

As I headed south on Pearl, the two Dodges trailed along a block behind me. When it became clear that I was not being followed by anyone else, I pulled over, got out, and signaled for the cop cars to pull alongside.

Bowman, being chauffeured in the front car, rolled down his window. "Jumpin' Jesus, Strachey, was that *Pug Lenihan's* house you went into back there?"

"Yeah."

"Well, what kind of half-assed stunt is this anyway? Criminy, man. If word got back I was up here poking into Pug Lenihan's business without him asking, I'd be hung by the gimmeys in Capitol Park at high noon. Now goddamn it, when and where is this attack on you supposed to happen? If you want my cooperation on this, you're just gonna have to fill me in before you get a single 'nother iota of my valuable time."

I said, "Forget it."

"What?"

"Let's skip it for now. I have to check on a couple of things and then I'll get back to you."

"Don't bother," he said, thrusting his gray squid up at me. "The next time we meet, I'll be bothering you—*plenty*." He rolled up the window and they left me standing in the slush.

I drove back toward the Hilton. I was not being followed and I could not understand why. Mrs. Clert certainly would have notified Terry Clert—presumably her son, or husband, or great-nephew twice removed—as well as Mack Fay of my appointment at Pug Lenihan's. It would have been their first certain knowledge of my whereabouts since Timmy and I had abandoned our house the previous week. Why would they let the opportunity to get at me slide by? Had they been tipped by someone in Bowman's crew that the cops would be surveilling me? That possibility made me unhappy.

Or did Fay and Clert know that Pug would insist that I return to his house with the money later in the day, and that after I spoke with Joan Lenihan I was sure to do as I was told? Although Pug had seemed genuinely unaware of Fay's recent efforts to retrieve the money for him—*if* those efforts had been on Pug's behalf at all. Fay and Clert, it now appeared, had been running their own scam to make off with the two and a half million—diddling Pug while he thought they were helping him.

But if that was the case, how could they hope to snatch the money from me if not at Pug's house? If they had been tipped that I would arrive with the cops in tow on my first visit, how could they be sure that I wouldn't also have Bowman with me on any subsequent visit? Mrs. Clert had seemed relaxed, confident, secure—not the demeanor of a woman whose family's elaborate act of larceny was in serious jeopardy.

In room 1407 I bolted the door, dragged the five bags out

of the closet, unlocked each one, and opened them. The two and a half million was intact. I locked the bags and stacked them back in the closet.

I dialed Joan Lenihan's number in Los Angeles. After twenty rings there was no answer. I called my New York Telephone contact, who told me that three calls, each lasting approximately four minutes, had been made from Pug Lenihan's number to Joan Lenihan's phone in LA during the previous thirty-six hours. The most recent call had been at 6:15 the evening before. I hung up and tried LA again. No answer.

It was just after noon in Albany, nine in LA. I figured both Joan and Gail were working seven to four, or they'd worked the night before and had unplugged the telephone and gone to bed. I'd try again in the late afternoon, and if that didn't work, ask Kyle Toot to track Joan down and ask her to call me. I figured I now knew what the key was to trigger Joan Lenihan's cooperation, and the thought of it made me sick.

Before heading out for lunch, I checked my answering service, which had what was described as "an extremely urgent" message from Timmy. The message was: *I am in the company of Messrs. Fay and Clert involuntarily. Bring the you-know-what to our house at midnight tonight, but do not come accompanied by you-know-who. This is no joke. I repeat, this is no joke. Sorry about this.*

Now I had done it. *They* had done it. And I had done it. "Did he say where he was calling from?"

"All he said was to take down his message carefully and to get it to you as soon as possible. But you didn't leave a number. We didn't know where to reach you."

Timmy knew though. And he hadn't told them about our room at the Hilton. They didn't *have* to have the information, because they had him, which they knew was as good as having me and the money. Still, he hadn't told them. I ached to be able to thank him for that. But I didn't know where to find him.

TWENTY

I SPED OVER TO TROY THROUGH THE slush and parked in front of Flo Trenky's place. The green pickup truck was nowhere in sight, so I trotted around the corner and down the alley to see if Fay had parked out back. He hadn't. Workmen were removing the debris of the collapsed back porch and using a power shovel to load the splintered lumber into a dump truck. I went back out front and pressed the door buzzer.

"Yeah? What can I do you for?"

"Mr. Mack Fay, please?"

"Mackie ain't in right now. Who should I tell him dropped by?"

"I'm Phil Downey, Mr. Fay's parole officer. When do you expect him back?"

She had a pretty cracked face under a load of rouge and purple eye shadow. Her orange wig had bangs combed up like eyelashes, and her actual eyelashes were thick with some type of black muck. Broad-hipped and ample-bosomed, she stood facing me in chartreuse pedal pushers and a low-cut yellow sweater. On the side of her neck was what appeared to be a twelve-hour-old red-and-purple hickey.

She looked at me suspiciously and said, "You got some ID?"

"Are you Mrs. Fay?"

"No, I'm Flo Trenky, Mack's fiancée. Mack didn't say nothin' about no parole officer stopping in."

"This is a routine check. Could you show me his room, please?"

Her look hardened. "You got a search warrant? I need to see papers. If you got an ID and you got papers, you can come in. If you don't, you better talk to Mackie first. But Mackie ain't here."

"Look, I like Mack and I don't want to make any trouble for him. Tell me where I can locate him, I'll go there and fill out my report and that will be that. If I have to call in that Mack can't be located and might have left the state, it'll be his neck, not mine. I've just got a job to do."

She hesitated and seemed to loosen up, then got a puzzled look. "Where's your briefcase?"

"At the office. This is my lunch hour."

"Listen, wiseass, I never saw a parole officer without he had a briefcase glued on his arm. You're no parole officer, buster. What if I told you where Mackie went is none of your beeswax? What if I told you to scram? What if I told you you'd be in hot water if you didn't move your butt offa my premises?"

I sighed. "Flo, I have a confession to make."

"Come again?"

"Could we just step inside? You're going to catch a chill standing out here without a coat on and—well, this is going to shock you, but—my relationship with Mackie is kind of personal, and I think now is as good a time as any for you to hear about it." I took out my wallet and presented her with my membership card in the National Gay Task Force.

"What? What's that there?"

"Mackie has stolen my man, Flo. I want him back. Maybe between the two of us we can make Mackie see the light and then he'll come back to you and give me my man back. Down at Sing Sing Mackie stole my honey away from me."

She blinked hard and a chunk of something black fell off one eyelash, ricocheted off her left cheek, and plummeted into her cleavage. "You shittin' me? Mackie ain't that way. You're shittin' me."

"I think we should have a tête-à-tête, Flo—get to know each other. And see if we can figure out a way to get Mackie back on the straight and narrow. Maybe it's just a phase he's going through, but you never can tell."

This did not fit with what she knew and she didn't want to believe it. But here was a woman who had been lied to by men before and her fund of mistrust was ready for tapping. I was not proud of myself for being the four hundredth man to mislead and abuse Flo Trenky. But I had to do what I had to do. In a shaky voice she said, "I'll kill that Mackie," and led me into the house.

The living room, overlooking the street, had a worn couch and a couple of electric-blue easy chairs with doilies on the arms and a coffee table with two Schlitz empties and a glass ashtry full of butts. A big Sears TV set with a vase full of paper geraniums atop it occupied one corner, but the focus of the room was a large cardboard fireplace with bricks painted on it and a cellophane fire that turned over a spit on a red light bulb.

Leaning in a stand next to the electric fire were a brush, a shovel, and a cast-iron poker. The brush and shovel looked as if they had stood undisturbed for a long time—like Timmy's and mine, Flo's fire produced no ashes—but the poker appeared to have been recently cleaned and polished.

"My friend's name is Jack," I said. "Perhaps you've met him. It's possible Mackie even brought him here. It'd be just like him, that wild and crazy guy."

She flinched. I thought about spitting it all out, telling her who I really was and why I had come into her home, and why I was now so desperate to locate Mack Fay. But she might have panicked and thrown me out—I had no way of judging how much she knew or didn't know—and I had to do what would work.

"Last week," she said in a tremulous voice. "That must've been the fella Mackie brought over last week. Him and Terry."

"Terry Clert?"

"They was buddies in the correction facilities. Mackie and Terry came in with this fella and said they need my place for some private business. Why, Holy Mother—is *Terry* a fruit too?"

"Yes, but he and Mack are just pals. 'Sisters,' people used to say and I suppose some still do. But it's my Jack who's the one Mackie's got the crush on. You say they might have been together here last week. Was the man you saw slim, about five-ten, going bald, wearing glasses, dressed in jeans and a dark-blue pea coat?"

"That's him. Oh my God."

"What night was that?"

She bit her lip and said, "Tuesday night. I had to miss part of *Riptide*, but June filled me in. They came in and said could they use my place to talk business, it was private, and I says sure, why not, so I went over to June's, my sister's, and watched my programs over at her place. Mackie said it was business, but—are you tryin' to tell me Mackie and that guy Jack was in here—*doin' it?*"

"Yeah, the rotten creeps, they probably were. I was home Tuesday night, so they knew they couldn't use our place. Usually I work nights, but last Tuesday I was at home, so they must have come over here for their lousy cheating. So, you were gone for how long?"

"I went out about nine o'clock and got back about a quarter to twelve. June and I had a couple of drinks and chewed the fat for a while. When I got home Mackie had gone out and didn't get back till God knows what hour. Why, that two-timing so-and-so! He must have been ashamed to look me in the face! Why, that—Mackie never even *told* me he was AC-DC. He must've picked it up in the facilities, that's all I can figure. Why, that—right under my roof he does it! Wait'll I get my hands on that lying son of a bee!"

"I hope none of your other tenants saw what was going on and are laughing at you behind your back. Was anyone else in the house that night?"

She fumbled with a pack of L&Ms and managed to insert one into the side of her mouth. "Unh-unh. There was a salesman here for a while on Sunday, Jim O'Connor, but he left when the back porch fell off. My back porch broke down on account of all the snow, but that was Sunday. Last Tuesday the only other person in the house was Mr. Frye in 2-B, and he never goes out of his room, just to the mental health on Monday morning and then pick up a box of sandwiches and root beer for the week over at the store, so he wouldn't've seen any funny business that was going on.

"Why, that Mackie! I should've known. In the morning the place looked like they had a party in here and cleaned it up. I just should've known. Men! You gotta keep an eye on 'em every minute. Though let me tell you, mister, *this* is a new one. *This* is a real big surprise. I'd've never believed it if you hadn't told me. Not Mackie." She lit the cigarette with a butane lighter and shook her head in nauseated disbelief.

"What made you think they had had a party?" I said. "I'm surprised, because Jack is a Jehovah's Witness and doesn't drink or smoke."

"Oh, it wasn't much," she said abstractedly. She was having trouble keeping her thoughts focused on this minor matter. "Back in the bedroom they must've spilt something on the rug and then tried to wipe it up, but it left a stain I can't get out. Wine or something. Busted the bottle too, I guess, 'cause there's still glass slivers. I got one stuck in my big toe yesterday. I mentioned it to Mackie, but he just said never mind the rug, he was gonna get me out of this dump anyway, take me to Atlantic City and put me in a condo. But that's just bull. Mackie can't even leave Troy till his parole is up in '87. Hell, he don't even have a job except driving some old coot around.

"Say, lookit—" She dragged on the cigarette and her expression had turned quizzical. "Tell me somethin' then. If you think Mackie's playin' around with your boyfriend, why don't you just give your boyfriend a piece of your mind? Tell him to shape up or ship out. What do you want to go botherin' Mackie for? Jeez, you might get him in trouble with the parole office for perversions. Listen, fella, *I* can handle Mackie. If he's gonna keep gettin' between my legs he's gonna have to quit foolin' around with degenerates who might give out that new disease that came up from Hades. What's it called?"

"AIDS."

"That's the one. I heard it can make you awful sick."

"That's why I want to find Mack today, Flo. I think Jack is with him right now, and I want to find them and talk some sense into Jack before it's too late. Do you think they might be at Terry Clert's house? Terry lives over on Third Street in the North End of Albany, I've heard."

"Yeah, they might be. Mackie went out early this morning and said he was picking up Terry and they had some work to do. But maybe that was just a line. Do you think?"

"Yes, I do. I think that was just a line."

"Men! You can't believe a word they say."

"No. No, I guess you can't."

I parked in front of the Clert house on Third Street at ten till two. The green pickup truck was nowhere in sight, nor was any other vehicle I had ever seen before. I watched the house for fifteen minutes and saw no sign of life. I knew Mrs. Clert would still be at Pug Lenihan's, though Corrine had mentioned a Kevin Clert who stayed with Pug overnight, and he could have been asleep inside the ramshackle frame carton I was looking at.

Slogging through the melting snow, I moved to the rear of the house and popped the lock on the back door with a credit card. I walked in with my revolver drawn. I'd never shot a human being and didn't want to now. But I knew I would do it if it meant saving Timmy or myself, both of whose lives I valued more highly than Mack Fay's or Terry Clert's. I knew now the kind of people I was dealing with, and if they were badly hurt and suffered exquisitely during whatever was coming next, I could learn to live with it.

The house was silent except for a dripping faucet and a humming refrigerator in the kitchen where I stood. If Timmy was in the house the leaky faucet would be driving him crazy, so I gave the handle a hard shove. The drip-drop-drip continued. The washer was shot but I didn't take the time to replace it.

Finding no person, awake or asleep, in the downstairs rooms, I climbed the stairs and checked the bedrooms. There were three, each recently having been slept in, all unoccupied at the moment. One room, neat, feminine and freshly Airwicked, was obviously Mrs. Clert's. The other two, malodorous and chaotic, with pants flung over chairs and soiled twisted sheets on the beds, apparently belonged to the two male Clerts. I poked through the debris but found nothing incriminating or helpful.

Back downstairs I went to the telephone on the kitchen counter hoping to find an address scrawled on a notepad, as in *Boston Blackie* or *Martin Kane, Private eye*, but there wasn't any.

I did not know where to look next for Timmy. A jar of instant coffee was next to the teakettle on the gas range, so I fixed myself a cup and sat at the kitchen table drinking it in the trapezoid of dusty sunlight that shone in the back window. I did not at all want to do what I decided to do next, but it seemed that both survival and neatness required it.

Back at the Hilton, I made nine telephone calls to acquaintances in New York City before I was able to complete the arrangements I had in mind. I skimmed off fifty thousand dollars from the two and a half million in the closet, stuffed it in my coat pockets, went down and picked up the car, and headed south.

I was in Manhattan by six, out by six forty-five, back in Albany just before ten. That gave me two hours before I was to meet Timmy and his captors at our house on Crow Street. From the hotel room I placed several more phone calls, the first of which was to my friend the narc.

TWENTY-ONE

THE TEMPERATURE HAD DROPPED BACK to three degrees and was headed, the radio said, down to eight below. For once, that was good. I picked up two friends at their house on Chestnut Street and drove them over to Rensselaer and back. Then I drove them over to Rensselaer and back a second time.

"On the phone you said you needed our help, but all we're doing is riding back and forth across the river. What is it we're supposed to do?"

"Pant."

"No, really."

"I want rapid breathing. Pant for me."

Casting nervous glances at each other, they panted until I dropped them back at their house.

"Thanks for your moisture."

"Don, are you okay?"

"My feet are cold, but my faculties are intact."

"Why don't you try turning the heater on?"

"Ah, but then I wouldn't have your frozen breath preserved on my window glass."

"You aren't going to go somewhere and lick it off, are

you? I would consider that low-risk sex, but I suppose the ultra-cautious might insist it constituted an exchange of body fluids."

I shoved them out into the cold night and drove over to Crow Street, peering through the peepholes I had scratched in the film of ice. No lights were on in the house and Mack Fay's truck was nowhere on the street. With one window rolled down I backed into a space half a block from the house. I turned off the ignition, shut the window, and waited invisibly. It was 11:26.

Two cars rolled by in the next twenty-four minutes, their headlights brightening the icy opalescence in front of me, but neither car stopped nor even slowed. At ten till twelve a third vehicle moved slowly up the street with a fourth close on its tail. Through the peepholes I made out Fay's green pickup, which backed into the last available space on the block, forcing the car behind it—the beige Buick I'd seen in front of my office the week before—to park alongside a fire hydrant.

One man emerged from the truck and three from the car. Of the three, the one in the middle—Timmy's height and build, and wearing Timmy's coat—wore something that covered his face and head, possibly a pillowcase. The two others were leading him by the arms. The party of four met in front of the house and moved up the front steps. The door was unlocked and they entered, shutting the door behind them. After a moment, lights went on behind the living room draperies.

At three minutes till twelve I retrieved a bundle from under the car seat and, moving quietly, attentively, walked down the block. I opened the door of Fay's truck and inserted the bundle under the driver's seat. I thought, this is not perfect justice, but in an imperfect world, it will serve, it will serve.

At midnight precisely I walked up the front steps of my

home and stomped the snow off my feet. I glanced up and down the street and, satisfied that no one had observed my recent odd actions, entered the house.

The four of them were seated around the picture of the fire. Two stood up as I entered. "I'm glad you got my message," Timmy said, remaining seated. "It's been an unusually long day." His smile was sincere but lacking in joie de vivre.

"Did they mistreat you?"

"Not to any lasting effect. I'll have to have these pants cleaned and pressed."

"We didn't want to mess him up too bad," Fay said. "Not with him being worth two and a half million. You got an expensive little girlfriend here, Strachey. Hey, you didn't know that before, did you?"

Fay had a two-day stubble of beard, nicotine-stained teeth, and dead black eyes. He grunted smugly and glanced at the other two to see if they were having a good time too. The younger Clert, Kevin, I figured, was a chunky gimlet-eyed youth who closely resembled a kid I knew in the eighth grade who sat in the back row sticking a pencil in his ear. The older Clert, Terry, was taller, rangier, better-looking and twitchier, and he kept his finger on the trigger of a sawed-off shotgun aimed at Timmy's midsection.

"You two must be the Clert brothers," I said, "Bert and Ernie. And I guess you're Mack Fay. It was hard to recognize your voice without a six-pound pile of shit stuffed in your mouth."

They all made stunned, ugly faces at me, and Timmy winced.

"What's in your coat pocket?" Fay snarled. "Kevin, shake him down."

I lifted my arms as Kevin removed my Smith & Wesson and examined it as if it were a moon rock. He carried it away dumbstruck.

"See," I said, "I didn't have an erection, I was just glad to see you guys."

More stunned, ugly faces. Timmy gave me a pleading look.

"Where is it?" Fay snapped.

"Not far from here."

"For your girlfriend's sake, hopefully it's in your car."

"The money is in a hotel room downtown."

"This asshole told you to bring it *with* you, you dumb fuck! I was right there when he said it on the phone. Now you get your ass downtown and bring it back here! You got fifteen minutes, *you hear me?*"

I checked my watch. Timmy was looking increasingly distraught, but this wasn't going to last much longer. I said, "I can have it back here in ten minutes. But first I want an explanation in return for the money. Why did you have to kill Jack Lenihan?"

A dumb coy look. "Who says I did?"

"You found out about the existence of the money in Pug Lenihan's house from Mrs. Clert—or was it from your father?—and you were planning to make off with it, but Jack stole it first. You grabbed him when he came back from LA, but he didn't have the money with him. You took him over to Flo Trenky's place Tuesday night to try to force him to get it for you. But why did you have to kill him? I want to know that."

Fay shrugged and grinned stupidly. "He told us you had it," he said mildly. "The dumb fuck wasn't gonna tell us anything, but he changed his mind when we told him some things we knew about his mom—some interesting shit I picked up over on Pearl Street. Then he spit it out real fast, oh yes, he sure did. He told us you had the money. And then he started thinking and putting two and two together and getting very pissed off and mad at the world and going kind of nuts on us and—shit, we had to protect ourselves, didn't we? I mean, shit, that guy was fuckin' apeshit. I suppose you could say it was too bad what happened had to happen, but I think you have to admit, Jackie was kind of a weirdo anyways. He could have been a real pain in the ass if he was around. So, what can I tell you, good buddy?" He shrugged again and looked at me with his lifeless eyes while the other two stood around looking bored. Kevin was picking his nose and sticking the produce behind his ear.

I said, "How did you know I wouldn't arrive here with the cops? Why were you so sure of that?"

The dead eyes watched me. "'Cause then the cops would know *you* had the money and you wouldn't get to keep it. You'd lose it too."

"Maybe I'd rather see it go back to Pug than turn it over to you."

"Hey, did you hear that one, Terry? Shit, Pug can't take that money back from the cops, and you know it. Old Pug can't say it's his 'cause old Pug can't explain where it came from, right? The state would keep it. You aren't such a dipshit you didn't figure that one out the same as we did. And if you were gonna bring in the cops, you'd've done it right away. But you didn't, did you, Strachey? Shit, mister, I had *your* number from the day one."

I said, "The money properly belongs to Jack Lenihan's estate. He inherited it from Al Piatek. There's a legal will. The money is Jack's, and with him gone, his mother, his legal heir, gets it. The cops would have to turn it over to her."

He sneered. "Shit, Joanie'd just give it back to Pug. He'd end up with it for damn sure."

"Why?"

"Hey, just ask her, good buddy. My dad told me the dirt on Miz Joanie. Oh yes, Miz Joanie would have that two and a half million back on Pearl Street in no time at all. Hey, just ask her if she wouldn't do that."

I looked at my watch again. "The money is in a room at the Hilton. The desk clerk will hand over a key to either Timmy or me. One of us can drive over and pick it up, or we can all go over there together. However you want to do it."

"We'll just jang around here," Fay said. "You got fifteen minutes. Miss Timothy here can bring out some liquor if you got any in the house, and when you get back we can all celebrate."

"And then what happens to Timmy and me?" I said.

"Hey, friend, what can I tell you? Look at some TV? Call an ambulance? It's none of my business, right?"

My watch now said it was twelve-fifteen. I walked to the front door and opened it. Six clean-shaven men in flak jackets strode in wielding automatic weapons of assorted shapes and sizes. Two others came in the back door simultaneously and moved rapidly across the kitchen, through the dining room, and up behind Terry Clert, who spun around a couple of times but didn't shoot anybody. Fay and the Clerts made more ugly faces, out of which came vulgar protestations. Shiny DEA badges flashed in the light of the picture of the fire.

"What the fuck *is* this?" Fay whined. "Narcs? You guys are fuckin' *narcs?* What is this fuckin' shit?"

Someone read Fay his rights and made reference to a glassine bag of white powder under the seat of a truck parked outside and registered in Fay's name. The discovery was made, Fay was told, as a result of an anonymous tip. Fay's parole officer—one of the six armed men who had entered through the front door—had a legal right to enter Fay's vehicle to investigate, and he had done so. He said he was surprised and disappointed that Fay had taken up this new line of criminal endeavor, but there it was.

Fay repeatedly cried, "Setup! Setup!" and demanded access to a telephone so that he could arrange for an attorney.

Timmy, who had placed atop the mantel the sawed-off

shotgun previously aimed at his gut, asked, "It's not a toll call, is it?"

Kevin Clert, drooling and trembling, said, "Hey, I didn't off that faggot! Shoot, I wasn't even there. I was at work that night."

Terry Clert, mum until now, found his voice. "*I* didn't hit him. Mack hit him!"

"Hit who?" said a narc.

"Hey, man, let's you and me go someplace and talk, huh? How about it, huh? We can deal, huh? How about it?"

At that point somebody suggested that Ned Bowman be called, and I volunteered to wake him up. Out of habit, Bowman spewed forth a stream of sour invective, but then I got a word in and he became quietly alert.

TWENTY-TWO

TIMMY SAID, "MY BED. I AM ACTUALLY lying in my own bed again. Oh, this is sweet."

"You sound as if you doubted you ever would."

"There have been times in the past week when I wondered if I'd ever lie in *any* bed again."

"I'm sorry you got dragged into this. I probably should have sent you off to Poughkeepsie after I got the first call from Hankie-mouth—Fay."

"What do you mean, 'sent me off'? What am I, your foster child?"

"I hope not."

"Well, there wouldn't have been any problem if I hadn't stopped by here this morning. That was my own fault and I feel pretty dumb about it."

"Good."

"To tell you the truth, the whole time they had me in

that motel with the shotgun aimed at me, I never really believed they were going to hurt me. I was outraged and my pride was offended, and I was nervous about the gun going off accidentally. But I kept telling myself it was the money they wanted and they wouldn't shoot me as long as they didn't have it and could still use me for making you lead them to the money. That's why I didn't tell them where it was hidden."

"Oh? I thought you were just being loyal to me."

He laughed. "You would think that, wouldn't you? Hell, it was all enlightened self-interest. I didn't give a crap about the two and a half million and your big plans for it. Not at that point. I was interested in staying alive, period. Anyway, the subject of the suitcases full of money is all academic now. When you went downtown with the feds, did you stop off at the hotel and hand the money over to them?"

"No, I told them I didn't know what had become of it. That Fay was mistaken in his assumption that I had it."

A little silence. We'd been lying belly-to-belly, but now he backed off and stared at me big-eyed. "No."

"Sure, why not? The governor says the state is running a surplus this year, so he won't need it. And if the feds ended up with it, it'd just go for a lid on another MX silo. Hell, the money can be put to better uses than that."

"But it's evidence. It turned out Fay and Clert *were* dope dealers."

"Yes, it's true that they were in the narcotics business." I looked away and would have lit a cigarette if I had not recklessly quit smoking six years and two months earlier. "But the point is, the two and a half million had nothing to do with that probably. You heard it all—the money was Pug Lenihan's, illegally obtained in some manner."

"Sure, dope trafficking. It was a family operation. Pug, Jack, maybe even Dreadful Ed. Fay heard about it at Sing Sing from Jack's former associates who were caught, and they got Mrs. Clert positioned as Pug's nurse so that she could tip them off on large amounts of money moving through the house. They were going to steal it—probably to finance a big buy of their own—but Jack grabbed it for his civic-reform program. It's all as plain as day. The feds will piece it together and they'll start searching for that money methodically and relentlessly. And guess who they'll come to first asking about it. *You*. Don, hand it over now, or—God, you could actually end up in *prison*. Really. Don't you understand that?"

"That's the tenth or twelfth most ridiculous story I've ever heard. Pug Lenihan dealing drugs? To him, dope is a Commie conspiracy. You might as well accuse him of shipping spare parts for MIGs to the Sandinistas."

"But look at the *evidence*. Tonight the narcs found fifty thousand dollars' worth of cocaine in Mack Fay's truck. Jack Lenihan dealt drugs in a big way and just barely escaped going to jail for it. Everywhere you turn in this thing, it's drugs, drugs, drugs. From some of the things Mack Fay said tonight, it even sounds as if *Joan Lenihan* was in on it. I mean, think of Hollywood and what's the first thing that comes to mind after movie-making? No wonder she was so wrought up and closemouthed about the whole thing. Joan is probably in it herself up to her teeth. Listen, lover, forget the money. Turn it over to the cops and extricate yourself from this mare's nest before it's too late. I know how badly you want to diddle the Albany machine, and, God knows, I sympathize, I understand. But using a dope ring's boodle is not the way to go about it. It is dangerous, it is wrong, and it won't work."

I said, "There is a certain logic to your conclusions, but they are the wrong conclusions. Of that I am certain."

"How do you know?"

I figured if I told him I had planted the coke in Fay's truck he would (a) have me arrested and testify against me, or (b) pack his bags and enter a monastery in the morning, or, at the very least (c), recite to me long passages from Cardinal Newman and then sleep on the couch.

I said, "There are no Irish dope dealers. You should know that. Narcotics is not as satisfyingly depraved as prostitution, it's not as socially useful as bootlegging, and it's not as lucrative as owning city hall. The Irish don't need it and they don't want it. Dope is for the blacks, the Italians, the Jews, and the go-for-it WASPs. The Lenihan family wouldn't be interested in it."

He let his head fall back on the pillow and gave me one of his full-body deep sighs. "So what are you going to do next? Have the Mafia launder the money so that you can turn it over to Sim Kempelman?"

"I've considered that, but I've decided the risks are too great. Anyway, that would be immoral. I'm not sure yet how I'll clean up the money for Kempelman. I'm determined to find a way, but first I have to take a trip."

"Another one? How come? Where to this time?"

"LA again. Want to come along?"

"I'd like to, but I'm still a public servant on the state payroll, as far as I know, so I'll pass. Who are you going to see out there, Joan Lenihan?"

"Yes."

"Why?"

"To threaten her. I'm going to threaten her with a proposition she's going to hate."

News reporters from eight radio stations, three television stations, and two newspapers phoned between six and eight in the morning. I told them Mr. Strachey was out and that I was the Bulgarian cleaning lady.

Over his Wheatena, Timmy said, "Despite your clever disguise, I take it you're going to be of little assistance in straightening this place up. I think I'll just go ahead and call a cleaning service."

"Right, a cleaning service or a building contractor. Sure, go ahead. It's a business expense and I can pay for it out of the suitcase money."

He shuddered. "Do what you're going to do, but don't tell me about it. Don't mention the money to me again for a while, okay? Until I ask."

"Fair enough. Are you sure there isn't anything you need though? A word processor, a new stereo, a snazzy little BMW?"

"Don, come off it," he said, but he had the *Times Union* spread out in front of him and a minute later I caught him studying an ad for a twelve-hundred-dollar compact disc player.

The phone rang.

"Mr. Strachey?"

"Diz da klinning leddy, Miz Pronck."

"Ha, ha. I congratulate you, kid. I just heard on the news that you assisted in the apprehension of some bad apples last night. You are a resourceful fellow, and I want to be among the first to thank you for a job well done. Your presence in this benighted city of ours raises its moral tone, though don't tell me the dirty deeds you performed in order to accomplish what you did."

"Don't worry, I won't. I suppose, Sim, that you're also calling about the cash donation for your organization's good efforts in the upcoming mayoral campaign. Well, let me just say that I can write you a ten-dollar check and stick it in the mail today, but if you had a larger amount in mind, all I can say is, I'm still working on it."

"Yes, well—" He hesitated now, the cheery demeanor all gone. "Maybe we'll just have to let the larger amount go by the boards this time around. I hate to say it, kid, but if you've got hold of that two and a half million, I think you might be stuck with it. There's no way I can possibly imagine our accepting money gotten in the illicit trafficking of narcotics. No matter what kind of shenanigans we went through to clean it up, that money still has been where it's been and it is what it is. I'm sorry. You'll never know how sorry I am."

I said, "What makes you think that's where the money came from?" My palms were beginning to sweat.

"I didn't have to go to law school to put two and two together and come up with four-minus-ten-percent-overhead, Mr. Strachey. Last night three men were arrested in your house for possession of a large amount of cocaine. One of them additionally has been charged with the murder of Jack Lenihan, who previously was arrested though not convicted on narcotics charges. Mr. Strachey, I can see what I can see, and I wouldn't touch that money if it was presented to me by the national chairlady of Hadassah. It is irredeemably tainted, though it breaks my heart to speak the words."

Now I was sweating all over. I said, "I think I've made a mistake."

"And what would that be?"

"I can't tell you. Hell. I'll be in touch. Give me a few days."

"No, there would be no point to it. But let's have a teriyaki again one day at that charming but rather loud young people's establishment off Madison Avenue. Maybe in a year or so, when you are no longer a name in the news. And again, my sincere congratulations on your accomplishment as a crime fighter. Would that there were a few like you in the Albany police department."

"Yeah, would."

"Good day, then."

"So long, Sim."

I picked at my stale muffin. Timmy said, "What was your mistake?"

"What?"

"You told him you thought you'd made a mistake. Which one was that?"

"None of your business. Crap. I'm going out." I got up and flung my muffin in the trash. After I left Timmy would retrieve the muffin, wrap it in a bread bag, and place it in the refrigerator until garbage-pickup day so that it wouldn't draw ants or mice.

"When will you be back?" he said, making a mental note of the improperly discarded baked good.

"In a day or two. If anybody calls, just say—anything, any damn thing at all."

"I'll just say that you've got a hair up your ass and you've gone to the Mayo Clinic to have it removed. In that saying, do you think it's *h-a-i-r* or *h-a-r-e*? *H-a-r-e* sounds more uncomfortable, which is probably your situation right now. You're the expert, which is it?"

I realized, of course, that Timmy was not to blame for my shortsighted clumsiness and there was no reason for my taking out my anger and frustration on him. In fact, he had been through an ugly experience that I had caused to happen, and, if anything, he deserved sympathy, gratitude and sensitive forbearance on my part that day and for many days and weeks to come. I said, "You'll have to call the library on that one, sweetheart," and left.

From the Hilton I phoned Ned Bowman and asked him several questions that had been nagging at me, and he answered them. He said he had a lot of questions for me too, but I said later. I got out the money in the hotel-room closet, skimmed off another thousand, paid for two more nights of storage, and drove out to the airport. I was in LA by 12:15, California time, rented a car, and drove over to Joan Lenihan's apartment building, where I waited.

TWENTY-THREE

AT TEN TILL FIVE IN THE AFTERNOON the two of them drove into the parking lot beside the building. Joan was at the wheel, Gail seated beside her. I thought they might enter a side door and get away from me, so I trotted through the spray of the lawn sprinklers and met them as they stepped out of the car in their shiny whites. To Joan Lenihan I said, "We need to talk."

"Do we? I don't think so."

"We thought you went back east," Gail said, looking powerfully ambivalent about my presence. "Why are you— didn't you go back to Albany?"

"The men who killed Jack are in jail on both murder and narcotics charges. I thought you would want to know that, Joan. Or has Corrine called?"

Her face froze in fright and confusion, and she said, "Who is it?"

"An ex-con, a car thief, by the name of Mack Fay. He had two accomplices, Terry and Kevin Clert. The Clerts are the sons of the nurse who looks after your father-in-law. They were after the two and a half million, but Jack got to it first and they killed him. One of the remaining unanswered questions is, where did that money come from? Apparently it was kept in Pug Lenihan's house and he considered it his, but where did it come from originally? You know, don't you, Joan?"

'Where *is* it? Where is the money *now?*" She was trembling with rage. Gail Tesney stood stricken, looking at Joan, then at me, then at Joan again.

"The money is safe. I have it."

"With you?"

"In Albany."

"It's not yours. You have no right."

"Whose it is then?"

"Give it to me."

"Is it yours?"

"Just give it to me. It doesn't belong to you. You *have* to give it to me."

"You're going to turn it over to Pug Lenihan, aren't you? That's what you would do if you had it. Are you going to tell me why, or am I going to tell you?"

She paled and began to blink, panic rising. "Gail, why don't you go on up. I'll be up in a little while."

"Joan, what is *wrong?* What is he *talking* about?"

"She'll be all right," I said. "Go ahead. We'll come up to the apartment in a few minutes."

Joan waved her away. "It's okay. I'll be okay. Go ahead. You go ahead."

Gail stared at us both for a long moment, looking hurt and abandoned, then turned and walked quickly into the building. Joan and I found a dry patch of grass under some eucalyptus trees and sat on it. I said, "I'm offering you a proposition. Either you tell Gail or I'll tell her."

She fumbled in her big leather bag, found a pack of cigarettes, and lit one. "Tell her what? What is it that I'm supposed to tell Gail? You go around telling people how to run their lives. Tell me what I'm supposed to tell her."

"That you killed your husband, Dan Lenihan, eighteen years ago this month."

She didn't flinch. Drawing on the cigarette, she leaned back against the tree trunk, then exhaled mightily. She looked at me and said, "Yes, I killed Danny. Did Pug tell you?"

"No."

"Who did?"

"You did—with your irrational fear of Pug Lenihan,

who's nothing but a vicious, cracked old blowhard. He's been holding this over you for eighteen years, making your life miserable every time the subject of Albany came up, threatening you, extorting cash to pay for his nursing care, using you as a lever against Jack after Jack made off with the famous two and a half million last October. You're so scared of Pug you can't even let him find out you're gay, for fear of the bigoted browbeating you think you'll have to take from him. The truth is, for eighteen years Pug Lenihan has been blackmailing you with his knowledge of your husband's death. Except, I don't quite believe it. What happened?"

"What happened? Danny died, that's what happened. I killed him." She dragged on the cigarette and gazed toward the setting sun, which was huge and lovely in the smog above the horizon.

"How did you go about that? I'm told Dan Lenihan was drunk and passed out in the street, where he froze to death in the middle of the January night."

A slight shake of the head. "No. Not on the street."

"Where?"

"On the front porch."

"That's not murder. That is horrible bad luck."

"No."

"He had gone out drinking, to Mike Shea's on Broadway. As he did—every night?"

"Every night. Yes, every single solitary night of the nineteen years of our marriage. Before Corrine was born, I went with him. Every night."

"And he left Shea's—when?"

"At three. He always left at three because Mike knew when to shut him off and Danny would still have enough strength left to make it home on his own steam. Mike would call me at three—wake me up—every night at three in the morning for nineteen years. And I would go down and unlock the door so Danny could get in. Danny never carried his own key because he'd lose it. So I'd go down and let him in—open the door. Every night."

"And Mike called that last night, as usual?"

"Of course."

"And what did you do?"

"I went back to sleep."

"You mean you were exhausted and you dozed off."

"No. I mean I went back to sleep. I said to myself, maybe if I go back to sleep Dan will pass out on the front porch and freeze to death. It was the deepest, most restful sleep I'd had in years."

"Had he beaten you?"

"Every night."

"Before he went out?"

"No. When he came home. Every night at three in the morning I'd let him in and he'd hit me. He never hurt me much. He couldn't—he was too drunk. He could barely walk."

"According to the police report, Dan's body was found on the sidewalk near Sacred Heart Church, not on your front porch. He never even made it home that night."

Now she looked at me with no expression I could identify. Her face was set and grim but her eyes were full of tender sadness. "Early that morning someone found Dan on the porch and dragged his body down by the church. That's where they discovered him, but that's not where he died."

"This person who moved Dan's body must have been someone who understood what had happened and wanted to protect you. Who was it?"

Her expression did not change. "Hell will freeze over before I tell you that." She flicked away the cigarette, which had burned down to the filter. "So now you know. Jack trusted you and now I've trusted you. Will you give me the money, please? So I can return it to Pug?"

"How did Pug know what really happened? How could he be sure?"

She shrugged. "Was there ever anything that went on in the North End that Pug didn't know about? I doubt it. He checked with Mike Shea, who told him I'd been called to let Dan in. He checked with everybody on Walter Street who he knew stayed up late or got up early and might have seen something. One of them had—Howie Fay, Mack's dad. He saw Dan's body being moved."

"And he never mentioned it to the police?"

"No, just to Pug. Pug told him to keep his mouth shut. Danny was already enough of an embarrassment to Pug, and to have word get out that his son had been murdered by his own family would have been the final humiliation."

"His own family?"

"Wife. His own wife."

I studied her, and she looked away. I said, "So that's why you can't cross Pug—and why you tried to stop Jack from crossing Pug. I take it Jack did not know the true circumstances of his father's death. Otherwise he'd have been more careful in his dealings with Pug."

She nodded, watching me.

"Where the hell did Pug Lenihan ever pick up two and a half million dollars anyway? Or might I guess without trying too hard?"

A grunt of sour laughter. "From 1926 until 1974 Pug handled the finances for the Boyle brothers. Kickbacks, bribes, loans, gifts—it was always 'one for the party, one for me.' The Boyles must have gotten theirs too. They didn't die in big fancy houses in Latham, so you can probably assume that there are suitcases full of money under three other beds in Albany—or were. That's where he kept it, you know, under his bed. Mrs. Clert must have known about it, and old Howie Fay. I found out from Danny, who worked for his dad when he was young, and Danny told me about it when he was drunk one time. And I made one terrible, terrible mistake." Her eyes were wet now.

I said, "You told Jack."

She nodded. "Last summer I told him. In October Jack took the money out of Pug's house when he was working out there. He was going to give it back, he told me. To the people of Albany."

"I'm sorry."

"When Jack was out here last week to pick up the laundered money, I removed the cash and stuffed newspapers into the suitcases Jack was sending to you, and I did what Pug told me to do on the phone, which was to send the money to Mack Fay, who was Pug's driver. Mack was supposed to deliver the money to Pug. If I had told Jack the truth about his father's death and what Pug was doing, he'd have killed Pug. I *know* he would have. He hated him enough to do it. We all did. Don't you see now what an evil man Pug Lenihan is? And why you have to return the money to him?"

"No, I don't. What can he do?"

"Why, he can have us arrested! And charged with murder! There's no statute of limitations on homicide cases. Pug told me that and I know it's true. We could go to prison!"

"Joan, listen to me. The Albany police *know* the whole story. They figured it out an hour after your husband's body was found. Only by using the most tortured legal logic can you be charged with murder in any degree. No jury could be found that would convict you. And in any case, the cops *knew* Dan Lenihan and are inclined to think of his death as a piece of ugly bad luck. It's just another sad story out of the old North End and not a police matter. Once in a while Irish fatalism has its uses, and this is one of them.

"Maybe you're going to feel just a little bit cheated by this, but Pug Lenihan has nothing on you or anyone else in your family. Nothing at all. I spoke with Ned Bowman about it, and he told me nothing Pug Lenihan says anymore is taken seriously by anybody downtown. He's a has-been, a relic, a fondly regarded old cipher. He'll get a big flowery tearful funeral, but in the meantime he has no appointments to make and presumably no cash that is legally disbursable, so he's just a revered shell, a monument for the pigeons to crap on. Why is he so hot to get the two and a half million back anyway? What could he possibly be planning to spend it on?"

She said, "On his deathbed he's going to hand it over to the archdiocese to reopen Immaculate Conception School."

"Ah. A benefactor of institutions of character building."

She was looking at me dazedly. "Are you telling me the truth? About—what the police said?"

"I am. I spoke with Ned Bowman about it this morning. You have nothing to worry about from the Albany police or DA. Nor does any other member of your family."

She quickly stood up and began to pace back and forth. She walked over to a car parked at the edge of the lot and suddenly pounded a fist on the hood. Trembling, she came back to where I was seated on the grass, and I was afraid for an instant that she was going to pound her fist on me. Raging and weeping, she cried, "He raped me! Before I left, he *raped* me."

"Pug did?"

"He *brags* about it. On the phone he calls me a cheap slut—his last piece of ass but not his best. I let him *do* that. For *eighteen years* I've let him—" She collapsed.

After a long dinner, they drove me to the airport. At the boarding gate, Joan said, "I still don't think I want to go back to Albany for a while. Maybe never. But Corrine is coming out here in two weeks for a long visit. I'm so happy that she's finally going to do it."

"It'll be good for both of you. She needs you. And there are some things she might need to talk about."

She looked at me evenly. "Oh, no," she said. "Corrine and I never talk about that."

TWENTY-FOUR

"I'M NERVOUS ABOUT THIS," TIMMY SAID. "Maybe you should have hired an armored truck. What if we're in an accident and this stuff goes flying? 'MOTORISTS' MOOLAH MANIA—Two Albany Men Held After Dollar Storm Causes 300-Car Thruway Pile-Up.'"

"We've got five suitcases and only three seat belts back there. What can I do? I'm driving very, very carefully."

We passed the Woodstock exit on the way south. The sky was blackening in the west, but if the forecast was accurate we'd make the city before the snow began to fall. Anyway, New York was expecting rain, not the foot of snow predicted for Albany, where the newspaper said a group of Jamaican scientists was expected to arrive soon to study what life in the tropics would be like in the event of a worldwide nuclear winter. I figured in Albany the catastrophe would hardly be noticed.

Timmy said, "After all you've been through—and I've been through—I guess I am kind of sorry you couldn't find a way to clean up the money and get it to Sim Kempelman. I'd have loved to watch the machine kicked around by its own misplaced left feet. They'd never have known what hit them."

"Yes, they would. Larry Dooley would have explained it to them."

"That would have been even better."

"The millennium in Albany will have to wait a couple of years. It's okay though. In a lot of ways I like Joan Lenihan's idea even better."

"It's just a shame though that we can't make the presentation in Pug Lenihan's name. Get his name in the Albany papers one last time."

"Too risky. Questions would be asked, maybe investigations launched. Also, the news might have finished Pug off—a stroke, or coronary, or something. What we're doing is safer, surer, and a reasonable approximation of justice."

"Are you sure their office is open on Saturday? We can't just leave the suitcases on the sidewalk."

"I phoned. Somebody'll be there."

Timmy became thoughtful for a couple of minutes, then said, "I am glad I decided to take a few weeks' vacation, I really am. I had the time coming, so why not use it? But I'm still a little unclear about why you wanted to travel so far away. I mean, it's awfully expensive. And it's so far south too. Even though it's summer down there, don't you think it might be kind of chilly in Patagonia?"

"That's just the thing. It's off the beaten path. We'll avoid the crowds of noisy nuclear families from New Jersey and spend time in a place uncontaminated by overdevelopment and so forth."

He nodded but remained, I suspected, curious.

Our flight from JFK was due to leave at four, and we arrived on West Twenty-fourth Street just after one. No parking spaces were to be found in the vicinity of the Gay Men's Health Crisis headquarters, so we double-parked in front of the building. This wasn't going to take long.

We dragged the suitcases out of the car and toted them past the signs advertising the organization's lobbying, social service and fund-raising efforts on behalf of AIDS victims. On the stairway we put on our ski masks, then hiked up to the reception office.

"This is not a holdup," I told the startled chap behind the counter. "It's an anonymous donation."

Before he could speak, we dumped the suitcases, turned, and fled.

In Patagonia it snowed, so we left after a day and a half and flew up to the Yucatán, where we climbed up and down Mayan pyramids for ten days. Timmy got sunstroke and I got dysentery, and the place was awfully hot.